SETON Girls

CHARLENE THOMAS

DUTTON BOOKS

CONTENT NOTICE:

This book is a work of fiction, but it depicts many real issues, including racism, sexual harassment, and sexual assault.

DUTTON BOOKS
An imprint of Penguin Random House LLC, New York

First published in the United States of America by Dutton Books,
an imprint of Penguin Random House LLC, 2022

Library of Congress Cataloging-in-Publication Data is available.

Printed in the United States of America

ISBN 9780593529348

1st Printing

LSCH
Design by Anna Booth
Text set in Maxime

For Mom and Dad

It isn't easy to create change that lasts.

In fact, it's really, really hard.

But we did it, here at Seton. And we believed we did it together.

Don't you remember the stories? All the tales passed on from seniors to freshmen year after year?

Cooper Adams. Who he was. What he meant. How he came in and changed our whole entire world.

The tales I've heard go like this:

Once upon a time, thirteen years ago, the heavens placed upon us Cooper Adams. He had dimples that could seduce a housewife and threw a spiral that could dent a brick wall. He inherited a pretty good football team in a really good division, and he led that team to undeniable greatness. An undefeated season that no team—not Billingsley, not St. Mary's, not Anderson Prep—had ever seen before. And as he did it, he united a school that had only ever cared about football to care about its girls as well. He was our ally. A feminist before it was even cool.

How, you ask?

Well, the tales say that during the summer of 2006, just before he would take over as Seton Academic High School's Varsity quarterback, he sat in his basement and penned a cheer. When it was finished, he taught it to his team. And then, at Seton's first game of the season, right after halftime, the entire football team stood on benches and faced the crowd—faced *us*—as they recited the legendary *Seton Girls* cheer for the very first time.

Cooper Adams did other cool stuff, too. He convinced the school to create Seton Girls swag to go with all the Seton Football stuff sold in the online bookstore. He donated the proceeds from the football team's Season of Giving bake sale to a women's shelter, instead of to another junior football league.

Cooper Adams saw us. Cooper Adams *loved* us.

Why, you ask?

Because he couldn't have had his perfect season without us.

Those were his words. On October 27, 2006, in the very first center spread quarterback feature that Seton ever ran, he was asked why he cared so much about the girls. What was it that made us special? What did he want the rest of the world to know?

And he said: "I want all those girls to know that we couldn't have had this perfect season without them."

I read the quote myself when I was researching whatever the hell it is I'm writing now, which I know is the exact opposite of the "I-cannot-tell-a-lie/Isn't-he-a-hero?" quarterback feature that all of you were expecting to see. I want to say I'm sorry, but I'm not. I just want us to be okay.

I imagine, at the time that Cooper's words were first published, Seton girls everywhere sighed longingly and collapsed into the nearest arms like they were at a BTS concert. Because Cooper was so perfect. Because he was, and continues to be, our star.

Every year that followed, Seton quarterbacks stood on the foundation of what he built. Undefeated season after undefeated season, like we were *magic*. But Cooper was only replicated, never duplicated.

Until now.

Because we get to have his kin. His *blood*. His brother, with his own delicious dimples and killer spiral.

But if you thought, like I did, that that made us the lucky ones . . .

You were wrong.

What it is.

<u>August 25, 2019</u>

Our skin glows a dull purple in this bowling alley with all its neon lights. Nelly's "Ride Wit Me" is blasting from the team playlist that the manager happily plugged in as soon as we got here. The playlist Seton has had forever, that only our football players know the password to.

The music is so loud, J had to get up with me, follow me from the plastic seats to our lane, and lean into my ear just so I can hear all this unrequested sideline coaching.

"But Alz, if you just, like—"

"I can't."

"If you use your wrist, though . . ."

"J."

"And your forearm . . ." He trails off.

"Look at my forearm. Look at my forearm compared to your forearm."

We hold our arms out next to each other's, forearms facing the sky. His has veins the width of pipe cleaners. My arm could lay on top of his twice.

He sighs and slides his hands into his pockets.

I know how much he hates it as I lean over like a little kid bowling, and maybe that's partly why I do it. I swing the pink marbled ball between my legs with both hands and push it down the slick lane. I stand up straight as the ball takes out four of the nine pins I didn't knock out the first time.

I smile up at J.

He's still watching our lane, until he looks at the screen above our heads to check my score. He nods a little to himself and winces like he's waiting for a doctor to finish giving him a shot.

I laugh and shove him, but he barely moves. "*Relax.*"

"It's just that *you're an athlete,* Alz—"

"No, you're an athlete."

"But you're a part of me. I'm a part of you," he argues.

"Did Thoreau say that?"

He wraps his arms around my shoulders, and I rest my face against his chest, my ear against his red *Seton* T-shirt, soft enough to melt because it's been washed so many times. He kisses the top of my head through my fluffy bun and declares, "Yo, you talk enough smack to be an athlete."

I laugh and he does, too, as we walk back to our group of tables now that my turn is officially over.

Our crew takes up three lanes. There's a crowd of people we don't know at the door, waiting for spots to open up, some who were waiting even before we got here, but the staff figured out how to make room for us despite our lack of a reservation. The guys just wanted to hang out tonight, get as much of the team together as they could without it being a house party like normal. One more chance to make a memory before this summer is officially over.

Parker has his arms folded in front of him when we get back to the tables where the wings and the pizza and the cups of beer that

the manager let him order are waiting. The lights are making everything about him skew a different color. His green eyes are almost orange. His pale skin is blue. His brown hair that's sometimes buzzed
short but right now is long enough for Michelle to push her fingers
through—and a lot of times, she does—looks like dust.

J, in real light, is a compilation of different shades of brown. Me,
too. So, tonight, he's a fun array of purples, not a neon rainbow like
Parker.

The boys are debating like they always are. It's anything from
the best burger in town to the best touchdown ever scored. Right
now, they're going on about superpowers. Which one they'd want
if they could have any one in the world. It's Parker's turn to choose,
seconds after J takes his seat on the bench and has me sit on part of
his leg so there's enough room for me, too.

Parker sucks his teeth. "Yo, I don't need a superpower. I *am* a
superpower."

Everybody laughs, the guys louder than the girls. Nudging each
other and bumping each other, and Parker's smiling, too, but he's
saying, "*Yo. No, yo. Shut the fuck up. Yo, hear me out,*" while he slaps
their hands and grips their shoulders and makes sure everyone is listening. "I'm being deadass serious right now. I *am* a superpower. I'm
a fucking superpower. And you're a fucking superpower," he says,
clapping his hand against Charlie's shoulder. "And J, my man." He
reaches his hand across the table and J meets it with the same easy
handshake they've done for years. Fingers sliding and a snap to end
it. "You're a goddamned superpower if I've ever fucking seen one.
Everything we do, everything we've *done* is a certified superpower.
No one else can touch us. Check the fucking almanac—"

"This dude said 'the almanac . . .'" chuckles one of the guys at the end of the table.

"Yeah, I said it. I said check the motherfucking almanac. There's only one Seton football team and that's all there ever will be. Don't sit around crying about the superpowers you don't have when we're the goddamned definition of the term."

J's laughing into his lap, shaking his head to himself with his hand on my leg as he subconsciously picks at the hole in the knee of my jeans. I smile. Because it's *annoying*. And because he doesn't care.

"That's why we're gonna take States this year," Parker declares, the promise he's been making all summer. "First time in history. This team right here." He jabs his finger into the table, once with *right* and again with *here*. "I bet my fucking life on it."

It's like he shines a little brighter when he says it, his neon glow more radioactive, more untouchable. The boys smirk and nudge each other, and half of them start a mini-chorus of *He wants two*. Trophies, they mean. One for the season and another for the state championship.

"Does that just go for you guys?" Britt MacDougal asks, her voice breaking through their chant before it really has the chance to become one.

She's a few people down from us, from Parker, sitting on the tabletop. Her thick hair is frizzy and loose and gorgeous. She's wearing tiny cutoff jean shorts and a fitted long-sleeved black shirt with Timberlands. She's surrounded by her three friends—the four of them together like this weightless, perfect, intoxicating aura everywhere they ever go.

Bianca Patel sits on the tabletop next to Britt, both of them glowing shades of purple like J and me. Kelly Donahue is in the seat on the other side of Bianca, glowing neon like a girl version of Parker. And then there's Michelle Rodriguez, more blue than purple, with her long dark hair coiled up in a ballerina bun, her perfect body on display in a pale pink romper. She's Parker's girlfriend, and she loves him, just like he loves her. But I've always had a feeling that she loves Britt a little more.

Michelle sits in the seat next to Kelly, resting easily between Britt's legs, her elbows on Britt's kneecaps. She watches Parker as Parker smiles and watches her back. His girl. His *girls*.

"What do you mean?" he asks Britt.

"Your whole self-righteous superpower title," Britt answers him, her gray eyes still gray, even in this lighting. But they burn more. "Does that just go for you guys or does it go for us, too?"

"Like you girls?"

"Me, B, Kel, Mich. Aly. Any girl here. Any girl who exists."

"I know you're super-powerful when you get drunk and hungry." Parker smiles.

They talk to each other like that. Like family.

Michelle smiles at him warningly from between Britt's legs. "Don't be a dick."

"How many times do I have to tell you that you're the best girls in the world?" Parker amends.

Bianca seems to think about it. "Maybe try one more time?"

"Louder," Kelly demands, smirking as she does.

But Britt shakes her head, looking at her friends. A conversation they're capable of having with just their eyes because they've mattered to each other for that long.

She's talking to Parker, but almost anyone at our table is listening, too. Watching. Those girls are distracting in the most addictive way.

"*Best* is an adjective," she informs him over the music. "We deserve to be nouns."

What it is.

Best *is an adjective. We deserve to be nouns.*

It's been playing through my head since Britt said it last night, and again now as J and I wait outside of Seton's main doors. Britt and her friends have so many moments like that, moments when it was the four of them that I just *remember.* That pop into my head like a song lyric and make me smile to think about all over again. Last night, Parker laughed and said, "Fine, you guys are beautiful dolphins, what do you want me to say?" but nobody cared about that part. The part that had mattered had been theirs.

"Hmm?" J asks, offering me a French toast stick from the breakfast tray he got from the cafeteria when we first pulled in this morning. Around 6:55 a.m. Traffic wasn't too bad.

He puts it right up to my mouth. I shake my head and yawn. "I have to get used to being up this early again before I can eat." He makes a face like I just told him birds can't fly, but dips his stick in syrup and takes the bite for himself.

It's the first day of school, and J and I have been waiting outside for the past twenty minutes, sitting on the shallow brick wall that borders Seton's main entrance. There are red and white streamers wrapped around the trees outside and a hand-painted banner hanging above the main doors—red letters on white paper that read *Let's make it 13!*

If Parker and the Varsity team can go undefeated this season, it'll be our thirteenth perfect year in a row.

But for now, it's just Monday, the blue sky is cloudless, and the parking lot is filling up with cars that belong to Seton-proper kids. Some go inside, some linger in the lot, and J and I share his cord-attached earbuds while I hold my Seton-issued iPad on my lap and download the course packs I'm gonna need for today. We're listening to the *Rent* soundtrack off J's phone because he had a pre-assignment for his music history elective to watch a musical over the summer, and that was the one he chose. After he decided it was the deepest thing he'd ever seen, he downloaded the soundtrack, and it's been part of the shuffle ever since. He nods to himself and sings along to "No Day But Today" the same way he does when it's Drake.

The team starts to congregate outside, too, as their cars pull into the lot. Some of them pass a football around that randomly (at least, it seems random to me) gets tossed J's way every now and then. He manages to anticipate it every single time, then throws it easily back across the lawn.

"Do you wanna come with me to Walgreens when we get home tonight?" I ask as the ball whizzes back over to him.

He catches it with one hand and finishes another French toast stick with the other. "For Glade PlugIns?" he asks, because he knows how much I love a good Glade PlugIn. For a while we had to use them, when they were paving the road near our house and it made everything inside smell like tar. That's over now, but I'm still obsessed.

"Yes," I answer.

"Of course."

"That means you probably can't play football with Cory."

"I could probably do both." He lets the ball soar back to where it came from.

"No, because Cory is gonna want to play forever."

"That's not true."

I roll my eyes. "Yes, because he always does. Because he thinks he could actually play for Seton, too, one day."

"He could."

"He drops *every pass* you throw at him."

"Yeah, but he's your kid brother, Alz."

"So what?"

And then J nods, picks up another French toast stick, dips it in syrup, and takes a bite. "You know what, you're right. Let's gag him and throw him in the basement when we get home tonight."

I make myself look down at my iPad instead of at him so he can't see me trying not to laugh.

But his voice makes me sure that he's smiling anyways as he leans his shoulder into mine and says, "I promise we'll get your Glade PlugIns."

For a little while, it's quiet, besides all the noises that are supposed to be there. The boys. This *Rent* soundtrack. The voices of everyone else as they walk up the steps to the red double doors, wide open like they always are on the mornings when the weather is nice enough. I check the WiFi connection on my iPad because this course pack is taking forever to download.

But I look up when the yelling starts.

"Mich, *what are you doing?*" Britt insists, calling at Michelle over the roof of her car.

Michelle is halfway across the courtyard, and Britt's car is still running. I'm not even sure that the car actually stopped before Michelle got out if she's already gotten this far.

"What are *you* doing?" Michelle spins around to face Britt across the sidewalk. "Seriously. What are you doing?" Her voice is strained. Almost frantic. Like something awful has happened. The kind of awful that gives a mom the strength to lift a truck off her toddler.

"You can't just jump out of my moving vehicle like you're Laurence fucking Fishburne!" Britt storms over to her, leaving her car door open, leaving Kelly and Bianca to rush out of the back seat, and turn off the car, and get Britt's keys, and shut the door behind her. The car isn't even in a spot yet. "You're not invincible, and you're not replaceable, so you can't do that, okay?"

"No," Michelle says.

"No to which fucking part?"

"*You* can't." Her voice is shaking as she presses her fingers against the middle of Britt's chest. And that's when Parker—who'd been sitting on the steps, a part of that whole random ball-throwing circle with J—stands up slowly, approaching them like he's just as lost as the rest of us. "You can't say nothing while half my squad is telling me that you hooked up with my boyfriend this summer and then drive us to school like the world isn't on fucking fire."

Parker stops dead in his tracks.

Bianca and Kelly have caught up with them now, like the perfect volunteer firefighters, here to put out the flames. But it doesn't matter that Bianca is squeezing Michelle's arm and whispering something in her ear that only they can hear, or that Kelly has Britt's elbow and is trying to pull her away.

"It doesn't have to be on fire," Britt says.

In the daylight, the two girls are back to the colors they're supposed to be. Michelle's long, almost-black hair is shining and effortlessly bent at the ends. Her eyes are dark brown again, her skin back to sepia. She's wearing a collared, long-sleeved baby-doll dress—Ralph Lauren–looking and perfect. Pretty like a princess, as always.

And then Britt, this wild girl of all our dreams. With her gorgeously thick mane, and her eyes that are the same color as frozen lips, and skin that's a little bit browner than mine. She's never wearing Ralph Lauren anything, and today her non–Ralph Lauren look includes cutoff black shorts and an oversized white sweater with holes in it. We've all generally accepted that Britt is probably the most surreally gorgeous girl we'll ever see.

"Then say something," Michelle pleads.

"What can I say?" Britt asks.

"Say that it isn't true."

Britt watches her, and they both look so miserable. It aches all the way to where J and I are sitting. And aside from being transfixed, because I've watched these girls for the past two years as we ended up at the same parties and sat a lunch table apart from each other, I can't even begin to comprehend how this happened so fast. How twelve hours ago, they were woven together at the bowling alley with the rest of us, and now this accusation that my brain can't even process.

"I can't say that, Mich."

And Michelle scoffs, and shakes her head, and declares, "So burn me alive." She turns around and keeps walking, across the courtyard. Bianca exchanges a quick look with Kelly before she follows.

Michelle passes Parker, and he tries to intercept her, but she shakes him off, and Parker looks at Britt as he backs away in the direction Michelle went. "Britt, what the hell was that?"

But Britt doesn't answer him, and for now, he makes the decision to jog after Michelle and Bianca instead.

That's when Kelly takes Britt's face in her hands, and looks at her dead in her eyes, like she knows how to get the truth out of her. The last thing I hear her say is "Tell me what the hell is going on."

And the rest is whispers, the kinds of secrets they've always had.

What it was.

The team was in Cooper Adams's basement, even though no one else was home—well, no one besides his five-year-old brother. He was there, but it didn't matter, because he was always there, and he was busy on the steps with the football their dad had gotten him for Christmas, spinning it on the polished oak floor, trying to shove it through the bars along the stairwell, throwing it in the air and catching it with both hands. He was distracted, but Coop gave him headphones and his iPod anyway. Not because his brother was a snitch, but he could be a parrot sometimes.

Cooper sat behind his dad's big mahogany desk in the leather chair that stretched a full six inches over his head like a throne. On the wall behind him was the professional portrait his mom made them take after his brother was born, when he was finally old enough to wear one of those little-kid suits from the Neiman Marcus catalogs she kept stacked in the bookcase next to a bunch of copies of O, The Oprah Magazine. It was the four of them, with their sandy-brown hair and emerald-green eyes, and the dog in a bow tie, and Coop's boys gave him hell every time they saw it, asking if they thought they were the White Huxtables or some shit.

Coop always loved it, and always laughed about it, but it was even funnier when they were high like they were now, the guys on his team sprawled across his leather sectional and the leather

armchairs while some of them sat on the floor, and they played
Grand Theft Auto and puffed and passed two blunts they'd just
rolled. His mom always bitched for days when they made the upstairs smell like weed. So his dad told them to just keep it in the
basement or the car to spare him all the goddamned grief.

"Are we trying to roll through Jimmy's tonight or what?" Brad
asked.

"His sister's fucking *crazy*, man," Tanner answered, slamming on
his controller with his thumbs as he stared up at the TV from the
floor. "The girl tries to rape me every single time I'm there—"

They laughed harder than they should have. Each one's like an
echo that could bounce against these basement walls for as long
as there was weed left to smoke. Cooper's brother looked up from
his football, peering through the wooden rails, smiling out of pure
dumb interest. Coop winked at him and tapped his ear to remind
him to keep his headphones on.

"Yo, *same*," Tommy said, punching the cushion as he did.

"That girl would fuck fucking anything." Brendan laughed so
hard that he started to cough into his elbow.

Wyatt slapped him on the back a few times to keep him alive,
and it only made Coop laugh harder.

"She's fucking gorgeous, though," Brad declared.

And they all nodded and slapped hands in somber agreement,
busy thinking about Jimmy's horny but gorgeous sophomore sister.

"Hey, what if we didn't lose to Billingsley this year?" Coop asked.

All eight of the guys in his basement looked at him. Maybe it
seemed random to anybody else, going from Jimmy's sister to talking about their upcoming season, but for them, it wasn't. For them,

football was a topic that was always imminent. Like a thunderstorm in the summertime.

They were the Seton Varsity football team now, and in seven weeks, they'd play their season opener. They were the most promising team Seton had had in years, and everyone knew it. Local sports radio had been talking about it for weeks. There was always a buzzyness right before the season started, this hopeful *What if* among all the elite locals who'd been rooting for the same schools since they'd been the ones attending. But this year was different. Cooper was better than the quarterbacks who had come before him. A quick thinker with fast feet who knew how to make plays. *He's Special* read one of the headlines that had run not too long ago.

But Billingsley was special, too. And people talked about them *all the fucking time.* Debating if Cooper was really good enough to handle a Varsity-level Billingsley team. Debating if Cooper was really good enough to handle Varsity pressure at all. He sat up in the dark while his laptop screen glowed against his face, and googled his own name, clicking through all the hits, texting his boys everyone's opinions about who he was and what he could do.

He told his team every time: *They have no idea what I can do.*

"What if we didn't lose at all?" Coop went on. "Now, or ever again? What would you say?"

He still had all their eyes, while his little brother sat throwing a football into the air.

"You do know when they tell us to fly, they don't literally expect us to jump off a fucking building and fly, right?" Brad asked.

Cooper smiled. Years from now, once he'd left Seton and he and his old teammates were laughing about the times they'd once had, he'd explain to them that he never actually loved football, not in any kind of life-changing way, at least. That was the part people didn't understand, that they'd never understand. It wasn't about some intense love of the game for him; it was about how it felt when they wrote articles about him like he was some kind of anomaly. It was about how his aunts and uncles looked at him when his dad would brag about what a local legend he was. It was about the way his guys were looking at him right now.

"Yeah, I know," Cooper answered. "But that doesn't mean we shouldn't do it anyways."

"You're talking about going undefeated in *our* conference?" Jason spoke up. "Coop, it's not just Billingsley. AP's trying to get Garvey into Navy next year. They've been running that triple option all summer just to prove to recruiters he can do it."

Dylan Garvey was another one they wrote about all the time. He was at Anderson Prep, and they didn't have a whole lineup like Billingsley did this year, but they did have Dylan. And Coop would say all the time how much he'd love to break his legs.

"I'm not saying what if we beat them. I'm saying what if we *won*?"

"Someone get this kid in an English class . . ." Brad insisted.

"Hear me out." Cooper smiled, standing up behind the desk, resting his hands on the shiny wood. "You're my boys, right? I've never done you wrong, right? Are you gonna hear me out?"

"Talk to us, Coop," a few of them encouraged.

"Last year, shit changed, right? Okay, *how* did it change? Playoff model. We don't make it to States anymore just because we have a better regular season record than everyone else. We just need to be good enough to make it to the playoffs. Which means teams can lose twice, three times, even, and still have a chance at States—we saw it last year. Hamilton lost *three games* but still made it in because they had a better record than anyone else they played that year. So, if that's what's going on . . . if we can get people to see that that's what's going on, then we have power. Because if we have something they want, they *need*, more than they need a win, then they'd be stupid not to make a deal with us."

They'd stopped passing the blunts, the smoke hanging in the air like the best medicine they'd ever had.

"You mean like we trade them something for a win?" one of the guys asked.

"What the hell can we trade for a win?" another pressed.

Coop could tell his team anything, and they'd listen to him no matter what he said, because that's what their team was all about. But maybe this was different somehow. Maybe, this time, they'd think he'd gone too far.

Except, Cooper had lived a mile away from Seton for his entire life. His parents had prepped him for those entrance exams since sixth grade, and his dad and Coach Gentry had played nine-hole rounds together over at Nappahawnick since before Cooper was even born. He'd been in the same football practices his little brother was in now—from the moment he was big enough to hold a football and not topple over—and he knew his town better than he knew anything else in the world. He knew how things got done. He knew what kinds of people got them done. And while he spent the past years in the hallways and at the parties and on the field, and googling what people were predicting about who he'd be this year, this idea was never so ridiculous that he didn't want to try it. And he said it now with that kind of confidence, that kind of smile on his lips, that kind of eagerness and giddiness to finally get it out to the people he did everything with—these guys who were his family.

That's the funny thing about family. At least, the kind of families they belonged to, that existed in the worlds of Anderson Prep and Billingsley and Seton. That even if you are crazy, they'll still tell everyone else you're sane. Keeping up appearances. It looks better that way.

But that day wasn't about appearances. They really didn't think he was crazy at all. In fact, they looked at him like he was a genius. Like he was making them some offer they didn't even deserve—a Mercedes for their birthday when they'd just flunked chem.

"What do you guys think?" he asked.

They looked around at one another, and Coop peeked at his little brother. He was busy rolling the ball across his knees, and his headphones were still on.

"What if we get caught?" was the only question anyone had.

"Then my dad." Cooper looked at Brad. "Or your dad." He smiled at Tanner. "Or this motherfucker's dad will get us uncaught."

And Cooper stood there, with the kind of confidence that was instilled by the Porsches sitting in the garage, a DUI from his sophomore year that never saw the light of day, and his dad's Harvard Law degree hanging on the living room wall upstairs.

Then he promised, "We're not getting caught."

What it is.

It took J and me forty-eight minutes to get to Kyle Samuelson's to-night, which isn't bad, but we still have to park around the corner because there are already that many cars parked along the curb. We leave J's decade-old Ford Explorer behind (J got his license this summer, and now his dad officially shares the car with him on weekends) and walk the inky-black road that heads back to Kyle's giant home in Seton-proper.

J's laughing at me, and I'm trying my best to be pissed at him for it, even though it's so annoyingly hard not to laugh anytime he is. All because Mom group-texted us this stupid picture she'd found in one of our old photo albums of J and me sleeping next to each other with my mouth hanging open, drool everywhere. Mom loves send-ing us my drool pics, because she and Dad actually think they're adorable, and J thinks they're hilarious.

"What are you still laughing about?" I insist, our bodies close but not touching as we keep walking. J has a bottle in a paper bag that he's holding around the neck in the hand that's farthest away from me.

"Nothing, Alz." He wipes his mouth with his free hand. "I'm just happy to be alive." He looks up at the sky. "Grateful you never drowned me."

I shove him. "Do you want me to hate you?" He laughs and

grabs for me apologetically as I go on. "Is that what you're trying to do right now?"

He kisses me on the mouth and then lets his laughter die off into my hair. "Every day," he quips, and kisses me again before I can threaten him anymore.

"Yo, check my boy, J!" Chase Wilson calls out, and even though these houses are acres apart, he's a little too loud for the kind of night this is. Warm. Cloudless. The stars shimmer like diamonds do in commercials—the kind of stars I used to count.

Chase stands up when he sees J and me coming, his arms spread and a big grin on his lips as he waits. Vic Balon sits in one of the two foldable chairs at the collapsible table, set up on Kyle's stone patio. J and Chase slap hands and bump chests, and then J and Vic fist-bump and slap hands, too.

"And the missus," Chase says to me, bowing.

I rub his head. "So dramatic."

Vic smiles and stands up to give me a hug. Then he tells J, "You sure were walking up here slow as shit."

And with a smirk on his lips and a pen in his free hand, as he leans over and signs his name on the sheet in front of Chase, J says, "Man, we got a game tomorrow. I don't need to be wasting my energy jogging up some steps."

All three of them laugh while Vic hands me a different pen so I can sign in on the sheet in front of him, instead.

"That right there is exactly why we're about to go undefeated next year, too." Chase taps the side of J's head and declares, "Because this kid is fucking *logical.*"

I smile at J, but he won't meet my eyes. J hates compliments, even when they're just coming from his JV teammates on a Friday night at another Seton party. So, he changes the subject, instead. "You guys need anything from inside?"

"Nah, we're good." Vic sits back down and slides his hands into his pockets.

"Alright, well, text me if you want me to grab you guys something later. I'll come back."

"We know, man," Vic says, and even though this is just what we do—tonight, it's Vic and Chase who have to sit outside to manage the sign-in sheets, and soon enough it'll be J's turn again—Vic has been friends with J long enough to know that J will move faster if he's nudged. "Y'all be good. Have fun."

"*Missus*," Chase croons again, bowing as J and I walk toward the front door.

All the lights are on once we're inside Kyle's house and "Between Me and You" by Ja Rule is playing over the speakers, the same password-protected playlist that the manager plugged in for us at the bowling alley when he put us on a lane despite the line out front. It gets played everywhere we are, as long as someone from the team is there to unlock it. Almost thirteen years of music. The guys on the team get to add whatever songs they want, but they can never delete one.

J and I stop to talk to people, so it takes us a few minutes to make it to the kitchen. But when we do, J pulls a cheap bottle of whiskey out of the paper bag and sets it on the enormous kitchen island. The marble is already fully stacked with booze, but we stopped at the gas station by our house that doesn't card anyway. The guys on the team always show up at a party with a bottle—it's their way of helping to host even on the nights when they aren't hosting.

Kyle's kitchen is full of enough alcohol to sterilize an entire hospital, and he isn't even on the team. The guys bring three times this much when we're hanging out at one of their houses.

I'm not sure how long it takes us to run into Kyle, but when we do, he's out on the deck with a bunch of other people, gathered around a table with an umbrella that's open but doesn't need to be. He's wearing a Seton Girls hat, backward, and it looks just like most Seton stuff does—red with white block lettering. Except for the word *Girls*. That's in twirly script.

Kyle slaps hands with J and gives me a hug and says thank God we're here. The boys are in the middle of debating what's the most famous dance of all time, and Kyle is presently drunk enough to be convinced he needs backup.

J's next to me refereeing this argument that gets pretty loud every once in a while as they make some pretty valid points like *The Cha-Cha Slide literally tells you how to do the Cha-Cha Slide so how can anyone not know how to do the Cha-Cha Slide?* but I'm too caught up in a conversation with Gina-Melissa to really follow it. She's a junior this year, like I am, and she's telling me about this short story she wrote about a girl who's the daughter of a famous journalist and a novelist so she spends her whole life writing because writing is all that anyone ever expected of her. She watches what's happening around her and writes about it. She listens to stories about people's lives and writes about them. And she's convinced she knows exactly who she is, until the day her pencil pricks her and she doesn't bleed. It's a metaphor, Gina-Melissa says, about the way we can appear so perfect on the outside and still be completely hollow.

She's telling me about it while this dance war rages next to us, I think because she hopes I'll care. And I can't stop staring at her as she tells me about this story because I'm mesmerized by the mere fact that she can even *do* this. That she can have these ideas in her head, and spin them into full lyrical productions from scratch. I can't even imagine writing like that. I can't even fantasize about where to start. But this is one of the things I love most about Seton. How ridiculously smart and talented everybody is—whether they're an athlete or a future Pulitzer winner. How Kyle can be drunk ranting on my left and Gina-Melissa can be reciting perfection on my right, and it's not weird, or ironic, or some wild juxtaposition. It just is. We all just belong here. And it just *works*.

"GM, that sounds ridiculous. Of course I want to read it," I tell her.

"Really?"

"For real. Email it to me, okay?"

And just as she's agreeing, I get bumped really, really hard.

And suddenly, I'm wet.

"Oh, fuck," Britt says.

She's standing in front of me now, in the direct center of the distance between Gina-Melissa and J. Her kinky curls are big and loose and beautiful and wild.

The open part of her cup is facing me, still dripping with the drink that isn't inside of it anymore, because the ice-cold whatever-she-had is seeping into my white shirt instead.

"Oh, shit," GM breathes, eyeing my stained top.

"Aly, I'm *so* sorry," Britt tells me.

"Oh God, don't be." I pluck my wet shirt away from my skin. "This shirt is super old. Did you get any on yourself?"

"No, I'm dry—"

"Hey, you okay?" J asks, probably sensing mild chaos next to him. His smile is lingering from the debate he's been monitoring. "Oh, what's up, Britt?" he adds, when his gaze settles on her.

"Nothing especially noteworthy aside from the fact that I just attacked your girlfriend with rum and Coke."

J looks down at the stain covering my stomach. "Aw, Alz." He chuckles sympathetically. "I bet I have a T-shirt in the car somewhere. You want me to get it for you?"

I consider it, but it's probably some half-washed thing from one of his practices, and Britt insists, "Let me help. Don't put on some boy shirt; you look cute tonight. Come on, I can fix it. Trust me?"

And, just like that, she's the center of everything, despite the fight to my left and GM to my right; her big eyes that are maybe gray or grayish brown capable of convincing anyone to do anything.

"J, I'll be back," I tell him.

"Alright," he says. "Love you. Let me know if you guys want me to get you that T-shirt."

"Love you," I echo as Britt starts to lead me away. Then, to GM, I add, "Please, email me?"

She smiles and promises me that she will.

Britt takes my hand so she doesn't lose me as she weaves us through the crowd, back into the house. People try to say *Hey, Britt*, as she passes, and even the ones who don't still notice us. Well, notice her. The way everyone always does. But she ignores them, or is maybe so used to the attention that she doesn't even realize they're there. Her Timberlands squeak on the tiled kitchen floor as she stays fully focused on getting me to the nearest downstairs bathroom.

She turns on the light and locks us inside.

"Bianca spills things obsessively, so I always keep these wipes on me." Britt pulls out what looks like a baby wipe, gets on her knees so my shirt is at eye level, and starts blotting my stomach.

It's so completely bizarre that Britt MacDougal is on the floor in front of me, trying to un-stain this top I got from Forever 21 freshman year.

"Where is Bianca?" I make myself ask.

"I don't think she's here tonight."

"You don't *think*?"

She shakes her head, and her hand slows down for a second. "Honestly? I haven't really talked to her today. Her and Kelly and Mich . . . it's kind of weird with us right now, so I don't think they're coming."

As soon as J and I were here for more than five minutes, it was obvious that Britt and her friends weren't around. Parker isn't around tonight, either. And it's noticeable because they're always everywhere. Together.

"Britt?" I ask.

"Yeah?"

"You really, *really* don't have to clean my shirt."

She peers up at me from her knees, her face this mix of sad and sorry and something I can't figure out, and I take the wipe from her because I have to. Because I can't just let Britt MacDougal, or *anyone*, get on her knees and start cleaning my shirt.

She rolls off her knees and sits on the fluffy pink rug, resting her back against the sink. She stretches her legs out in front of her, which she kind of has to do because her skintight dress is even shorter when she sits down. "I guess I just feel like I might be fucking everything up lately." She sighs and glances at me again. "And your shirt is my latest casualty."

I gnaw my lip. Even though Britt and her friends are a year older than me, she and I have still talked a million times before (as we existed adjacently but separately), just never about anything real. And, right now, the only thing I can think about is how opposite this moment is from Kyle's last party, on the Fourth of July, when Britt and Michelle did this silly, sultry dance on top of the pool table in the basement to that Nelly Furtado song "I'm Like a Bird." And they were so goofy and so pretty and so happy and so drunk, and the guys watched them do it and absolutely loved it, and halfway through the song, Zach Willis scooped Britt off the table and told her he had to have her, and she laughed and threatened to pee on him if he didn't put her down. But he was laughing, too, and he didn't put her down.

"What do you feel like you're fucking up?" I ask.

"You have to keep wiping or the stain's gonna set."

I don't really care about the stain, but I start wiping it again because I hope it will make her feel better. "What do you feel like you're fucking up?"

"Just the world as we know it." She sighs. "You know what really sucks, Aly?" She rests her head against the sink and stares up at the ceiling. Almost like she's only talking to me because I'm the one who's here.

"What?" I ask anyway.

"That right now, everybody's whispering about what Parker and I did or didn't do this summer. And it's not because they care about me, or about Michelle, or even Parker—beyond worshipping the ground he spits on. It's not because they care about what happens to us, or what's happening at all. They want the story because they feel like it's *theirs*. Because they feel like, since we take hits off the same joints on weekends or sign the same sheets of paper or wear red together like a cult, they have a right to anything that belongs to any one of us. I mean . . ." And she finally looks at me, squinting at the audacity of everything. "It's like they actually believe I owe them an answer—whether it did happen or it didn't. And the only reason why people can't stop talking about it now is because I won't say yes or no."

It's been the most consistently asked question at Seton since Monday. Some people salivating, others in utter shock. J and I talked about it while we sat on my front step with our school stuff everywhere, and J threw a football back and forth with Cory. We talked about it again, during our hour-long ride home one evening, while I pinched his earlobe every time he started to fall asleep. I was always the one who brought it up, the one who was thinking about it, the one who wanted to know how it was even possible for this perfect group of girlfriends, who had loved each other to death for as long as I'd been at Seton, to have a rumor like this. How Britt and Michelle could be so kindred, and all of us could see it, and for a week now, they haven't even looked at each other.

I slide to the floor next to her and lean against the sink, too. I keep blotting while we both look ahead instead of at each other. "Why *won't* you say yes or no, Britt?"

"Because it's really fucking complicated."

We face one another, her unsaid words clouding the air like we just burned grilled cheese on the stove. I don't *know* Britt. None of us does, really, besides those girls, maybe Parker. But she's always been good to me. She's always smiled at me in the hallway. She's always said hey if we were in the bathroom at the same time and made small talk while she peed and I washed my hands, or I peed and she washed her hands, or we peed at the same time. Sometimes she doesn't see me. But if she does, she never acts like she doesn't.

All her friends are like that, but it always seemed to come the most naturally to Britt. Like she never had to think about it. Like it was just the way she was.

So, I really mean it when I say, "Well, I care if you guys are okay."

She glances at me. "I know you're gonna think I'm full of shit when I say this, but that actually means a lot to me right now." Then she takes a deep breath and nods at my shirt. "Your stain's gone, by the way."

She's right.

"You're magic." I smile.

Her pretty eyes narrow in on me, and she gives me a little smile back. "White magic or black magic?"

Britt, herself, isn't scary. But she can say things in a way that makes it so hard to know for sure whether she's joking. And getting it wrong is the scary part. Ruining your chance with her because you mistook sarcasm for reality.

She laughs when I take too long to answer—not at me, but almost like she's making this moment safe. She rests her head back against the sink cabinets and stares at the wall instead.

"Gray magic," she softly answers for the both of us.

What it is.

It's Monday, and I'm sitting at one of the oversized iMac screens in the newspaper office, reading Gina-Melissa's short story. "Pencils," she's called it.

It's only my second week as editor of *The Seton Story*, and maybe that's why I still have impostor syndrome when it comes to the idea of people actually wanting *me* to read their stuff. I get why they want to be in the paper—that part's obvious. It's just weird that I'm the one who gets to decide whether they will be. Well, me and Principal Mitchell.

I don't know very much about other schools and their newspapers, just that *The Seton Story* is different. It's an institution, at this point, over fifty years after it was first printed. It started out as this covert operation by a bunch of Seton kids who wanted to write about the kinds of topics that the school wanted to ban—like the civil rights movement, Vietnam, rock and roll. They'd print the papers in the middle of the night and leave a ton in the quad or drop them off at storefronts. For months, Seton tried to figure out who was involved, but they never could. The students wouldn't rat on each other, and none of the articles had bylines. Instead, they just wrote a simple attribution at the top of every issue: *By Us.*

It took years and a new principal before the Seton administration was finally willing to embrace the movement. They eventually brought *The Seton Story* in-house and started a journalism class and everything. They created the office I'm sitting in now, with all its expensive computers. We even have an online version with thousands of subscribers, not to mention our classic print edition. And, just in case it wasn't already totally clear, a junior isn't supposed to be editor. That position, like every other significant position at Seton, is supposed to be reserved for seniors. But before we left for summer break, Principal Mitchell said I was ready. He's noisy like that—a kind of modern, cool-dad revolutionary.

It was his idea to start busing kids into Seton in the first place.

There's a knock on the office door, and I call out, "Come in!" I press Save and spin around.

School ended twenty minutes ago, and at this point, most of us are where we're gonna be for the afternoon. The people who go home have gone home. The people who have clubs are at their meetings. J's at practice. I assume it's Gary coming by to pick up one of the cameras to get pictures for the story he's working on about girls' soccer.

But it's Britt.

She's in high-waisted black leggings, a white T-shirt crop top, a black beanie, and Adidas sneakers. Her glow is just as powerful as it's always been—except I've never seen her in this office before in my life.

"Hey," she says, gently pushing the door closed before she starts walking toward me. "You busy?"

I shake my head. "Just reading. Are you okay? I thought you would be at practice . . ."

"Tuesdays and Thursdays, games on Fridays," she explains

easily, filling me in on the girls' field hockey schedule. She sits in one of the swivel chairs and peers over my shoulder. "What're you reading?"

For a second, I hesitate, but I figure everyone will read it soon enough. "This short story Gina-Melissa wrote . . . Do you know her? She's the girl I was talking to on Friday night when you . . . well. She sent me this story she wrote, and it's honestly amazing, so I'm gonna try to run it in the paper. She's an unbelievable writer."

"Well, you're an unbelievable writer, too," Britt reminds me. And it's not that I forgot, or that I don't think so (even though I'm not necessarily sure that I *do* think so), but Britt says it in this way that I don't even realize I need.

Best *is an adjective. We deserve to be nouns.*

The memory still makes me smile, and I tell her, "Thanks, but I can write articles. Essays. Fact-based stuff. Fiction is different. Making up an entire story and getting people to believe it . . . That's like . . ."

"A superpower?" Britt offers.

"Exactly." I laugh.

Britt gnaws her lip as she looks over my shoulder at the screen behind me, her eyes sliding from left to right as she swallows the lines. "I do know Gina-Melissa. She's a really cute girl. She used to date Dan Kiley on the football team before he graduated last year, right?"

"Yeah! That's her. I'm pretty sure they're still together."

Britt nods and takes a moment before she says, "I'm glad she has a superpower." She takes a deep breath and adds, "I'm also really glad you were around on Friday."

It was weird how it happened without either of us ever

expecting it to, but Britt and I hung out the whole rest of Kyle's party. We didn't talk any more about Parker or any of that, we just . . . talked.

I noticed today that she still wasn't with her friends in the hallway. And even though it isn't weird for people to miss lunch at Seton (there are always teachers hosting office hours), I also noticed she wasn't in the cafeteria today, sitting in my periphery with them like she has for years now.

"Me too," I tell her. She shouldn't have to be alone.

She takes a second, like she's deciding on something. And then she asks, "You wanna get out of here?"

We walk out the main entrance, passing the long window outside of Principal Mitchell's office on our right, and the wall full of trophies that Seton's won on the left—everything from debate competitions to cheerleading competitions to soccer tournaments. All the football team's conference championships glitter along the middle shelf, identical year after year. Twelve in total, one for each undefeated team. *I want two*, I can hear Parker say.

We push open the bright red doors, and the air outside is the kind of warm and moist that hurts to breathe when you're panting. I don't notice until now how gray the sky has gotten.

"You think J's gonna get wet today?" Britt asks, smiling a little.

I smile, too, and take a confirmatory deep breath of the damp air. "Yes." Then I groan and add, "Which would suck."

"He'll be fine. I don't think he'll melt. Not evil enough." She spreads her arms out, palm sides up, and holds her head back to sniff the air, her eyes closed for a second as we continue to walk. It's a more elaborate—more *Britt*—version of the breath I just took a second before. "Some of them might." She lets her arms fall. "But I think J's safe."

I can't help but wonder if that's a jab at Parker.

"I'm not too terrified about him melting," I answer. "We just have a really long ride home, and anytime he gets drenched at practice, we're both soaked by the time we get back."

"Right," she seems to realize, glancing at me. "You take a bus?"

I nod. "A shuttle that leaves at five every day. So, he doesn't really have time to shower before he gets on. Practice is supposed to end at four thirty, but they always go a little long." I stop myself, though, because this is Britt. *Britt MacDougal.* She's always with the team. "I mean, you know."

We walk a few steps farther when it hits me that we're heading toward her car. She drives a two-door, all-black Audi with an *S* for Seton decal in the back window that I've seen a million times. In this lot. At parties. The Monday when everything changed. It was always her with Michelle, Bianca, and Kelly, with the windows down and the music loud, stuffing bags of fast food into their mouths and whispering about stories that the rest of us would never hear.

I feel guilty about something I can't even explain, now that it's just her and me.

She goes to the driver's side, and I go to the passenger's. Our eyes meet over the roof of her car, a breeze pushing wisps of hair into her face, an affirmation of the storm that's on its way.

"How long is the ride?" she asks me.

"Like an hour. Or an hour and a half in traffic," I answer. "Which there almost always is."

And, as she watches me, I can't totally explain it—this enigma that is Britt—but she has a way of looking at you, and being with you, that makes you feel like you're the most important and interesting person in this world. It's the part of her that always made it so easy for me to chat with her through bathroom stalls or at a party where she saw me first. It feels so real, coming from her. And at the same time, like she could drift right back out of your life with the very next breeze.

"Shit, that's torture," she says, but it comes out like *I'm so incredibly sorry for your pain*. We climb into her car—this car I've never been inside—and she tosses her army-green satchel into the back seat as she starts the engine. "Maybe I could drive you guys? That way he can at least take a shower and dry off before."

I shake my head and promise, "You definitely can't drive us."

"I don't mind."

"I do. I really don't want you to do that for us. But . . . maybe you could drop me back off at Seton in time to catch the bus? That alone would be a huge help."

Britt sighs and shifts gears as she starts to back out of her parking spot. "Alright, well, if J gets pneumonia . . ."

I smile as I fasten in. "Can I ask you something?"

"I would ask if I need a lawyer present, but I'm probably smart enough to be my own." She shifts gears and starts to pull forward. "What's up?"

"Why are we using AC and seat warmers at the same time?"

She laughs, looking both ways as we turn out of the parking lot, and we pass a group of Seton girls on the grass, with their iPads and their laptops and their backpacks. "Well, Aly, because I happen to believe that life is made up of extremes. Hot and cold. Beautiful and shit. And if you encounter one extreme, like frigid AC, the most effective thing you can do is counteract it with the opposite extreme, like maximum seat warming. Balance by way of doing nothing isn't living. That's existing. And we're way too young to just exist."

We end up at this place called A Coffee Shop that I've never been to before, but it's only five minutes from campus, in the same parking lot as an Amazon Books and a Gymboree. Britt says it was started a few years ago by this guy who went to Seton, and then he went to Yale, and then he bitched about it, so his parents gave him the money to open up this shop instead.

"Do you drink coffee?" she asks as she pulls open the door and a bell jingles over our heads. Inside is the kind of cozy that makes me want a book and a blanket. Wooden floors, brick walls, a fireplace. People eating off of real plates with real silverware.

"I kind of hate coffee, to be honest . . ."

"Gross, me too. It tastes like pennies."

I smile to myself as we walk up to the counter, where there's no line and there's this display case of all the face-sized pastries you can order, shielded behind glass like jewelry. I look at the little cue cards propped in front with handwritten descriptions. Britt just orders.

"Hey, can I get two large apple ciders with extra caramel and two honey buns with extra icing, please? To go. Thanks."

Since she's ordered double everything, I realize one of the orders is for me.

"Thirty-eight seventeen," the barista tells her.

Panic completely devours my soul. As she unzips the little wallet on her key chain, I try to insist, "Britt, I really don't need food . . ."

But she doesn't even look up and tells me like I'm delusional, "Of course you need food. People die without food."

As she pays, I do the math in my head. I've basically just found myself owing a twenty-dollar debt for juice and sugar, which I could maybe pay back by the end of the month if I save up what I should be spending on my meal plan and J can get a little from his dad and call it gas money. He's for sure gonna call me out for spending that much money just to eat when the Dollar Menu exists, but it isn't just *to eat*. It's to eat *with Britt*.

"Can I pay you back when I get my allowance at the end of the month?" I ask. Not that I really get an allowance.

Her eyebrows come together, and she shakes her head as she leans against the counter to wait. "You don't have to pay me back."

"Britt—"

"Kind of like how I don't have to drive you home later, you know?" Her eyes gleam the way they do sometimes, whenever it's an argument she's going to win. A look I see her give the boys all the time. And even though I feel bad, and also kind of embarrassed, I'm more than willing to let her win today.

When I really think about it—Britt's world compared with mine—I guess I can accept that she probably should.

It starts to rain as we pull into Britt's long, uphill driveway. It's the kind of Seton house I'm used to, even though I've never seen hers. Stone with brick stairs and a little man-made pond out front. Huge.

We jog to her front door, using our cups and bags of honey buns as umbrellas that don't work. Britt lets us inside and flips on a light. It's chilly the way my house is when we get home after a few days at Grandma's house for Christmas, when Mom refuses to run the heat because we're not there. "My parents aren't home," she assures me, answering a question I never planned to ask.

"When do they get home?" I follow her up the steps. They're wide enough for me to hold my hands straight out at my sides and still not touch the banister or the wall.

"They don't," she answers, rounding the curve and starting up the second flight. "They travel all week, every week."

At the top of the stairs, she goes to the left, down a hardwood hallway. Even though I'm in Seton houses all the time, it's always for parties, when there are dozens of us here, when the playlist is blasting and the kitchen island is full of liquor that we girls never have to bring for ourselves. The lights aren't even on in Britt's house, and even though gray daylight is coming in through all the giant-on-purpose windows, it still feels *too* empty.

But Britt's room feels lived in, once we get there. She turns on the lights while I look around, and she does—what I assume is—her routine stuff: drops her school bag on the floor, plugs her phone into the charger. She says she'll be right back, and then closes the door behind her to her connected bathroom.

I'm still holding my raindrop-dotted paper bag in one hand and my drink in the other. She has plush white carpets and a lavender bed. There's a TV mounted on the wall over a desk with a MacBook on it. There's a snow globe on her nightstand that says *Niagara Falls* and a bunch of natural hair-care products—brands I've never used before and don't even know how to pronounce, like Aveda and Ouidad.

Above her nightstand, she has so many pictures—some framed, some not—of her and Michelle, and Kelly, and Bianca. Pictures of them all together, and pictures of just two or three of them, and ones that Britt isn't even in. She even has the clipping of Michelle's Who's Who article from *The Seton Story* on her wall—this series we run monthly that's like a fun interview-based feature on Seton's most interesting students. And I follow Britt on Instagram, so it isn't like I didn't already know that they take millions of pictures together. But I've never seen any of these before. These are the pictures of who they *are*, the life they've had for so long that belongs completely and entirely to them.

I wish every day that I could know what it's like to have girls like this.

But instead, it's just J and me. Our parents are best friends, and we're the only two people from our entire middle school who even got into Seton. Seton's only busing in twenty-two kids in the entire junior class. Most of them live at least thirty minutes away from us. And I'll admit—I did sort of have this stupid idea when I first got in that I'd come to Seton and meet *girls*. But it's hard when you live an hour away, and you don't have a car, and you don't have twenty dollars in spare change for a pastry, and you can't be at the coffee shop or the movies or the Galleria for pictures like these.

"This one's my favorite," Britt says softly, touching an unframed picture of Michelle and Kelly. I hadn't heard her come out of the bathroom. "It was when we all got super dressed up for prom sophomore year and then said fuck it and didn't even go." She hugs herself as she studies her wall.

"Have you talked to them at all?"

She shakes her head. And just the way she's looking at these pictures . . . I know that she loves them more than anything else.

And that's why this rumor doesn't make any sense.

She takes a deep breath and goes to her bed, grabbing the comforter and pulling it to the floor. She pushes her pillows onto the floor next. "You really like it here, huh?"

"Like it where?" I ask, going over to the place she's made for us on the floor.

"At Seton." She sits on her knees as she takes my bag from me and flattens both hers and mine into makeshift place mats for our honey buns. I sit in front of mine, across from her. "I mean, it takes a bus an hour to get you home. I don't even want to know how early that means you have to wake up in the morning. And I know Seton is a really good school. I get that. But you must really like it here, to leave your friends and your old school and deal with that drive every day. It's a lot to do for something you hate."

"I love it here," I tell her, and it's been that way from the second my and J's dads started taking us to the football games when we were kids, from the second J and I toured the school in eighth grade, from the second Principal Mitchell shook my hand.

She crosses her legs and picks up her honey bun and takes a huge bite. Chewing, she asks, "Do you ever think about how crazy it's gonna be next year, though?"

"What happens next year?"

"What happens next year?" She's talking to me like I'm a lunatic. "I mean, probably nothing too mind-blowing besides the fact that J is gonna be the next Varsity quarterback."

I laugh and insist, "I try not to think about it."

"Why not?"

I'm not sure how honest I want to be. It's not Britt—I actually believe Britt will sit here and talk to me about whatever it is that I say—it's me. I don't know if I want to admit how much more Seton football means for us—how it's not just some chance for J to be a permanent local legend, or to walk every year in the annual

Thanksgiving parade, or to be the only person who ever matters at career day. I don't know if I want to remind her that if J can keep playing like he has been and also go undefeated next year, he could actually get an athletic scholarship to a college that our parents would kill themselves trying to afford. I don't know if I want her to know that a part of me is nervous that J and I won't be able to do all the things that Parker and Levi and all the other Seton quarterbacks have been able to do when it comes to hosting parties or throwing in an extra hundred bucks on nights when the liquor runs out. Or remind her that J wouldn't just be the first Varsity quarterback who bused in every day, but also the first Black quarterback that Seton has ever had. And even though Britt and I, legs tucked under us on her comforter stuffed with duck feathers, have almost identical brown skin and hair that uses product, her products come in pretty bottles with unpronounceable names. It's not that I don't think she would talk to me about all those things for hours. It's that I don't want her to feel like she has to.

I don't want her to feel like we're different.

"I don't want to be a jinx," I tell her instead.

Thunder cracks outside, and it makes me jump. The sky beyond her window is as gray as her eyes.

She's watching me when I look back at her, and she seems to mean it when she says, "You're a sweet girl, Aly." Then she pulls her knees to her chest and starts gnawing on a chipped blue fingernail. "It's gonna be a really big deal, though. The Seton quarterback is the most powerful person in a twenty-mile radius. He's the most power-ful person in our entire world." She pulls her finger from her mouth and studies it analytically, still the prettiest, most captivating thing

I've ever seen, even as she dives back in for a hangnail. "You know what I'm starting to realize?"

Everyone at Seton is super smart, but Britt is irrefutably among the smartest. She tested in on three subjects—science, English, and history—which is practically unheard of. Last year, she got one of the best SAT scores in the state. My freshman year, there was a rumor that she got accepted to some accelerator program at Dartmouth, but she said no thanks, because she was smart enough to know she didn't feel like being *that* smart.

So, I ask, "What?" ready to hear her tell me anything.

"That the Seton football team is a lot like a corporation. I was reading about corporations the other day in my ethics book. And it was saying how corporations can legally be seen as an individual in a court of law. Like, as an actual fucking person. Which means that a corporation can be found guilty of crimes without a single person who *works* for the corporation being convicted of anything at all. And that's so insane to me, because *corporations aren't real.* I can't, like . . ." She reaches out and pinches my cheek. Not too hard. Just hard enough to feel. "I can't do that to a corporation. And I can't do that to the football team. I can do that *to the people* on the football team, but I can't do it to *the football team* because it's a concept, or a construct, or just like . . . this fucking idea we have, but it's not a real thing.

"Except they still feel corporation-big. And they still feel *so powerful.* And if they ever did anything bad . . . like court-of-law kind of bad . . . they'd be treated like a team. Not like a bunch of idiot guys but like a corporation. I just know it. I just . . . *feel it.*"

I don't know what to say. I agree with her, but I also feel like as long as we're talking in hypotheticals, it's okay to agree with her. They are a little bit like the center of the universe, but we aren't in court, we're at Seton. So maybe, at the end of the day, that's okay.

"I mean, think about it, Aly." She shifts and folds her legs under her, like it's easier to lay out the facts from her knees. "We even capitalize the word. *Varsity*. Like it's Apple or Spotify or . . . *Nike* or something."

"Well, it's in the Seton style guide," I explain.

She squints at me like I want to eat glue. "What the fuck is a *Seton style guide*?"

"It's how people like me or the yearbook staff or the main office . . . anyone who writes anything for Seton, really. It's how we know what it should look like. So we're all consistent. Like times are always written out and hyphenated. And *Varsity* always gets capitalized."

"*That's insane!* Aly. That is insane." She looks around her room like she's searching for a way to explain it. She gestures at nothing and tells me, "It isn't some royal title. It's just a word. Like *orange juice* or *yesterday* or *pina colada*." She shakes her head and softly insists, "They're just boys."

I don't want to make her upset. She has enough to be upset about. So I promise like it's no big deal, "Every publication has a style guide."

She shakes her head and shifts again—antsy, almost. She pulls her knees back to her chest. "It's weird, Aly. All of it. Seriously. They're a corporation, and we capitalize them like they are, and we worship them like they are, and Parker is the CEO." She reaches for her drink on her nightstand. "Parker *is* responsible, and Parker *is* in charge, according to every single ounce of logic and reality that exists on planet Earth. But not in corporation land. And I think that's where we are. And I used to like it here, too. I really, really fucking did. But now . . . now I think I hate it." Her eyes are glassy as she forces herself to swallow and stares at me over her kneecaps.

I've never seen Britt so sad about anything before. And she's still in her beanie and her crop top and her sneakers, so every other thing about her is still *so Britt*. But she's looking at me like she hopes I see it. Like she hopes I just see *her*. "What happened between you and Parker?" I ask.

She's about to say something that matters, I can feel it. In this room where her girlfriends should be instead of me, where she's probably texted back and forth with Parker a million times before making plans, I can feel that she's more ready now than she was on Kyle's bathroom floor.

But not ready enough.

She shakes her head and rubs her eyes and puts her drink back on her nightstand. "You know what we should do?"

"What should we do?"

"We should try and name as many girls as we can who've gone to Seton."

My nose wrinkles, and I smile even though I think she's crazy. *"Why?"*

And her answer is so simple that I feel bad that I even had to ask. "Because they deserve to be remembered."

She lies back on her fluffy white rug, facing the ceiling. She pats the spot next to her, and I lie down, too. It doesn't seem real, to be lying on the softest carpet I've ever felt, next to Britt, when thirty-five minutes ago I was sitting alone in the newspaper office. But here I am, and I could stay here for hours.

"Cassie Barnes . . ." Britt starts.

"Kiera Gregory . . ." *The Seton Story* editor before I was.

And we go on like that for longer than I even know, sipping our expensive drinks and eating our million-dollar honey buns, until we're both scratching our minds for names that we'd almost forgotten.

What it was.

Levi Jackson sat on the sideline bench, praying to a God his mom had taught him to believe in—in the fair-weather way that ultimately means nothing. Church on Christmas Eve and Easter. Grace at Thanksgiving dinner. The antique Bible on display in the library along with all the other collector's edition classics that existed to be owned but not touched. The entire Jackson family believed in divinity the same way they believed in 911 or Grandma and Grandpa's money—always there when times got bad, but otherwise not generally top of mind.

But right now, things were bad, and Levi prayed like they were. He leaned forward on his knees in his grass-stained uniform, his eye-black smeared down his cheeks like mascara tears, his helmet on the ground between his feet, and watched the field.

There were less than two minutes left in the game. They'd won three times already this season without needing any help. But this game was different. That's why Levi decided it was finally time for him to negotiate his first deal. He'd been paying attention to St. Mary's over their past few games and felt the bruises he would have before he even had them, every time he watched their defense play. Offenses couldn't drive past the fifty-yard line. Every running play got stuffed at the line. The opposing QB was on his ass almost the entire game. They were forcing fumbles and stripping the ball and knocking down passes every other play.

So, Levi would have to make a deal. Eventually, he knew he would.

He decided to go after their kicker.

All his boys on the team told him it was the wrong strategy. They told him to negotiate with that huge cornerback they had, or one of the defensive tackles. But Levi didn't think that was safe enough, wasn't sure enough about the kind of talent they had on the bench, and who they might be able to bring in instead if one of those guys faked an injury or started fucking up. He just knew one thing for sure: a team that put that much work into their defense wasn't about to lose it all if one of their guys went down.

Levi had been paying attention to their kicker for the past couple of weeks. He had a leg that was unbelievable. He was hitting field goals from the forty-yard line. And that was gonna be Seton's downfall when they played St. Mary's that year; Levi knew it. Because Seton had a good defense, too. A great defense, really. Which meant this was just gonna turn into a game of punts kicked deep, offenses getting stood up at midfield, and kickers trying to put three points on the board when they could.

And Levi's kicker wasn't gonna hit much if they couldn't get him to at least the twenty-five.

So, Levi decided to go for St. Mary's kicker instead.

His team said not to, but—ultimately—the decision was his. The way this whole thing was set up, there had to be one decision maker. One veto power. One person who was responsible for whether it did work or it didn't.

And for the past eleven years, it had worked every single time.

The St. Mary's kicker was named Alex. Levi invited him over after practice on Thursday, and they met in Levi's basement. He gave the speech he was supposed to, the one that would remind Alex that regular season wins don't matter for a school like St. Mary's, a school that was good enough to take a loss or two and still make it into the playoffs, where they'd all be back at zero. The speech assured Alex that Levi still understood, though: Alex was an athlete just like the rest of them, and of course he wanted to win. Of course he wasn't about to just hand over the game out of the goodness of his heart. And that's when Levi showed him what he could offer.

It was kind of surreal, seeing the moment when Alex started to get it. When he smiled and realized that this was how Seton had been doing it; when he shook his head to himself like he should have known—or maybe a part of him always had known—that something was going on. He laughed and rubbed his head and said, "*Wow.*"

But he slapped Levi's hand and agreed, and Levi told him the terms, how he couldn't tell anyone, how he couldn't show anyone, and had him sign on the dotted line before he handed him his flash drive.

And now it was Saturday, and Levi sat there on his team's bench, with his brothers on Varsity to his right and left, the JV team on the bleacher behind them. There were less than two minutes left, and the game was 8-6 Seton, and the St. Mary's offense had the ball. It was fourth and three, and they were on the thirty-nine-yard line, and they'd brought Alex out to kick, and he'd been making kicks like this all season long.

The crowd behind Levi was so loud that he could feel it through the ground. A thousand people. He only really knew a handful of them, but every one of them knew him, knew his name and screamed it, chanted it, whooped it anytime he jogged back out onto the field.

And Levi watched the field with them, for them, with his arms on his knees, cracking his knuckles. There was nothing worse he could think of than losing this game and facing that crowd who knew him when he didn't even know who most of them were, and being their quarterback for the first loss they'd seen in eleven seasons. There was nothing worse than facing his team and being the first quarterback in eleven years who couldn't get this done for them. Even death would be better. At least young people always die as heroes.

Coach had his hands in his pockets, standing forty feet away from the bench, the kind of solemn he got right before he lost his shit. He'd told their guys to watch out for the fake, but St. Mary's wasn't gonna fake. Alex's leg was the surest thing they had.

Next to Levi, his teammates glanced over their shoulders at their classmates, cheering and screaming and wanting this. Levi felt his team look at him, and he didn't know what they were thinking—if they were hating him or feeling bad for him, if they'd disown him if all this didn't end the right way.

No one had ever told Levi what happened if someone reneged on the deal.

He watched as Alex's teammates slapped him on the back, he watched as the teams lined up. He watched that perfect snap, that perfect hold, his team get stood up for the millionth damn time at the line. He watched Alex take his effortless steps and swing his leg into the ball.

Levi dropped his neck and rubbed the back of his head. He should have targeted that giant-ass cornerback they had.

"He hooked it!" someone said.

Levi's head shot up.

He was looking at the field again just in time to see the refs waving their arms in front of them, crossing one over the other—*no good*. Just in time to see Alex's teammates patting his shoulder as they walked off the field. Just in time for the crowd behind him to erupt.

The game wasn't over and they all knew it, but his Varsity team reached out to slap his hand, smiled, and told him to breathe. His running back grinned: *fly, baby, fly!*

Coach yelled at them to get back out on the field. He slapped their helmets as the offense jogged out and gripped the defense's shoulders as they jogged back in, losing his mind as he ordered them to stay focused. In the stands, every single person was on their feet, arms wide at their sides, flapping them in slow, smooth synchronization, like the Eagles that they were.

This was Levi's thirty-third game playing for Seton. He'd seen magic on this field—both authentic and negotiated—more times than he could count. And it always felt big, every time it happened. The crowd always treated Seton football like it was their own personal miracle. It was addictive, and Levi could feel himself getting drunk off of it in a way he never had before. Because it's one thing to witness magic. It's another thing when you're the magician.

Levi pointed up and looked toward the sky, wagging his finger and thanking God as he jogged the rest of the way into the huddle. Every single one of those guys knew what he'd just done, knew what he'd just proved, knew how much this meant. That they had their own Greg Patterson, or Billy Hopper, or Cooper Adams now.

"If anyone cries, I'm kicking your ass." Levi smiled, their heads bowed with their arms around each other's shoulders. Every one of them giddy-laughed like schoolgirls, and then Levi called the next play.

Two minutes of game-play later, Seton won 11–6.

It's nice—isn't it?—how God tends to show up for boys like Levi.

At eight o'clock that night, Parker walked through Brandt Taylor's foyer, the warm outside air and buzz of the crickets and cicadas replaced with Nest AC and the football team playlist. The girls had been with him a minute ago—Michelle, Britt, Bianca, and Kelly—but they were already gone, off causing trouble somewhere.

Parker smiled and nodded at his friends as he passed, promising to be back when they tried to stop him to talk. He had a bottle of vodka in his hand that he had to drop off on Brandt's kitchen island as his contribution for the night, and he also had to find Levi. Then he could make his rounds, go back and hang out with all the people he'd told he would. But first things first. It was an order-of-operations kind of thing.

He set the bottle on Brandt's white kitchen island, the size of a king bed. Parker slid his hands into the pockets of his Seton sweatpants and surveyed what his team had brought so far that night. He'd come back for his drink once he found Levi.

Order of operations.

He walked easily through the kitchen, this kitchen he'd been in enough times before to know which side of the two-sided fridge was the freezer, to know that the trash can was hidden in that cabinet under the basin sink, to know Brandt's mom was some kind of conservationist and didn't believe in paper towels. Brandt was on Varsity, and the guys on the team shared their houses with each other the same way they shared everything else. Weed. Test answers. Their girls.

Parker found Levi sitting on a couch in the main living room, with guys on his left and his right, some of the senior girls sitting on the floor on the other side of the coffee table while they played Circle of Death. Parker walked up behind the couch and put his hands on Levi's shoulders, squeezing them in a quick massage.

Levi didn't have to look up when he slapped one of Parker's hands with his own. "What's up, my man?"

"Just stopping by to give credit where credit's due," Parker said. "You want to grab a drink?"

Levi stood up, told one of the guys to take his turn for him, told the girls he'd be back. Then he walked with Parker back toward the kitchen.

Parker smiled as they went, in their matching Seton football sweats.

"You sore, dude?" Parker asked. Levi was walking with a little limp.

Levi laughed to himself, shaking his head. "That St. Mary's defense, dude . . ."

"Dude!" Parker laughed, bumping Levi with his forearm, the way boys like to bump each other around, treat each other like punching bags. And Levi laughed and crossed his arms over his chest and hunched over and took it. "You fucking perfected that shit today. Fucking Spielberg couldn't have written it better."

They reached Brandt's island—they were the only ones in the kitchen—while their classmates' voices carried through the open doorways and a new song played from their playlist. Bob Marley. "No Woman, No Cry."

"What're you drinking tonight?" Parker asked as Levi sat on one of the stools on the other side of the island.

"I'll do a tequila grapefruit."

"Cool, cool," Parker said, reaching into the bag of red plastic cups. He went to the refrigerator and opened the freezer door. He filled the cup with ice. "Yo, Kelly's here. Brought her myself."

Levi smiled, arms resting on the surface of the granite countertop. "Are you sharing that news for any particular reason?"

Parker smirked to himself, uncorking the tequila, pouring too much of it over the ice. "Just letting you know who made it tonight."

But Parker, just like everyone else, knew that Kelly and Levi had made out last weekend. He'd heard it from Levi, but he'd heard it ten times more than that from the girls. Michelle, Britt, Bianca, Kelly. The way they could talk about stuff like he wasn't even there sometimes, because they were so used to him *always* being there.

"Alright, well, noted," Levi said. "Hey, you had a good game today, too, man. Seriously. They're still training those JV guys to be one hell of a defense next year. That wasn't an easy match-up for your guys today."

Parker finished pouring the grapefruit juice into the cup and put the carton back into the refrigerator. He had played well. He always did. His JV team won 20–14, and he'd rushed both times at the two-yard line for the touchdowns. But the JV games weren't what mattered. That's why they didn't negotiate in order to win them.

"You made a deal with the kicker, didn't you?" Parker asked. He kept his voice low because he shouldn't be saying it. If he were anybody else, he wouldn't know anything about the deals and the

flash drives for another ten months, when it was the summer before his Varsity year, and Levi would pull him aside—quarterback to
quarterback—to let him in on the secret that Varsity had kept for
the past eleven years. And even though, for the most part, Parker
and Levi still respected that process, and Parker didn't know *exactly*
how things worked, *exactly* who had what, *exactly* what they had
in their arsenal, they both knew that he knew that the team made
deals. What they used to bargain with. He was the only guy Seton
ever had who knew it before his senior year.

Parker handed Levi his drink, and Levi took it while he left his
free arm folded on the island. He nodded as he took a sip. "Scariest
decision I ever made in my life."

Parker leaned on the island across from him and looked him in
the eyes. "You can't play when you're scared."

"You'll get scared, too, when it's real. It'll hit you."

But Parker always talked to Levi about how sure he was that it
wouldn't, the same way he was sure that his dad could always get
him out of any real trouble, or that his mom might yell but she'd
never actually follow through on any of her threats. The thing
was, Parker appreciated structure. He liked to know who was boss
and what that meant for everybody else. And right now, Levi was
the boss. And Parker respected Levi more than he respected most
other people in the world. So, he would find him first at every
party. He'd pull him aside to talk football. He'd make him a drink.
He'd ask the questions he could get away with. He'd listen when
Levi was willing to talk, and he'd remember what Levi said so that
he could learn.

But it was still different, sometimes—complicated. Because at the end of the day, Levi was like a president right now. Elected. In power for a set amount of time.

But when it was Parker's turn next year, he would be a king. Boss by birthright. The royal blood running through his veins.

It was one of the many, many perks of being Cooper Adams's little brother.

What it is.

<u>September 15, 2019</u>

There's a golf course not too far from Seton that J and I pass every time we're on our way home from a party. It's on the side of town where most of the Seton-proper homes are, a turn off one of the main roads that leads back to their flawless neighborhoods. At night, the stone sign that's illuminated by lights along the ground reads *Nappahawnick*.

It's a Sunday, and Britt and I have been texting since we both woke up this morning, a recent habit that hasn't lasted exactly long enough to be considered normal. But it's our new normal, at least, over the course of the two weeks that Britt and her friends have spent not speaking, and even though I'm still rooting so hard for the four of them to be okay, there's a part of me that does feel lucky to have her here with me.

Maybe because being a girlsfriend (Britt's term, so it never, ever gets confused with the less important role of being a *girlfriend*) comes so naturally for her. I mean, she's been one forever. But she's also super restless, like a puppy that needs more walks. And I don't know if that's new, because her three biggest distractors are presently MIA—or if she's just untamable.

It's probably the former, but it's kind of fun to imagine it's the latter.

She always wants to be with people, or talking to people, or up to something. She calls me sometimes in the middle of a text chain that never even stopped to ask me things like, *"What's the weekend number for Seton laptop support?"* and *"Is it stupid to go to Target for avocados?"* and, today, *"Do you guys want to go to Nappahawnick?"*

J's head is on my stomach and he has one arm around my waist as we lie on my twin-sized bed. We'd been looking at flash cards for the history test we have on Monday, with the door closed, because our parents are less suspicious about it when we tell them that we're studying.

He doesn't look up, but he nods easily, so I know he's down.

"Of course," I agree.

J and I have never been to Nappahawnick. It's private but the backdrop to so many of the Seton stories that we don't live close enough to be a part of, so I'm excited to finally see it. To see if it's really like the setting of *The Princess Bride*, which of course it's not, but it's all I've ever been able to picture when people at school say things like:

Last night when we grabbed dinner on the green at Nappa-hawnick . . .

That day when nothing was going on and we took the boat out on Nappahawnick . . .

Remember that time we managed to get a round in at Nappahawnick right before the tornado sirens started blaring?

J's making the turn past the sign in just under an hour after we leave my house. It's a little after four, and he's been yawning all day like he always is on Sundays after Saturday football games and Saturday night parties to celebrate another Seton win. We have the windows down now that the AC in the Ford only seems to really work at nighttime, and another *Rent* song just popped up on the shuffle as J takes an open spot in the first parking lot we come to, just like Britt told us to do when we said we'd see her soon.

I wasn't sure what to wear to Nappahawnick, so I just kept on what I was already wearing, because I noticed J looking at me with the same level of interest as a little kid examining worm guts when I jumped off the bed and started digging through my drawers. I'm just in a pair of jean shorts and a purple tank top; J is in khaki shorts and a white T-shirt and a backward Seton cap. And I guess it's okay, since Britt just has on an oversized army-green sweatshirt, with shorts that are almost too small to notice underneath. Her hair is in a ponytail, and she's wearing real Ray-Bans.

She bounces up to my open window as J turns off the car. "I'll drive us the rest of the way," she says.

It's a half mile farther before she pulls up to a guard post where a boy about our age takes a membership card from her. He glances at it so fast that it could've been a Baskin-Robbins loyalty card, and then waves her through.

The lot we park in with Britt is more crowded than the one where J and I left the Ford and is filled with foreign cars like hers. They're pulling in and pulling out, while little kids run ahead of their parents toward the main lodge in bathing suits and floaties and men walk through the lot with their golf clubs slung over their shoulders.

Britt goes to her trunk and announces as she shows us what's inside, "I ordered the fuck out of KFC just now."

There are wooden signs posted everywhere—*this way to the golf courses, this way to the kayaks, this way to the pool*—and as we start to walk, more than one person recognizes J from the team, rich white guys in polos clapping him on the shoulder with big grins on their faces and voices that boom as they congratulate him on the season so far. We don't know a single one of them and none of them feel the need to introduce themselves, but J thanks them anyway.

Britt takes us down a path that no one else is on. It starts out as a sidewalk, turns into gravel, and then becomes mostly dirt as we weave through trees and J carries the bags full of whatever Britt brought. They've been talking about *Ozark* for most of the trek, but I don't watch it.

We end up on the side of the lake opposite the water sports, where there's a small stretch of sand along the water before it turns back into grass and then back into woods. It's quiet—a few people jogging past every now and then and a lady playing fetch with her dog in the water, but that's all.

Britt pulls a blanket from one of the bags J was carrying and thanks him again for bringing this stuff down for us. She spreads it out and digs into the second bag to reveal what she got. A bucket of chicken. A bucket of tenders. Every dipping sauce that exists under the sun. Fries, macaroni, and mashed potatoes times three. Cookies that I didn't even know KFC made.

J's eyes legitimately twinkle as he asks, "Yo, are you trying to seduce us?"

Britt smiles, sitting on her knees, her sunglasses on top of her head, squinting against the sun as she looks up at him. "Is it working?" she coyly asks.

We try to offer her money, but she won't let us.

It's obvious she's done this a million times, the way she knew every obscure path to take just to get to this exact spot. But never with us. With the girls, I'm sure. Parker, too, and some of the guys on the team. Maybe more people from Seton-proper because it *is* just that easy when it's a call or a text and a five-minute drive. Nappahawnick has to have been the backdrop for so many of her stories, too, and I can't help but wonder what those are and how badly she misses them.

"Do you think you'll stay here forever?" she asks. She reaches for another tender.

"Well, we're not really from here anyways," J reminds her.

Britt shakes her head, pushes her hair out of her mouth, evaluates her chicken before she takes the next bite. "That's shit. You're still Seton. You still got treated like you were management when you walked in here today. Nobody cares where you're from." It's more than a compliment. It's a proclamation.

"Nah, I know, I know. We're all family, I'm not saying that's not it at all. But we'd have to get here in the first place in order to stay here." J's always been so much better at this part than me, talking about where we're *actually* from, reminding the guys on the team when they start debating whether Denver or Salt Lake has the best skiing that the only skiing he's doing is that game at Chuck E. Cheese. And they laugh and love him anyway.

Britt nods. "Are you trying to get here?"

J watches me as the sky over the lake turns a little more orange with the setting sun. "I mean, it's great over here."

"I love it," I agree.

"And our families are only an hour away," he continues.

"Close enough but far enough," I explain to Britt.

"I mean, I could see something like this being the goal," J concludes. "A lot has to happen first."

"Like what?" Britt asks. She pushes the bucket of chicken closer to him with her foot like she's reminding him to have more.

"Well." He takes another leg. "Hopefully, we have a good season next year, I can get some money to go to a good school, have four good years there and get drafted. Not get injured."

"So, you want to go pro?" she asks.

"I have to go pro." It's always like he gets ten years older instantly, the second he starts talking about this stuff. It's never in the flashy lights kind of way, limos and magazine covers and gold chains dripping from his neck. But more of a survival kind of thing. "Me and Aly's families . . . we're really close. We're gonna be together forever, and I'm an only child, but Alz has a little brother, and we don't have a bunch of family money sitting around or anything like that. Aly has this whole journalism thing going on, and I love that, and I want her to be able to do that a hundred percent. A *thousand percent.* But that's not gonna change stuff for us. Like, the money she'd make doing that isn't gonna get our parents a bigger house or get Cory through school, or even get *her* through school." J peeks at me, but we've talked about all of this stuff before. He thinks about it ten times more than he says it out loud. And we may never end up in Seton-proper, but he wants us to end up somewhere like it.

Me too.

"But football can." Britt fills in the part he doesn't say. "So, you want it more than anything, I bet."

J thinks about it for a second and then he agrees, "I want it more than anything."

"I mean, the crazy part is that it's not crazy," Britt says, leaning back on her elbows, stretching her smooth legs out in front of her. "We have athletes that go pro. Like Caroline Schaeffer? She's playing professional soccer. And Angela Robinson? She got that sick ride to UConn and now she's in the WNBA." Britt sticks her finger in the sand, absently watching as she draws a circle. I wonder if J even knows those names. I didn't. Not until the day we lay on her rug and remembered the girls. "But I guess maybe it *is* crazy how soon that whole journey starts for you. It's kind of starting now. An undefeated season for you next year would be the beginning of everything."

J makes me have a bite of his chicken because he loves to torture me when I'm full. "No pressure, huh?"

Britt keeps drawing in the sand. "It's a shit ton of pressure," she whispers.

J sighs a little, unimpressed with the tiny bite I had of his chicken leg and taking it back for himself. "Yeah, speaking of pressure . . . Parker is not playing around about States this year. He tries to fire us up about it every time we're in the locker room. Or at practice. Or anywhere. And if we get there, it'll be wild." He rubs his head with his free hand. "But then I'll have to figure out how the hell to get us there again."

I hug myself. J's never admitted that to me before, and I know it's the way that Britt can suck words out of you like a vacuum that gets him to say it now. But I realize how right he is, how much we love to win, how addicted we'd get to States if we actually get to have it this year. I can't even imagine what Seton would do. Probably declare a day off to celebrate. Erect a life-size statue of Parker on the lawn. And expect us to win it all again next year, too. I scoot closer and take a bigger bite of his chicken this time, in the hopes that it'll at least make him smile.

It feels like Britt gets it, too—how big States would be—by the way she's looking at J instead of at her circles. She squints a little. "You know you're better than him, right?"

A lot of people whisper it, but we never say it too loud. It's not about J yet; it's not his year. But they love his speed. They love how he can slip away from sacks and gain a few more yards. How much more accurate his passes have gotten since freshman year. But J reminds me all the time—quarterback is just what he needs at Seton to get enough game time, to get recruiters to care. He doesn't need it forever and says he probably won't be able to have it forever anyway. Some college team will turn him into a running back or a wide receiver, but he couldn't care less, as long as he's there and as long as it's free.

J watches her back. All of her Britt-ness swirling around him for a second that he can't immediately pull himself out of. But then he does. He would never agree with that statement. Not out loud, even if it does make me feel a little bit better about J having to follow a potentially State-winning performance from Parker this year. So, instead, he asks, "What's going on with you two?"

There's a part of us that already knows, because Britt hasn't been coming to the parties, and she hasn't been sitting with us at lunch, and Michelle looks sick every day. But there's a part of J that for sure knows more than that, because of Seton football, because he spends time with Parker without the rest of us every single day, because they've definitely talked about it. J isn't asking right now like a narc, because he isn't one. You can trust J more than you can trust anyone else in the world. But that same thing he has that makes it easy for him to remind people where we're really from also makes it hard for him to completely ignore reality.

"Parker and me? We haven't talked," Britt says. "We won't, until I say something for him that I'm not willing to say." She sighs. "And it sucks, you know? Because I still kind of believe that we really used to matter to each other."

J wets his lips, like he's getting ready to say more, but J's not a girl, and I'm the one who's seen Britt sad over the past couple of weeks after years of never seeing her sad once. So, before J can talk, I cut in and promise, "You did. You still do."

Because that's all she really needs to hear right now.

We stay until it's dark outside, and the full moon on its own would probably be bright enough for us to see, but there are still lights along the sand that start to pop on. Britt says that Nappahawnick closes at ten on Sundays, and that she knows J and I will probably want to start heading home before that anyway. But even once she says it, none of us moves. J leans back on his hands and nudges me with his foot and tells me to let him know when I'm ready.

He eventually dozes off next to me on the blanket, the same way he would have by now if we were still home in my bed. We need to leave soon, but I love how simple and easy and perfect this day is so much that I'm resisting it like a little girl who won't go to bed so Christmas Day doesn't have to end. I almost want to ask Britt if she'd invite us back here again, or tell her that J could always drop me off on a weekend and then go hang out with some of the guys on the team, but it's so weird to practically beg her for another date, and maybe it's not even fair to. She had a whole life here that had nothing to do with me until two weeks ago, and that life could be back any second. And she should be able to reserve the right to go back to that life as soon as it's available, because it was perfect.

She says I should at least touch the water before we go, so we leave J sleeping on the blanket with the carnage from our KFC feast and walk up to the edge of the lake. She slides out of her sneakers and so do I, and we step onto the damp sand—hard like a shell on top and velvet once my toes break through. I ask if she ever swims here in the summer, and she smiles at the memory as she tells me how they used to split the summer between the Nappahawnick pool and the lake, because Bianca preferred the pool and Michelle loved the lake and Kelly didn't really care as long as she wasn't wearing a white bathing suit. I ask her which she preferred—lakes or pools—and it's almost like the thought never crossed her mind.

The bridge of her nose wrinkles up a little bit as she looks out over the water and admits, "Whichever made them happy."

We walk out farther, until the water is up to our knees, and all the stringy lake stuff is under my feet, and the water is decidedly chilly, and it kind of creeps me out now that the water is as dark as the sky. But Britt is unfazed, so I decide to be, too.

"You know, I've never heard a boy and girl say they're gonna be together forever and believe them until today," she tells me.

I hug myself. "It almost already feels like forever, honestly. We've lived across the street from each other our whole lives, and our parents are best friends. Sometimes it's kind of like . . . Do you ever think about how what isn't can tell you what is?"

Britt looks at me, eyes twinkling. "I have no idea what that means, but I'm already very into this conversation."

I laugh, struggling through a logic I've never spoken to anyone else before. "It's sort of like . . . J and I know what won't happen. We won't ever have parents who aren't best friends. We won't ever not love each other. We won't ever not have these lives that are so mixed up with each other that we couldn't untangle them even if we wanted to. So, in a way, that kind of just leads us to what *will* be. You know? If we're never apart, then we're always together."

"You've deductively reasoned your way into your destined future." She smiles.

I do, too. "I guess that's pretty much exactly what it is."

"So, what happens when it's time for you to go to college, too?"

"What do you mean?"

"Well, everything we talked about today . . . J has a master plan of an undefeated season next year and then a football scholarship and then the pros." She lets her fingers skim the top of the water. "And once he hits the pros, I get how that helps all of you . . . Rising tides lift all boats, right? But you still have to go to college in the meantime. How do *you* go to college?"

"Like pay for it, you mean?"

"Sorry if that's completely none of my business, I just . . ." She glances over her shoulder, back at the beach where J's still asleep. "I sat there listening to this magical plan for J, and I just didn't totally get the magical part for you."

No one's ever asked me that before, especially when it comes to the Seton kids who don't think about money ever. Usually J starts talking about the future, and the whole Seton quarterback thing immediately hypnotizes anyone who's listening. J and I have talked about how he thinks my parents could probably take out loans and then he could use his football money to pay them back when we graduate, or maybe his parents can help if they don't have to worry about his tuition. But that's the muddy part of the plan for now. The part that pertains to me.

"I'm honestly not really sure," I admit. "My mom works at the hospital by our house and has been picking up more shifts . . . My dad's been working longer hours, too, and I know I'm why. They don't like to talk to me about it, though. I think it'll be really hard for a while. I don't know if I'm going to be able to just end up where J does when he's there on a full ride. I don't know if maybe I'm gonna have to take a gap year and work for a while, or . . ." Thinking about it puts a knot in my throat, all the immediate pieces of this puzzle that J hasn't planned for. That I don't know the answers to.

"You know you can do it without J, don't you?"

I look at her, and she gazes at the water in front of us, causing little ripples as she slides her foot along the bottom of the lake.

"I know that probably sounds like shit coming from me," she goes on. "You're probably like, yeah, that's really fucking easy for you to say in your stupid big house with your dumb car. And I get that. I don't want you to think I don't get that. I get that I don't really know exactly what it would mean to have to figure out the financial burden of college, or even life, really. So, I don't want you to think I'm saying this like some asshole rich kid with no appreciation of how hard it can be. Because that's not what I mean." She takes a deep breath and stares out at the night as she tries to decide what she *does* mean. "It's just that . . . you're an *amazing* girl, Aly. You've been so sweet to me with no good reason to be at all. Maybe J is about to be Varsity quarterback, but you're editor of an actual *newspaper*. As a *junior*. And that's big, too. Bigger than football. I know at Seton you'd never believe it, but it's true. At least, I think it is.

"And so I mean you can do it without J because you're *individually* amazing. And you would figure it out. And you would be okay or even better than okay, honestly, even if J didn't exist. Even if J never existed in the first place. So, that's all I really mean. I hope you don't hate me because I said it out loud."

I'm so relieved it's dark and she's avoiding eye contact, because the knot in my throat has started to tug at the little strings behind my eyes—these tears that are a mash-up of my fears about the future and Britt's ability to see them, and acknowledge them, for the first time anyone ever really has. "I only hate you for making me eat seventeen pounds of fried chicken today," I manage to say without my voice tripping.

And that makes her laugh, her head facing the sky as the moon shines down on her like a spotlight, her thick hair in its long ponytail stretching down her back. She drags her fingers across the top of the water and splashes me as I laugh and block it as best as I can. "That's not a reason to hate me," she insists. "That's a reason to thank God I'm alive."

What it is.

"I feel like maybe this is empty," I announce as J pulls up to Spence's house on Friday night. He parks along the curb at the bottom of his driveway.

J glances at where I'm tapping: the Glade air freshener that clips to the vents above the radio.

I say *maybe this is empty*, but I mean *definitely*, because I've been getting whiffs from the back seat of J's post-practice BO mixed with grass ever since we hit the parkway.

"You think?" he asks, watching the mirror on my side as he creeps backward, getting closer to the curb.

"Yeah. I don't smell a summer breeze anymore."

"You want to stop at Walgreens on our way back?"

"Sure," I agree, like tonight is fine or tomorrow is fine or next week is fine, or whatever. Even though it definitely has to be tonight.

"Works for me," he says, cutting the engine and unfastening his seat belt as I unfasten mine, too. I start to open my door, but then he says, "Hey, come here."

I take my hand off the door and turn back to face him, and he slides his hand behind my neck and leans across the brake and puts his mouth on mine. J and I have been kissing since the summer before we started at Seton, but there are still times when he does it—like when we finally have one of our houses to ourselves, and now—that make my stomach flip upside down and stay that way.

When his mouth lets go of mine, I open my eyes and smile at him, his hand still rubbing the back of my neck in the quiet car. "Why?" I ask. Because we aren't celebrating a house to ourselves, and we don't have time right now to finish anything.

"Because why wouldn't I love you a little more each time you shamelessly tell me I smell like shit?"

I laugh as he hops out of the car, taking his paper bag contribution for the night by the neck of the bottle. I open my door while he slowly starts his walk toward Spence's, and I insist, "I never said you smell like shit!"

He turns his head, and the corners of his mouth point toward the ground as he nods, the whole thing emanating this extra-strong *Sure, sure, whatever you say* vibe that he's not saying out loud.

I slam my car door shut behind me and run to catch up with him, banging my shoulder into his back. He laughs as he wraps his arm around me, and I insist again, "I didn't say you smell like shit."

"Okay, Alz."

"I said *your stuff* smells like shit—"

"So much better," he says, putting me in a fake headlock and kissing me on top of the head.

I laugh the whole way up Spence's brick stairs.

At the top of the steps, Nic Sanches is already sitting in one of the foldable seats at that night's collapsible table, in jeans and a Seton Girls sweatshirt. There's an open chair next to him, and tonight, it's gonna be J's.

Nic smiles when he sees us, the patio glowing underneath the front light. "Bro."

"What's good, my man," J answers as they slap hands. The tree behind them flickers with lightning bugs like a string of lights set on random.

"Alyson Jacobs," Nic says next, wrapping an arm around my shoulders and squeezing. "Why do they write it like that? *Alyson Jacobs*?"

J smiles as he rounds the table toward the empty chair. "You mean in the paper?" J easily assumes, because the whole team speaks the same language.

"Yeah," Nic answers, like he's been thinking about it for a while. He repeats, all proper sounding, "*Alyson Jacobs*."

"Because that's my *name*, Nic."

"Nah, maybe that's your editor name. You're Aly to me." He offers me the pen. "Autograph?"

I reach for the girls' sign-in sheet. "What happens if I sign it Alyson Jacobs?"

"I'll just have to vouch for you when the guys ask who the hell that is," Nic answers.

I laugh and set the pen down on top of the sheet after I scribble my name. "Kind of you." I reach for J's paper bag as I ask, "Want me to take this in?"

"Wanna take me in, too?" a voice asks from behind.

I jump just before Britt rests her chin on my shoulder and wriggles her fingers into my side. I laugh because I'm ticklish.

I'm so glad she's here that I swing my arms around her neck and squeeze so hard she wheezes in my ear. I've been trying to talk her into coming to another party for weeks now, and this morning was the first time she wasn't completely against it.

Still. It's Britt, and there was always a chance she wouldn't show up until the moment she officially showed up.

"Hey, Britt." J smiles, wrapping his arms around her shoulders next, giving her a hug. I take his paper bag from him while his hands are behind her back.

Nic slides his sheet of paper toward her and says, "I feel like I haven't seen you out with us in forever."

"Is that why I heard you were crying in the boys' bathroom the other day?" Britt quips.

He smiles and requests, "Signature, gorgeous?"

She glosses her front teeth with her tongue as she reaches for the pen and uncaps it. Her gaze skims the names that are already on the girls' list, and then she leans over to add her own. "Hey, Nic?" she says, not looking up from the paper.

"Yeah?"

"Do me a favor and stop staring at my tits, will you?"

I don't mean to laugh, and J rubs his head awkwardly as he takes his seat for the night next to Nic. The highest part of Nic's cheeks— the meaty part right below his eyes—starts to go red.

"Besides," she says, setting her pen down on the clipboard and sliding it back over to him. She rests her hands on the surface of the table, which, ironically, makes her boobs look even bigger in her fitted gray minidress. "I have a question for you."

Nic forces himself to keep his eyes on her face. "What's that?"

"Why do we sign in on these things, anyways?"

I cock my head a little as I watch her watching Nic. She knows the answer, because we all do. Seton's been doing this for years and years, to track who showed up each night. Recruiting is such a big thing at Seton, and if some bad pictures ever make it online, it could ruin the guys' chances at everything. So, the rule has always been no photos and no videos at any football party. And then, as a form of collateral, we all sign in so the team knows who was there and has a short list of who to blame if anything bad ever gets out. JV mans it so the guys on Varsity don't have to. A rite-of-passage kind of thing.

But I let Nic be the one to remind her of all that tonight.

"Insurance policy, Britt, you know that. To protect the guys inside," he says.

"Yeah, I know," she says, still resting against the table as she takes a second to look at Spence's big house looming over us, bright against the night sky. She turns back to Nic. "But have you ever thought about just *asking* us to protect you?"

The fact that Britt is a genius matters especially in moments like this. In the moments where she watches you relentlessly with these eyes that grip you like gravity while she asks you the most obvious questions that you realize you've never once thought about. It's not when I see her schedule riddled with AP classes, or hear about how her test score messed up another curve, that she seems like the smartest person I've ever known. It's moments like now.

J is watching her, too, with his hands in his pockets and his tongue poking a lump into his cheek.

Nic frowns a little and admits, "I don't know."

Britt reaches out and squeezes the redness on one of Nic's cheeks. "Shame. Because maybe we would have."

I always end up drinking more on the nights when J has door duty. Not on purpose or anything. Tonight, I blame it on Britt, and my first time drinking tequila on the rocks because that's what she feels like doing.

Spence's house is packed within an hour, and the phenomenon

that Britt seems to be so used to (where all our boys try to say something to her and the ones who don't, watch) happens like clockwork. Except it's even more obsessive than normal, I guess because they missed having her around, too.

When we find a bunch of the girls on her field hockey team hanging out on one of the couches, Britt exhales like she just escaped a corn maze. Her teammates and I know of each other, but Britt formally introduces us, and when she sits on the coffee table, it's decided. We're staying.

One of the girls is growing out dreadlocks, and another has pink hair. They talk about the games they've played, and the goals they've scored, and the girls they'll be playing eventually. Pink Hair mentions her girlfriend in the stories that she tells, and I eventually put together that she's dating a girl who goes to one of the public schools around here, one of the schools I've never even heard of because the Seton kids never talk about them. I don't know why it's so shocking to me that there are schools in Seton's periphery that aren't AP or Billingsley or one of the other schools on our football team's schedule. But it's kind of like being reminded that people in other countries are posting millions of videos to TikTok, too; they'll just never hit my feed.

I hug myself and smile as I listen to them talk.

"You know Aly's editor-in-chiefing *The Seton Story* this year, right?" Britt says, bringing it up like she feels like it's time to talk about me instead. "A junior's never done it before."

"I knew she was running shit this year, but I didn't know she was the first junior to ever be editor," one of the girls answers. She looks at me and says, "Congrats, Aly. That's fucking sick." And she says it like me sitting in the newspaper office, picking stories to run and finding typos, is really comparable to them bruising girls' shins and drinking whiskey from the bottle right now.

Britt nods, sitting on her knees on top of Spence's glass-topped table, her Chucks still on and everything. Her cup sits in the nook of her lap, and she starts to nibble on a chipped purple nail as she says, "I know, right? It's historical."

It's everything that made me tear up during our night on the lake at Nappahawnick, and now it's like she wants to prove to me how much my stuff matters by getting her fully impartial teammates to agree. In a way, it's working. But I'm also just as bad at getting compliments as J is, and that's why I uncomfortably promise, "It's not . . . *historical*," even if, by definition, that's exactly what it is. "I'm literally sitting in an office reading. You're kicking girls' asses on the field every day." I shake my head, absently rubbing my elbows as I hug myself. "Not the same."

"Who *cares* if it's not the same? I think what you do is cool as shit." Pink Hair unscrews the top of their bottle. "Us kicking ass doesn't mean you can't be kicking ass. You kicking ass doesn't mean we can't be kicking ass. There's room out here for all of us to be kicking ass." She swigs more of their booze, her own affirmational toast.

Britt studies her carefully as she talks, nodding slowly to herself like she's hearing the words of the Dalai Lama. "That's fucking beautiful."

Pink Hair nods like she knows it and takes a second swallow from their bottle. At first, I assumed that maybe they just felt weird about taking the communal booze when they aren't all that close to someone on the football team, so that's why I assured them they're more than welcome to have some of whatever is on the kitchen island—that the boys brought enough for all of us. But Pink Hair just laughed and patted my knee as if to say, *Thanks for the invite, doll, but I can get my own self drunk.*

"I think you should do something wild with this gig," Britt announces, as if me being editor is the equivalent of me being president. Her voice echoes into her red cup as she has some more to drink.

"What do you mean?" I ask.

"What *I mean* is that that paper is an institution. There's not a single literate person within ten miles of Seton who doesn't read it on a weekly basis. Do you know how big that is? How influential that can be? You could *change our world.*" Britt stares at me with her gorgeous face and siren hair, blindly confident in who I am. "You could change the world."

We're all quiet for a second. The inside of my stomach is hot with the tequila that I didn't eat enough dinner to soak up while "Pop Bottles" by Birdman plays over the whole-house audio system.

It's something about being with this group of girls, and the way I watched Britt rebel against our sign-in sheets tonight just for the hell of it, that makes me realize, "I want to."

"That's. The. First. Step." She congratulates me with a slap on my thigh for each word. "You'll think of something." Then she tips the end of her drink into her mouth and announces, "I need more. Come on, Aly." She says to her team, "We'll be back."

She slides off the table, and I get off the couch, following her through Spence's packed house. My feet are in that in-between phase where they're kind of dragging but I'm still kind of floating? I make sure she knows: "I for sure don't need a refill."

"I respect that. I'm not one to encourage anyone to drink more than she wants to. It's less fun for everyone."

I slide far less fluidly past a group standing in the hallway than she does. "I really like your team a lot."

She smiles, glad and proud. "Me too." She taps the bottom of her drink into her mouth even though there's only ice left, before she adds, "They always make me remember how fake this shit is."

We're almost to the stairs that lead back down to the kitchen when we start to pass a room with these wooden doors that slide from left to right. She slows down, backs up, and peers inside. It wasn't like anything happened. No one called her name. But she stops anyway—like some primal instinct that kept the dinosaurs alive—and so I stop, too, and look around for what it might be. Whatever *it* even is.

We're at this room with a white sofa and a white armchair and a sectional, with a coffee table and a wall full of books. But, more important than any of that, it has Bianca and Kelly and Michelle and Parker, sitting together around the coffee table. And it doesn't matter that we were having so much fun with the girls on her field hockey team, or that we were in this cool little world with them where they hung out with public school kids and brought their own booze to parties, because none of that will ever be the same as this.

One of the last times I remember seeing Britt and her friends all together at a party was a little more than a month ago, over the summer, right after all the seniors had officially left for their colleges, and Britt's class had formally taken their place. It wasn't one of Seton's blowouts—instead of sixty people there were probably more like twenty—and we'd all pretty much been hanging out in the basement that night. And I remember that it was around eleven and, for whatever reason, Britt and Michelle and Bianca and Kelly were set on leaving. They wanted to do their own thing. Britt and Michelle were leading the uprising, but Kelly and Bianca were fully bought in. Parker was willing to hand it to them—the rest of the night, that is—and get out of there, unfazed by their spontaneous revolution. He was used to how they were when they felt like being powerful. And even though everyone else was still partying, laughing, drinking, smoking, Joey Wilcox (the party was at Joey's house) really wanted them to stay. He argued a million points—*It's early. You guys got here late. We only have a couple more weeks before summer's over. This is one of our first nights as seniors. My parents never leave me home alone like this.* But they didn't care. And the more they said no, the harder he tried. Because he was more than willing to fight for them.

Because it was *them.*

I watched the whole thing from the couch.

"We're *hungry,*" Britt told him, leaning in close. Bratty and flirty and charming, somehow, all at the same time. "We're not into this tonight."

"Food? I can do that. What do you guys want? I'll order it right now."

"You won't," Kelly challenged.

"I want phở," Bianca whined.

Parker laughed and shook his head.

"Come on, B, no one's delivering phở right now," Joey begged. "I'll order you guys whatever you want that's still open. Don't leave just to get food."

"Don't belittle our reason for leaving, Joseph," Britt chastised.

Joey smiled apologetically, stole an excuse to wrap his arms around her neck, and waited for forgiveness.

"Pizza," Michelle announced on their behalf. "From Bianchi's. With garlic cheesy bread."

"*Yesssss*. And chicken fettuccine!" Kelly requested.

"Get their fruit tart for B," Britt reminded her.

"Oh my God, their fruit tart," Bianca gushed.

"And chicken fettuccine and their fruit tart for B," Michelle added. She looked at the rest of her friends to make sure there were no other orders. When there weren't, she smiled stubbornly back at Joey and concluded, "Pepperoni and olives, please."

"*Black* olives," Bianca clarified.

Britt groaned and made a face like she'd just watched a baby projectile vomit. "We're out of here in a heartbeat if that shit shows up with some green olives on it."

Parker smirked at his girls and then looked at Joey to see what he was gonna do. Bianchi's was a four-dollar-sign Italian restaurant not too far from Seton. People went for prom and graduation. They'd just requested at least eighty dollars' worth of food, not including delivery or tip.

"Come on," Parker said, sliding his arm around Michelle's waist, pulling his keys from his pocket. "I'll get you guys some food."

"No, I got it," Joey said. "I got it." He held his hands in front of him to stop anyone from going anywhere. "I got it."

I lost track of the situation for a little while after that. But eventually, I went up the basement steps to go to the bathroom, and when I got to the top of the stairs, I found them in the kitchen, standing around the oversized island, with a huge pizza and an aluminum tin of chicken fettuccine and a loaf of garlic bread and red cups full of whatever.

Somebody's cell phone was playing "I Like That" by Janelle

Monáe while the football playlist blasted downstairs, officially separating their world from the rest of ours. And they were dancing while they stood there eating, while Parker sat on the island next to them, and Joey leaned against the countertops, talking to him. Lingering, like he was scared to let them out of his sight.

Maybe I watched for too long and that's why Britt felt me there, but she looked up and her eyes sparkled when she saw me. "Aly! Are you hungry?"

"Alyyyyyy!" Kelly drunk cheered.

Bianca smiled and mocked her, leaning against her shoulder, mouth full. Into Kelly's ear, she echoed, "*Alyyyyyy!*"

"Eat with us," Michelle said.

I wasn't hungry, but I went into the kitchen with them because I *wanted* to be there with them. Because there's something about them that's like the sun, that makes you bloom, that makes you warm.

Parker watched me walk over, amused, but he stayed busy with his conversation with Joey. And Britt and Michelle made room for me between the two of them, and Britt grabbed a giant slice of pizza from the box and dangled it over my head as she and Michelle danced next to me, and Kelly and Bianca danced next to Michelle, all of them selectively singing the words they knew, the words they could fit in while they weren't chewing.

"Say *ahhh*," Britt told me, and I held my head back and opened my mouth. She fed me a bite of pizza and laughed as she handed me the rest of the slice.

"Be flattered, Aly." Parker smirked at me from Britt's other side. "They won't even share with me."

———————

Tonight, Parker is sitting on the end of that white couch with his arm resting across Michelle's shoulders, and Bianca is next to her, and Kelly is next to Bianca, leaning across Bianca's lap, in Parker's face about something. He's always kind of been like that—their communal boyfriend. He drives all four of them around. Shows up to parties with all four of them. Walks the halls with all four of them. Takes crap from all four of them.

Well, used to.

There are more people here, obviously, standing around drinking, having their own talks and doing their own thing. But my gaze immediately goes to that couch—the one Britt would've been on if this was a month ago instead of now—like the way a black hole sucks up everything around it.

"Do you think they miss me?" Britt asks.

"*Of course* they miss you."

"So I should try to talk to them?"

If I'm being totally honest, there's a part of me that's not entirely looking forward to the moment when they all finally talk to each other again, because I'm sure there will be fireworks, and angels rejoicing, and bluebirds singing "Oh, Happy Day," and the result will be the extremely high likelihood that she just won't need me anymore. But there's also a *bigger* part of me that doesn't want to see them lose this incredible *thing* they have. This thing that's made up of all their beautiful gray magic and casts spells on me every day, just by watching.

So tonight, I tell her, "Yes. Britt, yes. Definitely. Maybe on Monday or something, you can go off campus for lunch—"

"I mean now." She looks at me. "Should I talk to them now?"

I blink at her. I'm drunk, yeah, and not ready to lose her in this very moment, but none of that has to do with how sure I am that talking to them after tequila on the rocks is a terrible idea. "*What? No.* Definitely not. Definitely Monday. Or Sunday. Or any day but *not* now."

Britt watches me, listening. She nods slowly, like she knows I make sense. Then she turns and says, "Mich," as she walks into the room anyway.

"Shit—" I blurt and jog in after her.

She stops a few feet in front of the couch while she watches them, and they watch her. I stop next to her, awkwardly, like a sound effects guy who stumbled on stage mid-act.

Parker laughs a little and says, "Hey, Aly."

"Hey, Parker," I answer.

We're all quiet for a second, just looking at each other. Until Michelle asks Britt, "What's up?" She sounds a little bit pissed. Maybe a little bit hopeful. Definitely a little bit ready to know what Britt wants.

"I wanted to see if we could talk," Britt tells her.

"What do you want to talk about?" she asks.

Britt shrugs, glances around the room, meets Michelle's equally pretty, yet completely opposite, eyes once again. "Global warming?"

Bianca smiles like she's missed her, but Michelle frowns and insists, "Don't do that."

"Do *what*, Mich?" Britt argues, holding her arms out at her sides and drunkenly smiling at the absurdity. "Try to talk? We can't just *not talk.* That's *nuts.* That's *certifiably insane.*" She drops her arms and looks at her, and like it's the only thing she's ever known for sure, she says, "We have to talk."

They're both quiet.

Then Kelly insists, "You guys do need to talk, Mich . . ."

Michelle glares at her like she just objected at Michelle's wedding.

"Probably not here, or now," Bianca cuts in, voice-of-reasoning this situation. "But maybe tomorrow. Maybe we can all get lunch or something?"

"*B*," Michelle snaps. And Bianca leans into her ear just like she did on that Monday when everything changed and says something that I have a feeling is really, really rational, but it's too soft for any of the rest of us to hear.

"You can't *do* this," Britt insists, cutting through Kelly's support and Bianca's attempt at logic. She slashes through all of it like the guy you can't kill in a horror movie, and for her—for them—maybe it should be that scary. "You can't just break up with me and take the kids and not even meet me in mediation. This is *inhumane*. It's practically illegal." She stands there, staring at Michelle. "I feel like I don't even exist anymore."

And it hits me in this way that breaks my heart that maybe she doesn't. Not right now. Not in the way we've always known her to, at least. As one of the perfect members of this perfect clique, as this girl who was part this and part that until she had more gorgeous, shiny faces than an emerald. Maybe that girl is gone because her friends decided she is. Maybe you're only real if people believe you are.

"Britt," Parker cuts in, and something about the way he says it makes me less nervous. He sounds like a veteran. Invested but calm, like he's witnessed explosive drunk arguments with them more times than he can even remember. "Will you just come sit down? Really. We shouldn't be doing this shit. You're miserable without them, they're miserable without you. And you can squash these rumors right now or not, I don't even care." Parker looks at Michelle and partly begs, partly insists, "Come on, stop pouting. We'll talk about this shit in the morning."

But Britt doesn't go over. She looks at him like he's the least impressive person on earth and says, "How can you talk like that?"

"Talk like *what*, Britt?" he insists.

"Like I'm just some fucking psycho. Like I'm *Gone Girl*-ing the shit out of this situation while you don't care at all—"

"Because I have *no idea what you're talking about!* Britt." Parker sits forward on the couch, his eyes pleading with her like the crisis counselor who doesn't want you to jump. "At the bowling alley, everything was fine. And then the next day, you started pleading the Fifth on this crazy rumor and wouldn't talk to anybody anymore. And I don't know what's up or what the beef is or if I did it, or Michelle did it, or we all did—I don't know. But you've been like my fucking sister for three years now. And you girls are obsessed with each other. And this is supposed to be *the best goddamn year of our lives.* But that's not happening because you're all too damn stubborn to just kiss and make up. And I'm tired of it." He looks between all four of them—down the line at Michelle and Kelly and Bianca, and then across the room at Britt. "So, get your ass over here. And kiss, already. Make up, already. And end this. Okay?" He isn't actually holding his hand out to her, but I imagine he is. I imagine her standing on the Bay Bridge and he's reaching out with his fingers spread so she can grab hold and come home.

She stares at him and declares, "You're a maniac."

Parker falls back on the couch and puts his hands in his hair and sighs. *"Jesus fucking Christ."*

Michelle hasn't stopped watching Britt since she walked in. "Why is he a maniac?"

"Because if the rest of us are crazy, that makes her sane?" Parker offers.

Michelle holds an arm out to stop him but doesn't look away from Britt. "Why?"

And Britt's voice is actually vibrating with this adrenaline that's making her shake when she says, "You are literally dating a guy, and sleeping with a guy, and *sitting next to a guy right now* who's capable of acting like the world *he created* isn't real because it's not the world he wants anyone else to see. He's *lying to you*, Mich. He's lying to you *about me*, and he's doing it under this guise of loving you and loving us and wanting everything to just be how it was when he should've been thinking about all of that the *second he had someone as perfect as you*, but he wasn't. You *know* he wasn't. He isn't that fucking great, Mich. He never has been. And he would rather sit here, and lie to you, *and destroy us*, than tell you the truth."

"What's the truth?" Michelle asks.

And Parker watches Britt carefully as he lets the question stand.

"You know the truth," Britt promises her sadly.

"If I know it, then why don't you just say it?" Michelle insists, and her voice catches because she's trying so, so hard not to cry. She stands up, leaving Parker and Kelly and Bianca on the couch. "You guys slept together. Right? It happened. There. I broke my own heart so you don't have to. Tell me why."

"Mich, that never happened . . ." Parker argues, but his eyes are locked on Britt as he does.

"Tell me why," Michelle repeats.

Britt watches Michelle across the awkward eight feet that sepa-
rates them. She twists her mouth, and she looks around the room,
at the mini-crowd that's noticing them, at me. Like she's deciding
something. Choosing something.

She looks back at Michelle. And she finally confesses, "Because
he didn't give me a choice."

What it was.

October 27, 2018

The thing that made cheering for Seton easy even when it felt like the world was on fire was the fact that cheering for Seton was a very methodical and predictable experience. There were just three basic rules, and it was these three rules that made it possible for Michelle to get through that Saturday's football games.

- **Rule 1.** JV games didn't matter. The JV boys treated them as scrimmages. The JV cheerleaders spent most of the time stunting in prep for competition in the spring. So, Michelle didn't have to worry about smiling for a crowd—not until next year.
- **Rule 2.** Only the Varsity cheerleaders got to stand on the track during the Varsity game, and *Varsity* at Seton was synonymous with *Respect. Invincibility. Seniors.* So, for the game that actually mattered, Michelle was on the bench for now.
- **Rule 3.** This covered exactly *how* and *when* to cheer at a Seton football game and was technically made up of a series of sub-bullets, but they were simple enough:
  - **Rule 3a.** Whenever it was time to source everyone's telekinetic energy to make something good happen, or to celebrate when something bad happened for the other team, the whole Seton crowd flapped their arms in slow motion. (They were the Eagles, after all.) The Varsity cheerleaders posed

with one pompom in the air and shook it until it shimmered. The JV cheerleaders held their arms in front of them and did spirit fingers from the bleachers. (Again, an easy enough task even if you're busy worrying about something else.)

- **Rule 3b.** Whenever Seton scored, the band immediately started playing "Hey Baby!" while everyone else swayed and sang along. The Varsity cheerleaders faced the crowd doing bouncy choreography as they clapped their glittery red pompoms. The JV cheerleaders stayed on the bench and rocked from left to right as they sang with coordinated claps and snaps. (And Michelle could sing "Hey, Baby!" and do the corresponding bench choreography in her sleep.)

"You sing like a fucking angel, Mich!" Kelly called out that night, as soon as the song stopped after another Seton touchdown and it was quiet for one of the few times it would be.

Michelle smiled for real for the first time all day, turning around and looking up into the crowd, at her friends toward the top of the bleachers. The stands were packed with red and white, but Michelle found them instantly. A gravitational pull kind of thing.

"When you bust out your shower voice? Mmm, we're not worthy!" Bianca called out next.

Michelle bit her lip. Her friends always cheered louder for her than they did for the boys. Stage moms gone completely berserk, without all the fat-shaming and future therapy sessions. It always made the base of her neck hot, which is how she knew it was getting patchy and red, but not in a bad way. It was like hearing a crush say they like you back. Or hearing the announcement that the one award that truly means something goes to you.

She looked to Britt last, because she knew Britt would say something. Her friends cheered for her the same way they did any- and everything else: together.

Slouching over her knees, Britt lifted her hands and cupped her mouth. "You're fucking unstoppable, Mich."

And even though Michelle hadn't said one word about anything yet, she was sure, in that moment, that Britt didn't need her to.

It was halftime, and the Varsity football team stood along the track, facing the crowd, in their cleats and their uniforms, their helmets dangling from their fingers by the face masks at their sides. They were the same boys Michelle had known since her freshman year, the same boys who were best friends with her boyfriend, who had crushes on *her* best friends, who'd sucked them into their special world where girls don't have to worry about things like finding a ride or bringing their own alcohol. But something about them looked different tonight as they stood there in front of everybody, changing. It was funny. Because Michelle realized in that moment that she couldn't decide whether change was gradual or instant. Whether the boys had been getting a little older, a little different, a little closer to leaving every second that she'd known them, or if yesterday they weren't and now they were.

It was Senior Night, the last game of the regular season, and it was officially time for their annual tribute. The Seton choir and the Seton marching band were in the middle of performing an impassioned version of "See You Again" by Wiz Khalifa, while hundreds of people and parents stayed on their feet, and the fluorescent lights drenched the field, and the Varsity cheerleaders faced the boys, their pompoms shimmering over their heads.

A few spaces over, the JV football team sat on the same bleacher as the JV cheerleaders, still dressed in their uniforms from the game they'd played right before Varsity, like they always did. Michelle looked at them, at Parker, as they grinned at the more famous part of the team, as they rocked on the bleachers to the beat of the song. She'd been zoning out all night, distracted by a million other things. Well, really just one thing. One thing for the millionth time.

Which was why she almost missed her cue, until her friend on JV pinched her bare leg just in time for Michelle to snap into character and cup her mouth with the rest of her squad. She chanted at the top of her lungs, her heart skipping an excited beat as she sang her favorite part—the part that came right before the chorus, the part about family being the only thing we really have—because she felt so incredibly lucky to have found a family here. To have a place that felt more like home than her own home, some days. To have these boys. To have her girls.

Sometimes, people cried on Senior Night. Especially moms and girlfriends, but even the guys on the team had a cute way of letting a tear fall whenever it was time to do this all over again.

When the song ended, the stands didn't clap, no one whooped or called out, not even Michelle's three best friends—who were always 98 percent likely to be the epicenter of rebellion. Everything was respectfully and honorably silent, even the wind.

They stayed that way for about a minute—the drummers would tell them once it'd been long enough. And eventually, they did, the snares and the basses creating their trademark go-go beat, the fans screaming out in excitement, the Varsity cheerleaders bouncing into their positions.

Because now that halftime was over, it was officially time for

Rule 3c. Arguably the most significant of any of the *How to Cheer for Seton* rules.

And those same Varsity boys, who'd stood like statues of fallen soldiers moments before, climbed onto the benches and bleachers, yelled into the crowd, and led the Seton Girls cheer with more commitment than any of them ever had before.

Because tonight was the last time any of them ever would.

When the game was over and the boys had won (24–10), Michelle leaned against the tall fences that separated the field from the parking lot, waiting for her friends. She was just far enough out of the way for the flood of people leaving the stands to get past without knocking her around, even though she probably wouldn't have noticed if they did. She hated that the same stuff still got to her so much, the stuff she had been seeing forever, the stuff she should be immune to by now. Wasn't that the way the human species worked? You get sick once, and the next time, your body recognizes it and fights better and smarter and faster. It hurts less. It destroys less of you. *Evolution.* You had a body that was smart enough to do that, or you died.

Michelle would've died. She thought about that a lot. If she'd been born *back then*, the universe would've deemed her genes way too unimpressive to deserve the right to stay alive and produce a new generation of incapabilities. She was blind without contacts, for starters, and raw fruit made her mouth itch. She could never spell *necessary* right on the first try. And she felt like her world was being forced through a meat grinder every time her parents—

"Yo, Mich!"

She looked up from the nothingness she'd been staring at a second before. Parker walked her way, in his red football sweats with

SETON on the front of his hoodie in white block lettering. He was grinning as he cut across the crowd to get to her, his football duffel on his shoulder. She anticipated how bad he was going to smell because all those guys were always so rank after a game, but he was still stupid hot. The kind of gorgeous that Netflix casts.

He took her waist in his hands and spun her around as she balanced easily on the ball of one foot, as her hair whipped across her shoulders in a breeze that was only theirs.

"You see my game tonight?" Parker asked, smiling into her mouth, kissing her as he spoke.

"I mean . . . I was kind of working."

"Yeah, right. Your entire job is to cheer me on."

Michelle's eyebrows came together skeptically as she went for the face palm that he deserved.

He caught her wrist and laughed. "Come on, Mich, for real. That thirty-yard pass before halftime?"

Michelle smiled as he waited for her answer. Parker had a handful of basic needs in this life. Food. Football. Her. And the Seton popular vote—the support, approval, and praise of all Seton-related humans at all times.

Michelle could tease him right now and say that pass wasn't that great, or that the real MVP was Terry Allen for actually hitting the field goal Parker's pass had set up, or that Levi's game looked way better anyway. But she didn't have the energy for it, the stamina to convince him she was just joking if this was one of those nights when he got all fussy and believed her.

"It was amazing," she whispered into his ear, and his hands found their way to the bottom of her tiny skirt, tugging it a little like a dad trying to make it grow.

"Come on and ride with Mac and me," Parker insisted. "We can hang out before we go to the party tonight."

By "hang out" he meant "have sex," and as much as the idea made her stomach flip—both because of how much she craved him and how much she craved the distraction—she shook her head and answered, "I can't. I'm riding with the girls."

"Aw, they won't care. And if you think they'll miss you too much, they can join us. How about that?" He buried his face into her neck and wouldn't let her go when she tried to pull away. "You, me, Britt . . . a sister-wives thing like that show you watch? Call it my gift for being the best boyfriend ever—"

"I will crush you," Michelle threatened, gripping his neck right across the Adam's apple now that she'd wriggled her arm free. She was smiling because he was, and because he was joking, in the smart-ass way that Parker Adams was allowed to joke about things. "And you will never speak again."

"Small price to pay," he said, taking her hand from his neck with an effort so minimal it was almost comical. "So, you're coming with me or what?"

But it wasn't a conversation, like some ice cream flavor she was considering trying but could be talked out of with enough effort and a delicious enough alternative. She let him lace his arm around her waist like a little boy who was trash at sharing, she let him weave his free fingers through her mandatory ponytail, and she said, "I'm riding with the girls."

"Fine." He accepted one of the only defeats he was used to. "Have fun and I'll see you girls soon, okay? Don't take too long. I *love* you."

That was how he always said it. I *love* you, with this emphasis on the word *love* like he was one-upping somebody she didn't even know. Someone who merely *liked* her. And it always made Michelle's heart spin in dizzying circles because of how powerful it felt to have Parker Adams say that to *her*.

"I love you, too."

And he kissed her one more time before heading back over to the guys on the team who'd been waiting for him as the crowd started to thin, and she took a deep breath of the crisp air that smelled like fall. In the next two hours, he'd go from smelly JV quarterback to Luigi from Mario Brothers for the party tonight.

"Mich!" Bianca called, and Michelle sighed in relief before looking over her shoulder to see her friends finally getting close. Bianca hopped over to her and wrapped her arms around Michelle's neck. Bianca's thick hair smelled like strawberries, just like it always did, just like it should. The same whiff Michelle was used to when she'd hold back B's hair to bong a beer, or when they'd drift to sleep together on the same pillow.

Kelly came next, popping her lips directly in Michelle's face, the same way she would if she had just finished putting on a new coat of lip gloss. She made her blue eyes big on purpose, the little brown freckles on the bridge of her nose close enough for Michelle to see how they kind of formed the outline of a teddy bear, which Britt pointed out first, years ago.

Michelle bugged out her eyes in return and tucked Kelly's brown hair behind her ears.

And last came Britt, sauntering up behind her two girls, letting them say hi first, like a patient mom. In some ways, Britt did feel like the mom, or maybe just maternal, when it came to all their friends. But in other ways, she felt like that rebel cousin who smoked cigarettes and passed a fake to get tattoos—the one your mom won't leave you alone with on Thanksgiving. Michelle would never be able to explain it, exactly what it was like to have Britt. But the same way you can look at the stars for too long and start to wonder if they're even real, Britt sometimes felt like the same undeserved miracle.

Britt slid her fingers into Michelle's ponytail and twirled the ends of Michelle's hair around her fingertips like she was the prettiest doll she'd ever seen.

And for no clear reason at all, she told Michelle in that moment, "Thank you for existing."

"You ready to bounce?" Kelly asked, taking Michelle's hand and walking backward as she led the way to the parking lot.

Michelle hoisted her Seton duffel off the ground and over her shoulder. "Who's whisking me away?"

"Well, I picked up Kel on my way, so all her stuff is already in my car," Bianca explained. "But if you ride with Britt, she doesn't have to ride alone?"

Britt placed her palms under her chin, prayer position. A smile with no teeth and blinking gray eyes that were part playful, part deviant.

Michelle linked her arm with Britt's and promised, "I'd never let you ride alone."

They split up, Kelly and Bianca toward Bianca's car in the student lot, Michelle and Britt toward Britt's car in the visitors' lot. Michelle threw her stuff into the back seat and climbed in front as Britt pressed the button to start the engine. Michelle fastened in while Britt did all her normal things next to her. Messed with the music, messed with the AC vents, turned on the seat warmers.

And while Britt did those things, Michelle watched the cars full of their friends drive off and knew that so many of them were about to do the same thing: go to one of their houses, get into their Halloween costumes, head over to Jake's for the party, get wasted. It was simple and maybe completely unexciting for some, but it was all she'd ever known Seton to be. They moved in droves here, like a school of perfectly synchronized fish, and she was one of those fish, grateful that she didn't have to figure out a bunch of stuff every other day, a bunch of plans or what to do or how to be. She just swam with them, and it didn't just feel easy, but safe.

But next thing she knew, Britt's hand was in her lap, palm facing up. Michelle looked at her—tearing her gaze from the moon and the stars and the cars she knew.

As Britt backed out of their parking space with her free hand on the wheel, she said, "Squeeze as hard as you need to. You won't break me."

It was some conduction theory Britt believed in and had been belaboring them with for years. That feelings—just like other forms of energy—could be transmitted from point A to point B. And whether it was true or not wasn't the point, because they all believed in it now—that they could share pain the same way that ice cools off a soda—and that was enough to make it real.

Michelle hadn't told Britt or the other girls anything yet, but they'd been using their group chat all day, and Michelle hadn't responded as much as usual. Britt called her a little before the game to say she was thinking about hitting up Melo, their weed guy, and wanted to know if Michelle thought it was worth it for tonight. But Michelle knew when Britt called it was about more than just Melo, that Britt had a feeling that something was up, and this was her call to check in.

Britt always had a way of just knowing.

Michelle told her sure, to hell with it, let's get an eighth.

"They hate each other again," Michelle confessed, her voice cracking in the dark car. She didn't have to clarify who she was talking about; it had been the same thing for years. A text her mom found on her dad's phone, a "colleague" who dropped her mom off at home—both of her parents testing the other like a toddler trying to learn the concept of boundaries. Her mom and dad had been together since they were sixteen. They'd both been caught doing more than they should be with other people. Their marriage counselor said they equated the friction with passion. They didn't know how to stop it even if they wanted to. So, it shouldn't bother Michelle, because they did it to themselves; they did it for the attention, or something ridiculous like that. But the screaming made her stomach feel like it was eating itself; the passive-aggressive way her mom would try to get her to hate her dad for the five minutes that she did, too, just to have an ally. The door slamming, and the tears that always happened after midnight because they couldn't fight in the daylight; it wasn't dramatic enough, romantic enough.

Anyway. Britt knew that story as well as Michelle did by now.

"Fuck, man," Britt reacted, like she was disappointed in the universe.

And then all the memories of the past day were swirling around Michelle's head all over again. The fighting they were already doing when she stumbled in, hungover, at 8:00 a.m. The glass she could hear someone throw and shatter from all the way in her bedroom, like their lives were some fucking telenovela. "It just *sucks*, Britt. It never stops. You think they had some breakthrough therapy appointment, or genuine truce, or even just some mind-blowing sex or *anything*. You always think it's fixed, and then it breaks and slices everyone up all over again."

"You guys have been bleeding over this for years."

"*For years*. I'm like . . . fucking hemorrhaging over here." Michelle pressed the heels of her hands against her eyes to keep her tears from falling.

And that was when Britt wiggled her fingers, her hand still waiting in Michelle's lap. "Squeeze, Mich."

And this time, she did. She took Britt's hand in both of hers and squeezed so hard—way harder than Britt deserved—and yelled, "Fuck this," as she slammed her head back against the headrest. It might've been science, or it might've been magic, or it might've been soul mates, or just resulting exhaustion, but—like always—it helped a little bit.

"Do you know what I think the worst part of all of it is?" Michelle asked. "Like, beyond the fact that they mess around outside their marriage. But the part that's even shittier than that is that they *want* to be caught. Every time. They want the drama, and the friction, and the—"

"They want to know how much love can take."

Michelle was quiet.

"I think you're beat tonight, Mich."

"Maybe I am. I kind of don't even feel . . ." But she didn't finish her sentence, because it didn't even matter how she felt at this point; it was too late, and the party was too soon.

"Like being the Josie to our Pussycats tonight?" Britt filled in.

The idea had been Kelly's, and there was never a proclaimed Josie. But Kelly had found these leopard-print leotards at Zara and sent the group chat a picture to see if the other girls would be game. They were.

"Just to, like, level-set this situation," Britt said. "That shit is totally optional."

Michelle tried not to smile—was surprised she even wanted to—as she answered, "No, it's not."

Britt squinted and smiled, too. "What?"

Michelle laughed. "Britt, it's not. We already got the outfits, we already promised Kelly and B. It's an ensemble look. We can't just bail on an ensemble look."

"Okay, first off, you're referencing *ensemble looks* like they're in Merriam-fucking-Webster's. And second off, a literal heart transplant is optional, so this is *absolutely optional.* Kel and B will get it. I can promise you that."

"But don't you want to go?"

Britt shrugged. "No."

Michelle believed her. "What would we do instead?"

"Whatever we want. I have our weed. Wanna do that?"

It sounded so good—skipping the party, getting high, not being alone but not being with everyone else. Michelle curled her legs under her and rested her head against the back of her seat, facing Britt. "Okay."

"Okay." Britt poked out her bottom lip, reaching for Michelle's cheek, pinching it between her fingers. Michelle smiled, and Britt smiled back. "Don't be sad. You know I can fix anything."

Britt texted the girls to let them know she and Michelle weren't coming. Michelle didn't ask what excuse she gave, and she didn't ask if they were mad, and Britt dropped her phone conclusively into the cupholder as soon as it was done. She offered to text Parker for her, too, but Michelle promised she'd text him later, once she was sure he was already at the party, too drunk to miss her.

Britt and Michelle stopped at the Safeway by Seton and bought a family-size bag of puffy Cheetos and Sour Patch Kids that they opened and attempted to throw into each other's mouths until a store manager who was way scarier than any parent either one of them ever had or ever met told them to pay before security dragged their butts home.

"We should walk somewhere," Britt decided once they were back outside.

Michelle looked at her, Britt's big curly hair (that Michelle had always loved a million times more than her own) wisping in the breeze like the beginnings of a tornado.

But it was like that r.h. Sin quote that Michelle loved so much that she had it on her Instagram and a Post-it on her desk. Britt *was* a tornado, but not the kind you run away from. She was the kind you want to chase.

"Walk where?" Michelle asked.

Britt reached out and pulled that too-tight band from Michelle's hair, her ponytail collapsing in waves onto her shoulders. Britt slid the hair tie onto her own wrist and shrugged. "Wherever we belong."

"Just let me put on pants?" Michelle asked.

"*Pants*?" Britt insisted as they started their slow walk back to her car. "You're tougher than that, Mich."

"I'm in a miniskirt."

"You were gonna be in a leotard."

"Inside," Michelle argued, leaning into her shoulder as they walked. "Drunk."

"With all those grabby boy-hands keeping you warm." Britt smiled, and Michelle laughed, because that was exactly how their boys were. Grabby. Touchy. Insistent, at times. But generally harmless.

Britt's trunk was full of options. She had field hockey sweats, leggings, windbreakers, and sweatshirts, and Michelle checked her cheerleading duffel, too. Michelle changed in the back seat—into sweats and one of Britt's field hockey sweatshirts—before the two of them headed the way that Britt wanted to go.

The sidewalks were full of ghosts and witches, parent groups taking toddlers and babies around in strollers for Halloweekend festivities. Michelle smiled at the adults she recognized—parents of their classmates and even a couple of teachers. She realized where they were going as soon as she and Britt made the left behind Whole Foods and they veered off the sidewalk onto the gravel path.

They'd found this park years ago with Kelly and Bianca, when the four of them were skipping class and wandering. But as many times as they'd come, they never ran into anyone else. So over time, it became theirs.

That night, they lay in the grass with their snacks and their weed, in the shape of a capital T. Michelle rested her head on Britt's stomach and faced the sky while she talked and Britt listened, while both their phones vibrated and pinged on the ground next to them with messages and missed calls that they ignored for now.

The smoking and the stars pulled it out of her, made the words come so much more easily. And Britt's fingers in her hair—that helped, too.

"Do you think they really know more than us?" Michelle asked.

"Your parents?"

"Just adults in general," she clarified. "I mean, we go home to them every night. We go to school to them every day. But do you really think they know more than us?"

"I don't think anybody knows anything."

Michelle waited for a second, and far away a group of kids screamed happily—scared in the kind of way that made you want to get scared again. "At all?"

"I just don't think any of us have any idea what we're doing. It just gets to be more obvious the older you get because there are so many less rules. I mean, we get to hide behind the fact that we have to go to school all day every day and can't do anything real until we're eighteen, and then we have to go to college. But after all that, then what? You're just the same clueless human with less rules to hide behind."

"So, you think it never gets better." Michelle felt Britt's fingers gently start to part her hair at the scalp.

"Or maybe it just never gets worse."

Michelle thought about it, tried to believe it; it was easier when she was high. But still, tonight, she had to ask, "What if it does get worse?"

"What's the worst possible thing?"

"What if my parents break up?"

"What if they do break up?" Britt encouraged.

"I mean, my dad would move out. I'd have to go between two different houses and have Christmas in two different places. I don't know. It would just be different."

"But they wouldn't be fighting," Britt reminded her.

"They probably wouldn't be."

"You might be able to sleep more nights."

"That sounds unbelievable."

"I don't know, Mich . . . Maybe it wouldn't be so bad."

"Sometimes I think it wouldn't be so bad, either." And Michelle dug into the open Cheetos bag next to them, in part just to make some noise so that maybe Britt wouldn't hear her voice catch. "Do you remember what you said in the car earlier? About how maybe they're trying to see how much love can take?"

"I do."

"How much do *you* think love can take?" Michelle sucked the cheese dust off a single Cheeto, counting the stars as she waited.

"Anything, minus one."

"Anything, minus one," Michelle softly repeated, not sure exactly what it meant, but it felt right—like a word she was trying to pronounce for the first time.

"Because people say that, you know? That love can conquer anything. And I've never been in love before, I mean, besides with you guys. But that's an anomaly. When we're talking about normal people, and normal kinds of *in love*, I just figure there has to be *something* it can't overcome. And maybe that something is different for everyone, but it exists. It has to. Because nothing is entirely invincible. That's impossible. And maybe love is just as close to impossible as you can get. So, yeah. Anything, minus one."

Michelle thought about it, and for the millionth time since the moment they'd met in sixth-grade social studies, she knew that Britt was right. "Anything, minus one."

They lay there quietly, just the soft crunching of Michelle's chewing and a wish on a star that they could lie together exactly as they were forever that Michelle was too embarrassed to say out loud.

"You're gonna be okay, Mich. I promise. You're the most amazing girl I know. You're gonna be like . . . a neurosurgeon one day. Or some huge entrepreneur or like . . . a recommendation in Reese's Book Club—"

"You're crazy," Michelle whispered.

"*Seriously*. You're like my favorite person who's ever existed. I think you're fantastic. I think you're magnificent. And every situation that you're ever in should enable that. You *deserve* that."

The stars blended into a ball of brightness as the tears pooled in Michelle's eyes. Britt said things to be funny sometimes, or to get her way, or to avoid the kinds of things she didn't want to deal with, but Michelle could always tell the difference, could always tell how much she meant the things that she really did mean. And she knew how much Britt meant this—how much Britt loved her, and how big her love felt, because it wasn't obligatory, like a parent's. Or transactional, like Parker's.

It was love and support and admiration entirely because of exactly who Michelle was, and she didn't feel like she deserved it all the time. She didn't feel like she was all that great all the time. And so she started to cry that night, in part because of how grateful she was to have a best friend who would stop swimming with her on a night as big as this one, and in part because Michelle hoped to never, ever let her down.

Britt wiped Michelle's tears with her thumb on her way to grab more Cheetos. "And, on top of having all of that going for you, you're a *Seton* girl. And you *know* that Seton girls know what's up."

It made Michelle laugh; it burst up from her stomach and out of her mouth like a match against a matchbox the second it catches a flame. The beginning of their Seton Girls cheer. The cheer Michelle wasn't really allowed to say until it was her turn to be on Varsity.

And even though it was dumb and it didn't matter, it also wasn't and it did, like everything else Michelle had grown used to around here. And Britt saying it now, while they were high in the grass at a park in the dark, when they should've been with everyone else, dressed as Pussycats for Halloween, felt bad the same way that passing notes behind a teacher's back feels bad. More fun because it seems dangerous, even if it's for no good reason.

"Because the Seton girls know what's up . . ." Britt went on, officially kicking off the cheer this time.

"From the front to the back," Michelle said next.

Britt bobbed her hips up and down, and Michelle rolled over to look up at her. "You even sound like a cheerleader when you say it."

Michelle smiled and shrugged as she went on, "Yeah, we know what's up . . ."

"From the left to the right . . ."

"Yeah, we know what's up . . ."

Britt twirled her hair flirtatiously (and satirically) around her finger. "Because we're Seton, and the Seton girls know what's up . . ."

"Aaayyyyeee . . ." Michelle laughed.

And they lay in the grass, and ate their Cheetos and their candy as they chanted the cheer that Michelle knew wasn't truly hers to say for another eight months.

But she said it anyway.

What it is.

Because he didn't give me a choice.

Because he didn't give me a choice.

Because he didn't give me a choice.

"Britt, wait—" I jog after her while "Just a Friend" by Biz Markie plays over the stereo, and the house around us is as normal as it's ever been, drenched with music we know and people we know even better in their Seton hats and hoodies.

But nothing's the same.

"Britt, please hold on." I catch up with her at the bottom of the stairs, and she turns around to face me just a few feet from the front door.

Her eyes are the same glassy they were that day on her bedroom floor. "Yeah?"

I really wish I had used a mixer with my tequila. "Are you leaving?"

She nods and hugs herself. "I don't really want to be here anymore."

"Do you want to go talk somewhere? Like outside?"

Maybe a tear falls, but she wipes it away so quickly that I'm not sure. "I would really like that." She opens the front door, and I follow her outside.

"Now push those two buttons down *together*," J's saying, leaning over Nic's shoulder as they stare at the screen of Nic's Nintendo Switch.

"*Oh shit!*" Nic says, bouncing in his chair and everything. They look up as the door shuts behind us.

J smiles knowingly when he sees me. "Snack time?"

"Wait, hold up. *She brings you snacks?*"

"When she misses me enough."

"*Wowww.*" Nic slaps J's hand like he's truly impressed. "Best damn girls in the world or what?"

They're so busy talking and dapping and messing around with Nic's game-thing that they don't even notice Britt speed-walking past them until she's practically at the steps.

They look at me, their eyes apologizing for what they're not even sure they did wrong.

"I didn't think about bringing out any snacks," I defeatedly admit.

"I was just kidding. I'm not even hungry," J says, which is a lie to spare my conscience, but I appreciate it. He nods in Britt's direction and tells me, "Let me know if you need me."

I jog after her down the steps and find her sitting on one halfway to the street. I hug myself as I go to sit down next to her.

"Are you cold?" she asks, offering me the bomber that's been tied around her waist all night like a guy you'd have a crush on in a movie.

It's not cold outside, but in the dark, there's a chill, and the answer to her question is *a little bit*, but it doesn't matter. "I'm okay," I promise.

"You're lying." She sighs as she drapes her jacket over my knees. "I always know when people are lying." Her kinky curls are flipping in the breeze.

"Aren't *you* cold?"

She shakes her head and stares across the street. "I like weather."

I pull her jacket farther up my lap so it doesn't fall onto the ground.

"I wish we had weed," she says longingly.

I look over my shoulder, back up the steps at Spence's mansion behind us, as bright, and practically as big, as a mall in the middle of the night. I don't smoke and neither does J, but I remind her, "I'm sure there's some inside. Do you want me to text someone?"

"It's okay. Thank you, though."

For a few seconds, we sit there quietly, and I can finally process what the hell I just witnessed. The way Parker lunged off the couch so fast that some of the guys who'd been watching had to dive across the table and grab him—controlling a pit bull before it had the chance to break loose. A vase on the coffee table shattered, and Bianca yanked Michelle out of the way. And while Parker snapped out of it—out of this rage I've never in my life seen from him except for when it's being directed at a bad ref—Michelle stared at Britt, radiating the kind of brokenness that exists in songs that make you cry.

Bianca was squeezing Michelle's hand down by her side and whispering more of what I can only imagine was her signature logic, while Kelly was busy shoving her finger in Parker's chest and telling him to "*Fucking stop.*" And while all of it happened around them—around Britt and Michelle—there was an unbelievable silence between them. Like nothing else existed, and no one else mattered, besides the two of them.

And that was when Britt left.

"What did you just say in there?" I force myself to ask, even though the echo of her words is still haunting me.

Her eyes stay fixed across the street. "Something bad."

I swallow hard. "Is it true?"

And her face scrunches up, an old lady teaching me an important life lesson. "The worst things always are."

I hug her jacket, unsure if my voice is too loud, even though I'm speaking as softly as I can. "But you said you slept with Parker. And you didn't have a choice."

She nods. "It sucks."

My stomach liquifies, and all my brain can do is recall a montage of all I've seen when it comes to Britt and her best friends and Parker—all these moments after football games and in the hallways and at parties just like tonight except they were happy, and they were good to each other, and I saw it. We all did.

At least, that's what I always thought.

But I also think about the way she looked on Kyle's bathroom floor, and how she looked at me on her bedroom floor, and how she looked at me at the bottom of Spence's stairs just now, and it hits me in a way that kills me that maybe this world that always looked so beautiful to me has been some kind of recent hell for her.

"I know that it's really complicated," I whisper. "And you don't have to explain everything to me tonight. But girlsfriends . . . they talk about stuff like this, right?"

"I thought so."

I scoot as close as I can get. The skin on our bare legs touches, and mine has goose bumps, but hers is soft and smooth and warm. I know Britt believes that I've been there for her for weeks. But as far as I'm concerned, it's been the opposite. Until right now.

I take a deep breath as she pulls a fistful of grass from Spence's lawn and lets it flurry like snow. "When you say that Parker didn't give you a choice . . ." My voice shakes a little bit. "Are you saying that he forced you?"

She waits a second, like she knows how much words matter. "Yeah." She looks at me, finally, her wet eyes glinting in the blue of the moonlight. "There's a lot that's broken here, Aly. And it's been broken for a really long time. Parker is a part of it. The *whole team* is a part of it, and they're gonna protect him no matter what."

"They wouldn't protect him from something like this."

"They protect him every single day," she says.

"Because they don't *know*—"

"They know, Aly."

"J would *never* protect Parker from something like this."

"I hope not J," she whispers.

I shake my head and promise her, "*Not* J."

I hope I can speak for more than just J—most of those guys probably wouldn't be okay with whatever happened if she just told them what actually happened. They're a team, not a mob, and they're her friends, too. But I can't promise on behalf of all of them, not about something that matters so much, as badly as I hope I'm right. So, I only promise for J. Because, with J, I really, truly know.

She sighs and absently starts to bite her pinky nail. "You watch the news, don't you?"

"I use our Seton subscription to *The New York Times*."

She nods, and slowly she tells me, "There are guys like Parker everywhere. Shiny, pretty, frat stars on the outside, with money or Ivy degrees or they can catch some stupid ball. They hurt girls at the parties they used to go to, or that they still go to now. They brag about it or belittle it or deny it or do all three in the midst of the same illogical defense. And there are these women, and these girls, who have bigger balls than these guys ever will, who are badass enough to say something anyway. Who just stand up like 'fuck you' and say something anyway. They tell their stories and play their tapes and sit on witness stands, and you know what happens to the guys? Sometimes they go to jail, but sometimes they still win their elections. Sometimes they're allowed to keep their jobs. Sometimes they get to keep making their movies and making their money and seeing their patients and teaching their classes. And you know what happens to the girls?" Britt shakes her head as she stares across the street. "I have no idea."

"But you still have to tell somebody." And I say it definitively, because even though this is a Parker I don't want to believe is real, and even though this would change everything in the entire world that exists, none of that can matter.

"I just tried to tell the whole fucking school." She gestures back at the house. "No one believes me; no one's going to. Parker's starting his smear campaign already, I'm sure. Even the girls are on his side."

"You don't know that—"

"I know that."

"How?" I insist.

"Because they're in there and not out here." She takes a deep breath. "I think I'm ready to go."

She says she's gonna walk home and asks if I'll stay over. Neither one of her parents came home this weekend, and she doesn't want to be alone. She says J should come, too, after he finishes door duty. And I agree without even thinking about it. I tell her to just give me a second to let him know I'm leaving.

I walk back up the steps, and J notices me the second I get to the top. Nic does, too, but J moves his wrist in a way that tells Nic he'll be right back, and then he walks toward me with his hands in his pockets.

When he reaches me, he wraps his arms around my shoulders and rests his chin on my head, a hug I really need. He lets me go and tugs on the sleeve of Britt's bomber jacket. I didn't even realize I was still holding it.

"She evaporate?" he asks, smiling a little.

It makes me smile a little, too. "She's on the steps. I think I'm gonna stay with her tonight. Can you come over, too, when you finish here?"

I'm expecting him to ask me why, or what happened, but he doesn't. Maybe it's because he's J and he doesn't really need the details; he's good enough at reading situations to get it when people just need him. But he might also not ask me what's going on because he already knows. Because he's already gotten a text from inside.

It's obvious he feels bad before he even opens his mouth to remind me, "Alz, I have a game I have to be back for first thing in the morning. I didn't bring any of my stuff with me . . . I'm not gonna have time to get it tomorrow if I stay up here."

I don't know how I forgot about the same Saturday tradition we've been honoring since we were little kids, but I did somehow. Seton football. What else is there?

And so we stand there for a second, waiting for each other.

"Will you be mad if I go with Britt?" I ask.

"Not at all."

This goodbye feels like it matters for some reason, but I can't figure out exactly why. It's a long drive home, and it'll be a late night for him because he's on door duty, so maybe that's part of it.

"Text me when you're leaving and text me when you get home," I tell him.

"I will."

But J tends to have the recall of a goldfish when it comes to remembering to reassure me he's alive, so I repeat, "Text me when you're leaving and text me when you get home?"

He laughs. "Alright, there was probably a fifty percent chance I would've remembered before, but we're at a solid ninety-one-point-three now."

I hold my head back and close my eyes and let him kiss me. "I'll be at your game tomorrow," I promise.

"I know it. When are we gonna go to Walgreens?"

"Tomorrow on our way home. Don't make an extra stop tonight."

"You got it, boss," he says.

We start to leave each other, him toward the house and me back toward the steps. Before we're too far apart, he asks, "You want me to let your mom know where you're at?"

I turn around, and he's facing me as he backs away. I keep backing away, too. "I'll text her."

To mess with me, he asks again, "You want me to let your mom know where you're at?"

I laugh, and he does, too. "I'll text her," I insist. And then I add, "Love you when you get home safely . . ."

I'm walking away again when he calls out behind me, "LOVE YOU, TOO, ALZ!"

I whip around to shush him, because maybe the Seton-proper kids can yell in this neighborhood after dark, but we shouldn't.

But he's already back with Nic, smiling and messing around, so I let it be and jog back down Spence's steps.

Britt's waiting for me in the street. "Sounds like he loves you." She's managing to smile. "Is he gonna meet up?"

"They have their games tomorrow . . ." I know she knows it, but she probably forgot just as quickly as I did. "So he has to go home."

"He can't just come for a little bit or leave early in the morning?"

I shake my head. "Home is far for us." I offer her my elbow. "Walk with me?"

She hesitates, like something's tugging on her, and I get it. But nothing good can happen if we stay here any longer, and it's like she realizes it the second I think it. So, she links her arm in mine and we walk together down the middle of the road, alongside all these other mansions, back to the one that's hers.

What it was.

(Sometime in) March 2019

It was one of those sleepy Saturday nights in Seton-proper, when the football season had ended months ago and no one wanted to party badly enough to plan one, so the Seton crowd congregated in their smaller, clique-y groups, buzzing around town with no true place to go. Some friends had gone to the movies, some had stayed in, some passed the day at Nappahawnick and stayed once it got dark, some hotboxed a car down in the Cedar Elementary parking lot. They weren't together, but Instagram and group texts revealed where everybody was like a blacklight that the teachers and the counselors and the parents couldn't access. Only the Seton kids could, with just a swipe of their fingers.

Britt had gone to BurgerFi with Kelly, Zach Willis, and Levi Jackson. They'd gone to the one off of the Georgetown strip because the one in the town center would probably be flooded with Anderson Prep kids that they didn't feel like seeing. It'd been a lazy and unplanned decision. Zach and Levi had been driving around with nowhere to go, the Seton blacklight revealed that the girls were at Kelly's house, the guys were hungry, and the girls needed comfort food, so Britt and Kelly agreed to take a ride with them. It was a spontaneous intermission from the night they had planned with Michelle and Bianca and a slight exploitation of Zach's willingness to drive.

The restaurant was packed, with three lines stretching all the way back to the main doors. They'd already ordered their food, so now they were waiting at a table for four while Levi and Zach passionately discussed which restaurant had better fries (Shake Shack or BurgerFi), and Britt and Kelly watched them uninterestedly.

Britt cut in and asked Zach, "If you're so obsessed with Shake Shack, then why the hell are we at BurgerFi?"

"Because he's not willing to defend this shit in the moment of choice," Levi easily answered.

But Zach laughed and told Britt, "Because this is where you wanted to go!"

Britt and Kelly reacted on top of each other, as naturally as blinking.

"*What?*" Kelly cried.

"You're drunk," Britt declared.

"We literally got a text," Kelly insisted, leaning across the table. "And then we got a call. And then we got into a car, devoid of any expectations *whatsoever—*"

"Hopeless," Britt confirmed.

"And *you said*"—Kelly was pointing at Zach while Levi smirked and Zach laughed—"'You guys wanna hit BurgerFi?'"

"Because I know how much Britt loves BurgerFi," Zach answered.

"You're sweet," Kelly decided, sitting back in her seat. "But we still could have made two stops."

"Nah, I know she doesn't want to hang out with me too long tonight," Zach said, smiling at Britt. "I know she wants to get back to rolling around with the girls in your bed."

Britt watched him across the table, arms folded, barely smiling. "Is that your actual visual?"

And Zach closed his eyes like he was drifting to sleep on a cloud. "Oh yeah, baby."

Zach was a 225-pound, six-foot-two-inch Seton Varsity defensive end who had a buzz cut and the ability to grow a soft beard, even though Seton made him keep it short. And this year, he was the boy allowed to pursue Britt.

Every year Britt had been at Seton, it was like the boys made some kind of truce with each other—that all of them could look but only one would be granted the right to try to touch, be her plus-one in plus-one kinds of situations, make out with her when she was drunk enough and wanted it, or wanted more than that. That year, the honor had gone to Zach Willis, a boy with the face of a teddy bear and the alcohol tolerance of an infant.

He'd been filling his chocolate milkshake with peanut-butter whiskey from a flask since the second they'd sat at this table, and he'd already topped off twice.

Britt reached for his keys, sitting in front of him on the table. They were heavy like a janitor's, with more keys than he could possibly use regularly, a key chain from Ocean City, and this black-and-silver flash drive like he was some fifty-year-old dad who'd never heard of Google Drive. "I'll take us back," she said.

"No," Zach answered, grabbing them back from her.

"You're drunk," she told him.

"Doesn't matter," he said. Then he amended, "No, I'm not."

She peered at him across the table, keeping his keys in his hands like he knew better than to give her the chance to take them again. "You call me eight thousand times a day and don't even trust me with your keys?"

Kelly smiled and Levi did, too. But to end the debate before it started, Levi took the keys from Zach's hand and decided for all of them. "I'll drive."

Britt was annoyed on the ride back to Kelly's, annoyed that she'd had Zach's keys and he'd taken them away, annoyed that he and Levi were in the front while she and Kelly were in the back. It was one of those compounding situations, not a moment but the mountain that moments turn into—the sign-in sheets at parties, the way the boys hosted any event that ever mattered, how the guys decided every year which one liked her enough to have her (despite her never being all that head over heels for any of them), and now, on top of all that, how Zach snatched back his keys like she didn't know exactly what she was doing when she announced she would drive them home.

But Zach reached behind and rubbed her knee, and Levi and Kelly kissed at stoplights, and Zach gave Britt his phone and let her and Kelly DJ the whole ride home. So, the girls blasted Lizzo, and Dua, and Ariana as Levi sped down the parkway. And even though all wasn't forgiven, everything was good enough.

In twenty minutes, they pulled back up to Kelly's house, a white manor with columns on top of a hill. The roads that led through Seton-proper existed with zero rhyme or reason (they all just curved in disorienting circles that led to one huge house after another), but the kids who lived there knew their way everywhere. Without GPS, sometimes without sobriety.

Britt sat on the grass outside of Kelly's house while Zach sat next to her, holding the bags of food that she'd take inside for Michelle and Bianca so tightly around the top that the paper had turned into a sweaty nub. But at least the food was still warm against her bare legs.

She was giving Kelly the fair and appropriate amount of time to make out with Levi in Zach's jeep, because that was what Kelly and Levi did these days.

"Did you check your bag?" Zach asked.

"Check it for what?"

"To see what all is in there," he said like some kind of genius.

"Oh. Yeah. I checked before we left."

"Did you check again?"

She looked at him, the drunk eyes that she was used to. "Why the fuck would I check it again?"

Zach laughed and explained, "Maybe someone put something else in there when he was holding all that food for you guys in the front seat. Maybe someone brought something along and slipped it in your bag for dessert."

"Like roofies?"

"You think I'd waste a roofie on a night I'm not even gonna be around to reap the benefits?" He smiled at her like it was a joke, the kind of jokes that Seton boys got away with.

"You're absolutely charming, you know that, Zach?" She groaned and meant the exact opposite.

"Just open the bag."

She sighed and looked inside to find a plastic baggie with a few partially smushed brownies.

She didn't want to smile, but she did. "Did you make these?"

"I did."

She held the bag to her nose and sniffed. "Are they hash brownies?"

"Nah, just chocolate. The way Betty Crocker intended."

She looked at the brownies in her hand, resisting the urge to mush them, to feel their gummy stickiness ooze through her fingers just because she could. Her life, her existence, was a series of impulses. Bubbles she was always tempted to pop and did, a lot of times. Just not always right away. There were right moments and wrong moments.

"Zach," she said, sliding her fingertips along the sharp edges of a blade of grass. Prepared to bleed but not actively trying to. "What do you think of me?"

He could have talked about that badass time she sprained her ankle scoring that field hockey goal in the rain, or when her essay on female oppression in *A Streetcar Named Desire* got that national high school award because her English teacher submitted it for judging behind her back.

But that night, Zach told her, "I think you're the fucking prettiest girl Seton's ever had."

She bit the inside of her cheek and nodded as she dropped her brownies back into her food bag. She cupped one hand around her mouth and called into the night, "Yo, Kel!"

The response was quick. The overhead light in the dark jeep flashed on as Kelly opened the passenger's side door, grabbed her bag, and smiled over her shoulder at Levi. She hopped up her front steps and offered Zach a hand when he stumbled trying to get to his feet. But he shook his head like it was an insult and got up on his own.

"You girls act like you have to worry about me," Zach called into the night as he backed away down the sloped lawn toward his waiting car. Loud because he could be, because the rules existed like tissue paper, surrounding them for decorative purposes when they were really just flimsy and disposable. "You act like I haven't been drinking longer than both of you were born!"

He was smiling as he went, as he bumped into the passenger's side of his own car.

Kelly looked down at Britt on the ground and rolled her eyes. She held her hand next to her ear and opened and closed it like a moving mouth.

Britt laughed out loud and chimed, "Blah, blah, blah. What a psycho."

Kelly giggled. "Do *you* need my hand?"

"I want your hand," Britt said, grabbing on and pulling herself off the grass. "Look what I got." She reached into her bag and revealed the brownies.

"Ooh." Kelly took the bag and dangled it from her fingers as she took a whiff. "Hash brownies?"

"Normal brownies."

Kelly's mouth twisted, mildly disappointed. "Zach made them?"

Britt nodded, and held her food bag open as she took a step back.

Kelly smiled and tossed the brownies back inside. "The psycho bakes," she playfully commended. "But I'll eat them."

"Oh, I will fucking devour them."

Kelly laughed, digging in her purse for her keys as they stood on the other side of her tall, all-black front doors. Even though they both opened, they usually went in through the right. "We're home now, so we can be as fat as we fucking feel like."

Somewhere inside, Kelly's parents would be in the midst of being as delectably familial as always. Perfect, as far as Britt cared.

On most nights, Kelly and her parents had the same dinner and then spent at least two hours watching the same thing on TV. Like, *together*. Her parents always called when one of them was on their way home from somewhere to see if anybody needed anything, and now that Kelly could drive, she always did the same. The whole family announced their plans to one another via spontaneous vocal updates that echoed through the house like Christmas carolers. *Sitting on the deck!* Or *Getting in the shower!* Or *Making iced tea!* Her parents knew when the girls were out, and they knew when they wanted them back—always 1:00 a.m. at the *latest*—and Kelly was right.

This was Britt's home.

When the girls had initially gotten the call to pick up food, the invitation had been for all of them. But they decided to divide and conquer to spare Bianca the stress of being social with anyone else that night, so Kelly and Britt tagged along while they left Michelle and Bianca in Kelly's room. The plan for the day had been Mind-Numbing Distraction, since Cramming, All-Nighters, and Ouija Boarding had yet to provide the desired SAT scores.

"This doesn't look like binge-watching . . ." Kelly accused, glancing at her paused TV as she and Britt walked into her room.

"We trusted you to babysit," Britt insisted to Michelle as Kelly bumped her door closed behind them.

"She just wanted to do, like, three practice questions . . ." Michelle explained, Kelly's MacBook guiltily opened to the College Board website on the carpet in front of her. Britt headed toward Michelle as she went on. "Not even really to practice but just to keep the muscle memory intact. Like a reflex kind of thing, you know?"

Britt set her food bag on the bed and sat on Michelle's lap on the floor as Michelle conceded, "Ugh, fine, I suck."

"B." Kelly sat on her knees on the carpet next to her friends. She pushed her laptop closed and set her food bag on top of it. "I'm about to put a lock on this thing if you can't chill."

To the side, Michelle was wrapping her arms around Britt's waist while Britt stayed on her lap, and Britt combed Michelle's ponytail. Forgiving each other for a fight that never was, smiley and giggly as they did.

"Maybe I'm a sadist," Bianca mused aloud, and Kelly squeezed her around the neck like a stuffed animal. "Like maybe I belong in a dungeon with a needle that I'm forced to prick myself with repeatedly because I'll never bleed out, and I'm really just designed for misery."

"Tomorrow will not be miserable," Britt promised her. "Tomorrow is gonna be fucking sick, B. It'll be one of those days they dramatize in your documentary one day. Just watch."

"Yeah, B, visualize your Netflix special and don't even worry about tomorrow," Kelly insisted.

"Maybe that is the strategy," Michelle said as Britt rolled off of her lap. "Maybe you just namaste your way through this thing. It's all in your head, B, you know that. You're a fucking genius. You're gonna be the chemist who invents an oral form of Botox, and we're gonna be like, eh, that's all she did today? Must not have had her Wheaties."

Bianca smiled as she pouted, grateful for words that she would always consider to be lies. But at least she was lucky enough to have liars. "Calories first?"

"Calories always, always first," Britt agreed.

"What are our options, ladies?" Michelle asked.

"Burgers on burgers on burgers," Kelly announced, unpacking one item from her bag at a time. Britt reached for her bag on the bed. "Britt has brownies."

"Hash brownies?" Bianca asked.

"Regular brownies," Britt said, dropping the Ziploc bag in the middle of their pile—comforters and pillows and remotes and phones. "Zach made them."

Michelle put her hands to her heart like it was the sweetest thing she'd ever heard, the way Britt knew she would, because Michelle loved all of their pseudo-romances. "That is *so. Sweet.*"

"No—nope. No. You're not—" Britt insisted as Michelle slid her arms around Britt's waist and squeezed with the glee of a mother during prom pictures. "He's literally drunk off of a peanut butter milkshake right now. I know you love Zach, but that is not adorable. That is sticky, and that is ridiculous."

Michelle smiled through a frown as Britt fed her a French fry.

"They are a mismatch," Kelly gently told Michelle. But deep down, Michelle already knew.

"All of Britt's boys are a mismatch," Bianca insisted as she unwrapped one of the burgers and peered into Kelly's lap to see if she might want something else instead. But she said it like there wasn't a single thing wrong with that.

"Maybe it's just hard," Britt said, putting two burger options in Michelle's lap. "Maybe it's just hard dating high school boys when you've already met your soul mates."

When the food was distributed, they resumed their original plan, sucking salty stickiness off of their fingers as they shoved sandwiches and fries down their throats, and *Euphoria* played in the background on Kelly's TV because this was their third time watching it anyway. So, they mainly just talked, in the unending, effortless way that they always could, about how drunk Parker was at the party last night, and how they should try to make banana bread after Bianca's test tomorrow, and how Zach's brownies weren't that bad.

"Do you ever feel really small here?" Bianca asked, when their empty boxes were scattered like debris and they lay heavy and full in the craters of Kelly's duvet.

Britt's eyebrows came together, her head in Michelle's lap as Michelle's fidgety fingers played with Britt's hair. Michelle's back straightened against the side of Kelly's bed.

Kelly answered on behalf of everyone, "You are not small."

"Because it's just like, we're one in a zillion when we're applying to these schools," Bianca went on as Kelly scooted closer. "We're literally just these stupid little guppies in these pools of essays and transcripts with no identity that anyone actually gives a shit about, especially for a school like Harvard—"

"*Fuck* Harvard," Britt insisted, but Michelle gently nudged her mouth closed, because Britt needed that sometimes.

It would never just be *Fuck Harvard* for Bianca. She'd wanted Harvard for as long as she could realistically want anything. For herself. For her future. For her parents, who'd both immigrated as kids and worked really hard so Bianca and her sisters could have the life they had today. And she'd done well on the SATs twice now, but not well *enough*.

"It's not just the Harvard stuff, though," Bianca promised. "It's everything. I mean, we matter at Seton now, but when we graduate, how long are people even gonna remember we were there? Like, do you even remember anyone who graduated our first year at Seton? Name five people who weren't on the team. And if they don't matter a couple years later, why would we? Even to the boys . . . Do you think they'll even remember us?"

"I hope Zach doesn't remember me," Britt offered, and it made all of them laugh, but it didn't undo the heaviness, the weighted blanket that Bianca had just wrapped them in. "Can I try again?" Britt requested. "To talk about this Harvard thing? I promise I won't say 'Fuck Harvard.'" So Michelle's hand gave Britt's face a little space. "It's just that, B . . . they should want *you*. You're fucking good at *everything*. From calculus to making those drunk banana splits that aren't even disgusting. And the way you've gotten Mich to turn off the parade *three years in a row* to go to the soup kitchen on Thanksgiving. You make me smile every single day. Seriously. Every single second, you make me smile. So, if Harvard would turn you down—a banana-split-making, volunteering, math Jedi like *you*—I don't *want* you going there. Because I want you to be somewhere that makes you feel like a giant fucking Macy's balloon, and that wants you, just as much as I do, every day. You know what I mean?"

Bianca rolled over and rested her ear against Britt's chest as Britt kissed her through her hair.

"Make room for me," Kelly pouted, eager to be a part of another one of the piles they were so used to creating. Piles and webs and human knots—as tangled as wired headphones—almost all the time.

"There's always room for you," Michelle promised, leaving one hand in Britt's hair and extending her other for Kelly.

"I'm three pounds fatter than I was forty-five minutes ago," Kelly warned, scooting over.

"I can't even breathe," Bianca promised, flapping a defeated arm across Britt's stomach.

They were quiet for a moment, maybe two.

Kelly softly said, "I don't think we're small, B. And I bet the boys do remember us after we're all gone." But she didn't say it like she was sure of it. She sounded like she was doing just that—thinking and betting, predicting based on gut and odds.

"But do we even want them to?" Britt asked, and she could feel Bianca breathing just like she was, synched up now that they'd been on top of each other for a minute or so. "I mean, they're gonna remember us. Of course they are. They're gonna remember the parties, and driving us around, and nights like this. Levi's gonna remember kissing you this year. Parker is gonna remember Michelle. But maybe that's enough. I guess it's like . . . maybe we don't need the same boys calling us to hang out five years from now. Maybe it's okay to be forgotten a little bit."

There were times when Kelly's room felt so big, nights when they stumbled in at 12:47 and collapsed onto rugs and pillows, laughing too hard to breathe and confident that everything they had and everything they knew was exactly right. Those were the nights when her room felt bigger than what they could ever need, big enough to fit their entire world.

But lately, there had been nights like this. They were rare, but they existed now, in ways they never had when the girls were just freshmen or sophomores. It was a subtle change. A slow and cautious acceptance that there was stuff that was gonna happen, and people they were gonna meet, and it wouldn't always be Seton, or Kelly's bedroom, or Michelle and Parker forever. It'd be different one day, and they'd slowly started peeking into that drawer of possibility, every now and then. In the same careful way you'd open a drawer full of hermit crabs, and then immediately slam it shut the second you saw what was really inside.

"I hope Parker and I can make it through freshman year," Michelle wished aloud, and Bianca, Kelly, and Britt listened to her easily, even though Michelle had been amending her desired timeline for their relationship for a while now. Some days she just wanted them to make it through the summer before they left for college. Some days she wanted him to be at her college graduation. "Because as much as I love him, I think I know Parker and I aren't gonna end up married one day. But I just feel like if we can make it through our freshman year of college and stay together . . . like, if he really, really tries like he says he will . . . it means that what we have is bigger than just some jock-meets-cheerleader teen drama. And I want to know it's bigger than that."

"I think it's bigger than that," Britt promised. "Just not big enough for forever."

Michelle sighed and rested her head against Kelly's bed, blinking at the ceiling. "Fuck. What even is forever?"

"Do you guys ever think about what you might want?" Kelly asked. "Like when you think about the kind of person you want to be with forever, do you feel like you know?"

"Besides us?" Bianca asked.

"Yeah. Like boy-forever," Kelly said.

"I think I want someone who's smarter than me," Bianca said.

"Not in a *Pretty Woman* kind of way, but just someone who I can fully trust has thought about things just as much as I would and then a little more."

"Someone who can handle his shit and your shit without you worrying about the house burning down," Michelle summarized.

Bianca sighed. "Exactly."

"I want someone who has a really good family," Kelly said. "And lots of siblings and cousins and they're all close and we can have these huge Thanksgivings where you guys are there and his whole family is there and there's just this long table that stretches through our gorgeous formal dining room and everyone is eating until they wanna barf. And I hope he's darker than me. Because I hate my freckles and the Donahue propensity toward skin cancer."

"We *love* your freckles," Michelle insisted.

Bianca promised, "And I already love my pale as shit, freckly nieces and nephews so much."

"I'm telling them you called them that . . ." Kelly warned, and Bianca laughed. She nudged Britt next. "Have you thought about what you want?"

And they were quiet for a second while they waited for her to answer.

"You know what I think I want?" Britt said. "Like really, really bad?"

"Tell us," they all requested.

"I want to meet the kind of guy who might live in California while I live in Maine. And for like, *a month* I'm telling him how excited I am to stream *Hamilton*. And how badly I want us to see it together for Christmas or something, I don't know. And he listens to me say that shit over and over again because he knows how high it gets me and so it's like a contact high for him, too. And then, the day *Hamilton* drops, I hope he watches it. I actually hope he watches the whole fucking thing, and loves it, and never even tells me he did it. I hope he lets me talk about that stupid play endlessly until Christmas comes, and then we watch it together like it's his first time. And I have no idea it's not, because he loves me in this big way that *actually matters*." She rolled onto her side so she could watch their eyes watching hers. "That isn't about not watching a fucking show for six months just to make me feel good about his streaming habits or give me something to brag about to a bunch of people who don't care. I want him to know that love isn't about that tiny shit, or about never telling white lies, or about doing every fucking thing on this planet together. I want him to protect my heart, not change his soul. And when the play ends, and I ask him what he thought about it—or, better yet, whenever I ask him what he thinks about *me*, I hope he never, ever fucking tells me I'm pretty."

And that was when they cocooned around her, and cooed and squeezed and told her how ugly she was, and Britt squeezed them back and kept them there, gratefully, on the floor in Kelly's room, that was just big enough for now.

What it is.

This is the time of year when Seton starts to feel special.

There's a way about us, this sort of order to things, that repeats itself annually the way the Earth laps the sun. At Seton, we love traditions. We love to do things because it's the way we've done things. We love to reinforce this world that's ours and that can never belong to Billingsley or St. Mary's or any of the other schools around here, because of all the nuances that can't be replicated. All the rules that only we know. All the patterns that only we keep.

And I guess it's kind of like that all year. But it's even more like that right now.

It starts with Zap the App, the first week of October every year, the week when seniors pledge to submit their college applications. The administration makes a huge deal about it—banners and streamers and surprise deliveries like pizza and doughnuts to the seniors' classes. The counselors stay late in case anyone needs a last-minute transcript. Anyone on the faculty will read and critique their essays and personal statements. And it's the one week all year when we run a mini-issue of *The Seton Story* every day, each one full of different college application and stay-sane tips.

When a senior finally presses Submit, they take their confirmation to Principal Mitchell's secretary and she gives them a string of red beads, Mardi Gras–style, one for every application they send in.

As soon as Zap the App ends, homecoming week starts—which is this massive celebration of the seniors getting their apps in and intense anticipation for the Varsity game that Saturday. For the record, it matters every second of every day that Seton hasn't lost a regular season football game in twelve years, but it's so much different when it comes time to play another homecoming game. The local news crew always stops by to interview the team and, especially, the quarterback. *The Seton Story* interviews him for this huge feature story, too. The editor always writes it. Tradition.

But in the background, or maybe foreground, or actually just *everywhere*, everyone buzzes about the game and who's going to win it. And then, when Seton does—because we always do—the team hosts this huge party at the beach to celebrate.

Seton doesn't do homecoming dances. We haven't in years.

Two weeks after that is our last game of the season until it's time for playoffs, and after that, it's the Week of the Girls. When all the guys on the team do really cute things for the girls all week, to thank us for all our support that season. Flower bouquets, boxes of chocolate, giant posters taped to desks proclaiming undying love and adoration. They tell us how perfect we are, how pretty we are. That we're the best girls in the whole world.

And we take their gifts and we accept their compliments, and for an entire week, we dare to believe that maybe we are.

"I am *so obsessed* with this story," Britt declares as we walk into Seton on Day One of Zap the App. "I want to name my daughter Pencils just in honor of this story." She has our special Monday issue of *The Seton Story* in her hand, folded to the page where we ran Gina-Melissa's submission. I decided to print it this week, along with the best recipes I've seen on TikTok lately and a word find, as a reprieve of sorts. To help the seniors think about more than just their applications. To help everyone think about more than what a weird year this has been so far.

I smile and insist, "You should tell Gina-Melissa that."

"If I see her, I will. I never see her."

But the thing is, GM is around just as much as I am. Her boyfriend played for us until he graduated, so she's with the team all the time, too. It's just that Britt is more looked-*at* than look*er*. I'll point it out to her the next time GM is nearby.

"How many people at Seton do you think would bleed if you pricked them?" Britt asks.

"Most, probably."

She makes a face like I'm losing it, her big hair loose today as we keep making our way down the hall. "Less than ten percent," she declares.

She went on a whole rant Friday night, once we got back to her house, going on again about how Seton isn't real; how it's a concept, a construct, a bunch of *V*s capitalized for no reason, and a perpetual calendar of unquestioned traditions; how she can't pinch Seton but she can pinch the people *in* Seton and how dangerous it can be when things get that big. I'm not sure who else she's talking about now, besides just the team, but the thought makes me anxious. Does she think I'm a part of the ninety or the ten?

Britt stayed home on Saturday, but still, she was everywhere. She was the only thing anyone talked about at the games and the party that night, like she was a legend they'd seen once upon a time—a mermaid, or Bigfoot. They had theories about whether Parker could or Parker couldn't, whether he would or he wouldn't, and debated it in the same way they would debate who's the best rapper of all time or which AP exam was more miserable. Maybe because they weren't with her, or didn't leave with her and see her the way that I did, but they've been treating it like gossip—and the good kind, at that.

Maybe that's why she thinks they don't bleed.

On Saturday, as J drove me back from the games, I asked him what he thought. Because of course I did. And because he thinks so much better than the rest of us. But it took him a second, and then he conceded that he doesn't know what to think yet.

"Are you Zapping the App this week?" I ask Britt as we reach her locker, changing the subject on purpose. I lean against the one next to hers with my backpack on my shoulder.

She starts to type in her six-digit passcode, and her eyebrows come together as she shakes her head like I'm wildly mistaken. "No."

I smile. "Why not?"

She pops open her locker and declares, "Because I have absolutely no idea who I'm gonna be this time next year."

She folds her copy of the newspaper smaller and slides it onto the top shelf. She seems like she's okay. When she finished spinning on Friday night, she popped popcorn and we fell asleep next to each other in her queen-sized bed, watching YouTube. She didn't cry again. She didn't say anything about it in the morning. We texted on Sunday and it never came up, and it hasn't come up today. Most of me is glad that she's alright. But there's another part of me that can't just ignore this flaming meteor that came crashing down two feet away from us Friday night and is still spitting fire this morning. We *have* to talk about it again. We can't just go on pretending forever like there isn't some giant flame ball to tend to.

I hug myself, and that's when I notice Kelly creeping toward us, sneaking up behind Britt while she keeps digging in her locker. Kelly winks at me when we make eye contact, a wordless request that I not say anything.

She stops behind Britt and places her hand at the bottom of her spine. She walks her fingers up the center of her back, itsy-bitsy-spidering her way to the base of her neck.

Britt closes her eyes, like she's taking a second to bask in the familiarity of those fingers. "Hey, Kel," she says, a moment before she actually turns around.

Kelly nibbles her lip. "Hey." I can practically hear all the things she wants to say whirring around her head like that disk that gets loud in your computer when you're trying to do too many things at once. She takes a deep breath and looks at me instead. "Hey, Aly." She seems so nervous.

I smile so that maybe she won't be. "Hey, Kelly."

It makes her smile, too, and she turns back to Britt. "You know, it's B's big deadline today. Hence the ensemble." Kelly does a little curtsy.

"Harvard early action." Britt nods. "You look like the best hype girl ever, Kel."

I wouldn't have thought she looked any more perfect today than she does any other day, if Britt hadn't mentioned it. But I realize that these Crimson-colored, miniskirted, corduroy overalls she's wearing aren't a coincidence. She has on a cropped white T-shirt underneath, and nude booties, and her hair is parted in the middle and in two fishtail braids with Crimson bows on the ends. It's a complete pro-Harvard uniform. And it's so extreme and unnecessary, but so beautiful and *right* because it's them.

I look at Britt and all the Crimson she's not wearing.

"Thanks," Kelly says like she means it. "I wasn't sure if you'd remember."

"Of course I remember."

"Do you think you might want to come with? I know she wants to have you there . . . You know how B gets. She set, like, five alarms for this morning just to make sure she didn't Rip van Winkle the shit out of today—"

"Kel, you know I can't come."

She frowns. *"Why?"*

"Britt, I'm gonna go," I try to tell her to the side, but she holds on to my wrist to stop me as she keeps her eyes on Kelly.

Britt evenly insists, "Because you guys didn't even come outside Friday night."

"Everyone was having a complete meltdown Friday night, but we called you and texted you a million times . . ."

"*You* did."

"And Bianca did, too, Britt."

The part they've left out hangs in the air like smoke, the kind that you're supposed to crawl under just to stay alive.

Kelly called.

Bianca called.

Michelle didn't.

"And so did Parker," Britt tells her, her gray eyes shining. "He texted me twenty-nine times. Calling me a bitch and a liar and a slut . . . a fucking homewrecker and a Michelle wannabe, whatever the hell that means. And it wasn't just these one-liner texts, Kel, like Tourette's of the thumbs. These were paragraphs . . . these were *dissertations* about what complete and utter shit I am, that he was sending me so constantly, and so insistently, and it was so *surreal* to see Parker's name on my phone sending me messages like that, that I actually changed his name to Vinny." Britt waits for a second, like she wants to make sure that Kelly gets it. And she does, I think, because her breaths are so shallow that I'm honestly not even sure that she's breathing at all. "And I don't fucking know why, or even know who Vinny is, besides the fact that he sounds like a guy who might talk to me like that. But I just couldn't deal with what it felt like to have Parker's name on top of this strand of texts that made me wish I never ever had to come back here. And I silenced my phone for a while. So, I missed your calls. But I saw them."

"Parker's a dick for talking to you like that," Kelly says.

Britt shrugs like that either isn't the point or isn't a surprise.

"And I would never talk to you like that," Kelly goes on. "Ever. *Ever* and you know that, Britt. I just . . . I just want to talk to you, that's it."

"Talk to me about what, Kel?"

"You *know*, Britt."

But she says it again. "Talk to me about what?"

Kelly's blue eyes get glassy. She looks up at the ceiling and then manages to look back at Britt. "I just *want you*, Britt. I fucking miss you so much it hurts, and none of this is normal, or okay, or what it's supposed to be, and we all know it. And I get that we haven't handled the past few weeks all that well, but it's because nobody knows *what to do*." Her lips are shaking a little; her voice is shaking a lot. And Britt watches her, transfixed. "We should've come after you on Friday, maybe you're right. We should've chased you. But also it's like you've been running from us *for weeks*. And I just . . . I would shatter Parker's fucking phone tomorrow if he ever tried to do that to you again. I really, really would . . . You know that, right? I swear to God, I'll do it right now. You know what I mean?"

I believe Kelly with my entire soul. Britt nods.

"And I just want to *know*, Britt. I just want to know what happened, and when, and how, and if you're okay . . . I need you to always *at the very least* be okay. I want you to always tell us instantly if Parker is saying a bunch of bullshit to you." She sniffs, still pretty as ever, even as she drags a finger under her runny nose. "And I just . . . I've been thinking about this since you said it Friday night. I've been replaying all these times in my head when I wasn't there or maybe I was and I was too drunk, or maybe things started out okay but when they ended, you were in a bad mood and I didn't ask why . . . I've been thinking about *everything*. And trying to figure out the moment when I became a shitty enough friend to miss something like this."

Britt swallows, her feet glued where they are like they're stuck in mud, like she's determined to not give Kelly the hug she needs so badly, or even the smile. "You're not a shit friend, Kelly. So, don't say shit like that, okay?" Britt shakes her head. She looks up the hall and hugs herself. "Kel, it's just that . . . you can't play both sides of the fence with this. You can't be cool with everyone right now. And I know that Parker is disposable in your mind, and that you'd break his shit in an instant if it would matter. I know that. But the thing is . . . Mich is still with him. And Mich is the one who needs to care about the answers to all those questions, and she doesn't. And while she doesn't, you can't play both sides. You're hers or you're mine. And I'm being really serious when I say this, Kel, and I need you to know that I'm not mad at you, and we aren't broken, and that we can fix this one day and we will . . . but you should go be with Mich. Because I'm miserable, but so is she, and Mich has always been a hell of a lot worse with misery than I am."

Kelly tries a few more times to pull her back, to say she's sorry, to undo this whole mess that isn't hers. But Britt never gets any closer, and Kelly finally accepts it, wiping her eyes as her cute suede shoes click away down the hall.

I see all of them (minus Britt) together for the first time at lunch. Michelle's Harvard costume is a high-waisted pair of black skinny jeans and a Crimson cardigan that's fitted and mostly buttoned and looks amazing on her, even though I can tell she isn't wearing more than a bra underneath. Bianca is in a plaid Crimson skirt and a short-sleeved Crimson turtleneck, and her hair is so flowing and perfect, it could be on a Kardashian. Even Parker's doing it with them, in a backward vintage Harvard baseball cap that I've never seen him wear before.

In the cafeteria, the seniors who got an early start on apps this morning are already beginning to wear their red beads; Bianca already has hers. And, looking at them, it's flawless. They're beautiful, color-coordinated magic—Bianca, like she's the lead in a three-girl girl group. But it's *not* a three-girl girl group, it was never, ever supposed to be, and everyone knows that.

No one at Seton commits to certain seats in the cafeteria every day, but everyone has a general area where they always are—including J and me, and the rest of the team, and the girls and Britt, before Britt stopped showing up at lunch. Our tables are round, welded to the ground, and seat five, and today J and I are sitting one table away from Parker.

The Seton cafeteria is huge. It's two levels with balcony seating and the kind of buffet you'd find at a Whole Foods. Seton is bigger than it needs to be for the number of kids who go here, so we're definitely not on top of each other whenever we're in the caf, but it still gets loud and hard to hear. Even when it's people sitting at the next table over.

So, I don't hear everything that was said to make Parker jump up like he does, standing awkwardly between the table and the seats. I can't hear everything he's saying as he grips the tabletop and leans across it and glares at Sam Klein like he could choke him and maybe, in a fit of insanity, really would. But the veins in Parker's neck get tight, and his face turns Seton red. His lips seem to growl something about how "we're not fucking talking about that shit, we're not fucking joking about that shit, because that shit isn't a joke."

Sam holds his hands up defensively and laughs uncomfortably and says something like he's "just messing around."

"Yeah, well, don't," Parker orders, and one of the guys sitting next to him claps a firm hand against Parker's shoulder. In a discreet effort to get him to remember where he is, to get him to sit down, to get him to stop yelling at one of our own.

It's the second time in three days he's blown up with an audience when it wasn't on the field, and I know that this time is about Britt, too.

Michelle has her back to him as she faces Kelly and Bianca instead. It seems like they're both trying to focus on her, but they keep stealing glances over her head at Parker.

And while the rest of us stare at whatever it was that just happened, Michelle just fingers her messy bun, and rolls her eyes like Parker's an idiot, and keeps talking to her friends like she couldn't give less of a shit.

It's like that all week—this unrecognizable Parker and Michelle. I knew a Parker-and-Michelle who flirted with each other like they just met the day before; a Parker who would let Michelle use the back of his hand to test out eye shadow shades in the middle of the hallway; a Michelle who once chomped the ice in their soda cube by cube and spit it back in the cup they were sharing (which wasn't even a little bit gross to either one of them) because they prefer their ice crushed.

Now, she won't even touch him.

I swear, maybe that's the most important part. I tell J more times than he probably even wants to hear it. But this isn't Michelle drawing a line in the sand, and choosing Parker over Britt, and saying she believes him instead of her. The fact that Parker and Michelle are still together is just a footnote at this point. It's the fact that the girls still aren't talking that's the real tragedy. And Michelle feels it, too. I know it. I can see it in the way she shudders when Parker reaches for her hand, and how her eyes always look like she might have just stopped crying.

This is limbo. Our in-between that feels like an in-between to anyone who knows what Seton is truly supposed to be.

And then homecoming week comes, and that ball of fire we've all just been letting hang out next to us since it landed last Friday night?

It explodes.

What it was.

<u>April(ish) 2019</u>

The road matched the color of the night sky as Levi walked down the middle of it with his hands shoved into the pockets of his Seton letterman's jacket. His warm breath blended with the cool spring air, proof that he was still alive four beers later than he deserved to be.

His lips tasted like Kelly's. Which tasted like the strawberry Skittles vodka they'd made that night (buy a ton of Skittles, separate out all the red ones, drop them in a three-fourths-full bottle of vodka, put it in the dishwasher and run it, and by the time the cycle is done, you've got the kind of vodka girls drink like water). He'd just walked the girls back to Kelly's house, up the wide brick driveway, past the his-and-hers BMWs, to her front door. He'd stayed there and kissed her a while, with his hands in his pockets, his neck dropped so she could reach him without trying too hard, while he smiled down at her and she smiled up at him and those smiles merged into kisses anytime her tiptoes decided she wanted them to. And the girls—Britt, Michelle, and Bianca—watched from thin glass windows that framed Kelly's towering front doors, heads stacked on top of each other like babies' blocks, while they tapped the glass and giggled and gagged and squashed their gorgeous faces against the panes.

Levi finally laughed and told Kelly she could go inside. And when he said so, she said, "No shit, it's my house," and he laughed and held up his hands in playful surrender. She opened her front door, and the girls whispered anxiously as he walked away.

One of them said, "Bye, Levi!"

Another one asked, "So who's a better kisser—us or him?"

A part of him was interested in the answer, but the door closed before he could hear it.

So, Kelly went inside, and Levi walked. Not because her friends were there—because her friends were always there—but because Levi had been doing this with Kelly for months now. Getting drunk. Making out. Leaving. He thought she was crazy cute, it wasn't anything like that. But Kelly Donahue was a good girl. Notoriously good. Worth a lot, if there was any chance he'd ever get her into bed.

But he knew he probably wouldn't. And that was why his boys always said he was wasting the year, that he needed to use his status as Seton QB to contribute to the greater good. Eventually, maybe he would. But for now, he liked her. Liked the chase. And sometimes, once he'd had enough alcohol to lose track of his own thoughts, he liked to compare her mouth with Justin's. Who was no one, really, besides this guy out west that Levi had met on a family vacation when he was just drunk enough, just far enough away from home. A boy he knew for a single night and then tucked safely in the past, two thousand miles away.

And so, that night, Levi let himself compare the two as he walked down the middle of the road from Kelly's house to his, with his hands in his pockets and a subtle smile on his lips. He always walked home at the end of the night, no matter what time it was or whose house they'd been at (unless, of course, it'd been his). Levi didn't drink and drive. For no particular reason—just one of those things he never really got into, like scrambled eggs or Post Malone.

He typed in the code for his garage door and slid between the cars to the door that led into the house. When he walked inside, the lights were off. It was 1:00 a.m. or something. Maybe 1:30 a.m.

He walked through the great room and past the study to the stairway, where he took one slow step after the other on his way to his bedroom. When he reached the top, his mom called out from his parents' bedroom down the hall. "Levi?"

"It's me," he told her, and closed his bedroom door behind him.

He didn't turn on the lights, but his blinds were open, and the blueness of the stars mixed with the streetlights made the room less dark. He kicked off his shoes on his way to his bed and fell face-first onto the mattress. His bed was completely made—sheets tucked in, comforter washed, nine pillows stacked in some perfect kind of order he'd never understand—because every day, after he woke up, the maid came by and made it for him.

Maybe it wasn't the second his face hit the covers, but it felt like it when his phone rang. With his eyes closed, he reached into his pocket, and then he glanced at the screen to see who was calling. Zach Willis. He closed his eyes and answered, "What's up, man?"

"I can't find my drive."

Levi rolled onto his back. "What?"

"My drive—dude, I can't find my drive." But Zach was unbelievably drunk that night. They had started pouring him shots of water at one point and he hadn't even known the difference.

"Bro, you'll find it in the morning. Go to sleep. Hydrate."

"No, dude—I'm not drunk right now. I mean, I am drunk right now, but I'm not saying this because I'm drunk right now. It was on my key chain. I'm holding my keys. The drive is not on my keys."

Levi sat up slowly. He felt it in his chest—this tightening that made it hard to get a deep breath. He felt it in his stomach—like he could throw up all those extra beers he never should have had. It's weird how a tragedy can sober you up. "Bro, if that drive isn't on your keys, we have a big fucking problem."

And instead of Zach laughing and saying he was just messing around, instead of Levi jumping awake and realizing it was just the worst nightmare he'd ever had, they both sat there, on the phone, trying to breathe—trying to stay alive—while their world threatened to crumble and crush them whole.

What it is.

I wouldn't say that Seton has a social media problem, but we do have a social media propensity. We post a lot of stuff, hence the need for sign-in sheets at the front door of all our parties. Seton even has a verified Instagram account that the yearbook team manages.

So, we see it quickly, we all do, when one of the guys at Billingsley comments on Parker's homecoming week post. Someone had taken a picture of him standing on the bottom bleacher of our football field, in his jersey and a pair of basketball shorts. His back is to the camera, and the field is completely empty, and you see him, but you also see the entirety of this field that's been his world for over three years. I only wonder who took it, because I don't think Michelle would do him those kinds of favors right now, but—either way—it's one of those cool, artsy shots. He captioned it:

> Can't believe this shit's almost over. First we make it 13. Then we're taking States. #HCW #FlyBabyFly #IWant2

Most of the county follows Parker on Instagram, and he got over a thousand likes and a bunch of comments within seconds of posting. There were so many #IWant2 hashtags in the comments, and Parker had gone through and liked them all. But then the Billingsley comment came through, and it was screenshotted immediately and mass texted the instant after that, and even though Parker had deleted it before it even got to exist for five minutes, the damage was done.

It said:

About to make it 13 years in the slammer if you don't get a handle on these rumors, big boy . . .

One of the guys on the team sent it to J before our bus pulled into the parking lot.

"I didn't even know Billingsley had heard about what Britt said," I whisper, now that J and I are walking toward the school and can finally talk again. There's this unwritten pact among teenagers on a bus at 6:00 a.m.—no one is allowed to say freaking anything.

"Billingsley knows everything," J says, adjusting his Tupperware bowl of cookies under his arm. He has a lot to carry this morning—backpack, football duffel, baked goods. "You know the walls bleed around here."

I'm honestly not even sure that it's a real saying, but for J and me, it is, and he does say it a lot. What he means is that something that happens at Seton gets to all of us. In the school, and even outside of it. It seeps from the walls, and it stains us like blood. "I know, but *this*?"

"Especially this," he says as we approach the wide-open front doors. "This is the only shit anyone's talked about in a week."

We walk inside and "Feel So Good" by Mase is playing over the same sound system Principal Mitchell uses to announce things like prom court and that code blue last year. There are collapsible tables with foldable chairs set up across the entire main entrance, red and white streamers and balloons taped to walls in the junky, haphazard way boys decorate things. Some of the balloons have already broken free from their strings and are nestled tauntingly in the nape of the peaked ceiling—at least twenty feet off the ground. This happens every year, and over time the helium leaks, and day after day the balloons drift back down to earth, until the tallest ones of us can jump up and grab the strings and pop them and throw them away.

It's homecoming week, and that's why a bunch of the Seton-proper guys on the team, who normally wouldn't pull into the lot for another twenty minutes, are already here. In their Seton sweats and Seton Girls T-shirts, dapping up J and giving me hugs as we walk through the doors.

They'll be here manning the entrance all week, greeting people and sitting at tables and dancing with money buckets for their bake sale as they officially kick off their Season of Giving. They'll do a bunch of stuff over the next few weeks before Christmas to raise money for charity, like car washes, our all-male beauty pageant called Mr. Seton Academic, this bake sale again every morning until the season ends, and then every Friday after that.

The reporters aren't here yet, but they'll come. They'll wander in on the bake sale all week and get their pictures. They'll shadow the team's practices and interview our coaches and the guys. They'll be at the game on Saturday. But for now, it's still just us and the guys on the team who probably think they're whispering to J softly enough that I can't hear them talking about the Billingsley comment this morning.

It doesn't look like Parker is here yet, even though he should be.

J is gonna have table duty this morning, so he grabs a seat next to Seth and takes the top off of his chocolate chip/Reese's Pieces/M&M cookies (Pieces and M&M's added with creative license after J channeled his inner Martha Stewart last night). They actually taste pretty good—they're doughy in the middle and only kind of burnt on the bottom—and honestly, that's part of this whole thing in the first place. The more shameful the dessert these boys make, the more people are willing to donate for it.

"Wow, these really look edible," Britt says, appearing next to me. She picks up one of J's cookies and starts analyzing it like the guys at the gas station when Dad tries to get them to break a fifty-dollar bill.

J smiles. "May give you food poisoning, but for sure won't kill you."

She smirks a little. "How'd you know my standards are so low?"

"Any girl who eats a bucket of KFC at a country club has good enough standards for me," J assures her.

Britt smiles to herself as she reaches into her school bag and pulls out ten dollars. She drops it into the bucket on J's table and declares, "You're a sweet boy, J Turner." Then she turns to me and asks, "Wanna walk?"

"Yes." I lean across the table and kiss J, his mouth waiting for mine expectantly even though he's dapping with one of his teammates who just got here off to the side. "I love you, bye."

"I love you, bye."

Britt slides past the table, our arms linked as we walk slowly down the wide hallway. She's wearing a soft pink sweatshirt dress today and a black beanie. We're the only ones going this way because everyone else is busy at the bake sale, and her sneakers squeak on the red and white tile.

"Have you been on Instagram today?" I ask, attempting to sound as conversational as possible.

She seems like she's trying to remember. "Not too much. Maybe three times. Maybe four. Why do you ask?" She has a bite of J's cookie, and I honestly can't tell if she knows exactly why I'm asking or has zero clue at all.

"Did you see anything . . . interesting?" I try.

"Some trending news about a potential Jonas Brothers reunion?" I can't help laughing, and she looks at me as she says, "Don't make me guess. You know you can tell me whatever you want."

It's so cavalier for her, such an easy promise, that it almost makes me forget about the Billingsley comment altogether. Because what I *really* want to talk to her about is the body I wish I had, and learn how she gets her hair to curl the way it does, and bitch about this girl in my World Sociology class who carries Chanel purses every day and always refers to Black people as *African Americans* even when she's talking about Black people from the U.K. or Canada or *South Africa* and how it makes me want to break something for reasons I can't even concisely explain. I want to talk to her about all the kind of stuff that J tries to be good at but just isn't, and—for a second— that whole Billingsley thing from this morning feels so far away.

"Will some of your boyfriend's cookie help?" She holds it close enough for me to take a bite and wiggles it in front of my mouth. We both laugh. "It's really kind of delicious, I don't get it," she declares as she takes the bite for herself instead.

But then she's being ripped from me—literally torn away—so quickly that I can't even process what's happening.

Parker has her waist in his hands, her feet not fully touching the ground, as he presses her back flat against our red lockers. He used to grab Michelle like this all the time—sneak up behind her and take her, with this cocky but lovable grin on his face—right before she'd gladly kiss him. But it's different now that it's Britt, and he isn't smiling, and his eyes are gleaming with a kind of hatred, and a kind of tunnel vision, I've never seen on anyone in real life before.

"Parker!" I grab for him. But he's so much bigger than us. Bigger in this moment than I ever realized before.

"I'm tired of this shit," he growls, staring her dead in the eyes.

"You think I'm not fucking tired of this shit?" she cries.

Michelle catches up to him and punches him in the side, the discreet way that you kick someone under the table when it's time to shut up. With her voice low and through clenched teeth, she demands, "*Put her down.* You look like a fucking lunatic."

He drops her, and Britt glares at him as she takes a defiant bite of her cookie.

"Let me tell you what you're not gonna do," Parker says, pressing his hands on the lockers on either side of her head. I reach for Britt's wrist so she'll keep walking with me, but she doesn't let me take her. "You're not gonna be out here starting rumors about me that make it all the way to other schools. You're not gonna be the reason why some newspaper gets some fucking screenshot, or why people start looking at me funny, or why I don't get a State 'ship this year, all because you and Mich can't just kiss and make up and move the fuck on already. You get that? You're not about to have some bullshit stories about me floating all over town because you're having some kind of mental breakdown, or because you're so fucking lonely at your own house that you've run out of anything else to do, or because it's hit you that once you finish at Seton, you're finished everywhere, because trust me—no one's gonna give a shit about you next year. There are a million girls just like you at every college in the fucking world. So, what you're not gonna do is take all that psychological bullshit out on me, and keep running your fucking mouth, and telling your fucking lies. There's no way in hell I'm gonna let you take this year away from me."

"What lies?" Her voice is so calm it sends chills down my spine.

He grips his hair like he can't believe his life. He punches the locker next to her head, and all of us jump but him. "It didn't happen!"

Britt swallows hard. "Yes, it did, you dick."

Michelle immediately slides between the two of them, and presses her hand over Britt's mouth, and looks her in the eyes and pleads, "Stop. Talking."

So I reach in to grab Britt again, to try and take her away, while Michelle elbows Parker in the abs because he won't back off. "We need to go," I insist, pulling Britt's arm. But I've only moved her a few inches, because she's so determined not to leave.

And when Michelle's hand slips from Britt's mouth by accident, Britt declares, "It happened! With sex once and other stuff other times, and if *force* is the word you're contesting, then you can contest it all day long. You can contest it on fucking Instagram, and you can contest it in these goddamned hallways, and you can contest it in a court of law, if that's what you want to do. I'm not scared of you or your bullshit, Parker. I know you way too well to be scared of you."

"You're not scared of me?" Parker insists, talking over Michelle's head as she presses her back into his chest. "You're not scared of me now and yet you were scared of me when I supposedly forced you to be with me? Yeah, Britt. That makes all the fucking sense in the world."

"*Why do you get to decide?*" she cries, ripping her arm away from me. "*Do not pull me away right now*," she demands, her finger trembling as she sticks it in the middle of my chest. She turns back to Parker, glaring determinedly into his eyes. "Answer me. Why is it up to you whether the way *I feel* about what *you did* makes sense? You don't get to storm over here like fucking King Kong and undo, or invalidate, what my experience was with you just because you think my reaction looks different from the ones you see in the movies you jack off to at night." Her eyes narrow on him the same way you try to recognize somebody from a hundred feet away, someone you think you know. "You can call me a liar. And you can prance around your fucking kingdom trying to be the good guy and reminding everybody who will listen how much you used to love me. You can do that forever if you want, and knowing how you are, I bet you will. But you're not gonna tell *me* to *my face* that what you've done 'doesn't count' because my response doesn't make sense *to you*. You can fuck off before you say that to me."

"Oh, get off your wannabe feminist mountaintop right now, Jesus fucking Christ, Britt. You're wearing a goddamned sweatshirt as a dress and you fuck with guys' heads like it's your job, and then you want to sit here and make me look like some asshole when I have the balls to tell you you're a walking contradiction? You're gaslighting. And I'm not falling for it.

"I mean, *why* would I even do it? Can you tell me that? Why the fuck would I even do it when I have the most amazing girlfriend standing right next to me, and I could get any girl I want? I could get any girl in the fucking world, so why the hell would I force one to do anything?"

"For the same reason you drive home drunk and you smoke your blunts with the windows down." Her eyes smolder as she watches him, and it hurts me to see how much she really loved him, by how much she hates him right now. "Because you think no one can ever stop you."

I don't know what would have happened if two of the guys on Varsity hadn't gotten to us at that very moment, at the very instant when Parker's fist was behind his ear and the pent-up energy in his arm was enough to throw a ninety-mile-an-hour pitch. I don't know where his fist would've landed, but forever and ever, Parker will get to say that it wouldn't have landed on her, because Scott Matthews grabbed it before the story could be written any other way.

"This is my fucking life!" Parker growls, spitty whiteness gathering at the corners of his mouth. *"And you're out of your fucking mind if you think I'm gonna let you destroy it. If you think anyone is gonna believe your shit . . . if you think you even have a fucking chance, you're out of your fucking mind!"*

But his threats get further and further away, because it isn't hard for Scott and Jeremy to pull him with them, no matter the fact that Parker is so red that there are sweat beads on his nose. Scott shoves Parker to snap him out of it, and maybe it does, a little bit. Because Parker jiggles his arms and rolls his neck like he's loosening up. Rubs his head through his backward Seton cap. He tells Scott and Jeremy that he's good. "I've just got one more thing to say," he tells them, and when Jeremy tells him he's too hot right now, Parker shakes him off and insists, "Just let me say this and I'm good." Then he calls down the distance between us, "Hey, Britt."

She doesn't turn to face him, and I try not to, either, but it's hard in an empty hallway, when the entire school is busy by the main entrance, dancing around and eating chocolate like we live in Neverland.

"Yo, Britt," Parker says again, and when she still acts like she doesn't hear him, he says, "That's cool, you don't have to look at me. Just listen. Listen when I tell you that you were right. That whole speech you gave about how you want to be a noun so bad? Well, good news—you are. You're a fucking atomic bomb."

And Parker slow-claps for her as he backs away, a shitty smirk on his lips as he does, and it's demeaning, and it's degrading, and it's heavy in a way that I can't completely explain. This reigning power-fulness of it all as Scott and Jeremy follow him. The three of them are laughing before they even reach the end of the hall.

I look at Britt and remember for the first time that Michelle is still here with us. Where she belongs. Because she can't follow Parker after who he just was. She can't just unlove her best friend in the entire world overnight. That's not what love does. It shape-shifts, maybe, or crumbles sometimes, but it doesn't just evaporate. It can't. It's not made out of the right stuff to just disappear, even when we wish it would.

That's what I'm telling myself, at least.

She's whispering into Britt's ear while Britt leans against the lockers, flattened. And for a few seconds, it's like the world is only theirs. The wreckage before the dust settles and you can see your hand in front of your face again.

"I can't even halfway reason with him. *He's losing his goddamned mind—*" Michelle's soft voice is a frantic hiss that I can only hear because the rest of Seton is busy bingeing desserts.

"Stop it," Britt snaps back. Her teeth are clenched and her lips barely move. "I'll call you later."

Michelle's gaze meets mine, and that's when she pulls away from Britt. There's something cautious about it, protective. I don't know. It reminds me of the way my mom gets when she goes to our front yard on Sunday mornings to pick up the paper and runs into a neighbor she didn't realize was there. The way she smiles but tightens her robe and pinches it up around her neck. She hates when anyone sees her before she wants them to.

Michelle doesn't smile, but she presses her lips into a firm line that almost resembles one, in the perfectly polished way that Michelle manages to do just about anything. And then she walks down the hall, in black and white booties, and a black miniskirt, and a white polo with a red cardigan tied around her shoulders. It's the opposite way that Parker went.

"I'm sorry I kind of yelled at you," Britt tells me. "I just can't walk away from shit like that, you know? Like, he can't just go unchallenged, leading with that kind of bullshit. Because then he can do that to you. Or Mich. Or any of us . . ."

The last part gets muffled into my shoulder, because I wrap my arms around her neck and squeeze. She's trembling in the steady way that J's Ford does at stoplights, and I close my eyes for a second and try to just *know*. Know *anything*. What to do. What to say.

"What were you and Michelle talking about?" We're still holding each other when I ask.

She doesn't answer me right away, maybe because she's trying to be okay. But after a few seconds, she says, "She just said she wants to go talk to Parker."

We don't let each other go. She soaks up my hug like a three-ply paper towel. And my head is spinning, so hers has to be, too. That's why she just said what she did about Michelle. Even though Michelle didn't even go the same direction as Parker, and I heard their whispers for myself. Because the dust is still settling, that's all.

Otherwise, she'd just be lying.

What it was.

Speed limits were more like a suggestion when you grew up in Seton-proper. Like washing your hands before dinner or not watching television right before bed—they existed as a recommendation only, designed to establish rules for the types of people who believe they reserve the right to ignore them.

So at night, the Seton kids sped down their roads and wove carelessly through their neighborhoods, with their seat belts off and their breaths wet with alcohol. And the local police, stationed in all their narky locations with their headlights off, would let them zoom past without even setting down their jelly doughnuts. Because they recognized the expensive cars as they went by, and smiled as they thought of the kids they belonged to.

On a night in early June, one of those cars belonged to Parker—a new, dark blue Ford F-150 that he handled like it was a dirt bike. And inside of that car, he had Britt in the front seat and Kelly and Bianca in the back while Michelle was out of town for the weekend at her grandmother's eightieth birthday party.

The windows were down, and it was one of the few summer nights they had left before things would get hot and sticky and damp. Where they lived—not just Seton, but the whole geographical area—had the kind of summer humidity that made it feel like a cloud had drifted down to earth and swallowed everything, a suffocating wetness that warned of the storm that was always somewhere, waiting.

"What are you gonna get us to eat tonight, Parker?" Britt asked, one of her knees pulled to her chest, her black Chuck Taylor digging into the brand-new leather of her passenger seat. A skinny black headband contained her mane while a few mischievous curls dripped onto her face.

Parker smirked, one hand on the wheel as he rolled through a stop sign. "We haven't even gotten there yet and you're already talking about what I'm gonna feed you when we leave?" He glanced at her and was laughing before he could stop himself.

She laughed, too, helping herself to his phone in the cupholder as she scrolled the team's playlist for the next song she wanted to hear. "Like you're shocked."

"I figured since this is at your man's house, you'd at least want to stay for a little bit." He was looking in his rearview now, looking at Kelly.

Kelly smirked at him skeptically. "He's your man. I just kiss him sometimes."

Bianca smiled proudly as Britt pressed Play on "Case of the Ex" by Mya and turned to face Kelly. "Fuck yeah," she commended.

"Yeah, whatever, you little Power Rangers," Parker dismissed. "Girl power, fuck guys, all that shit."

"Ooh." Britt winced, looking at him again, playful and mocking and addictive. "Someone's sensitive tonight."

"Maybe he misses Mich," Bianca suggested, sliding to the edge of the back seat. She wiggled her taunting fingers into Parker's ear to the beat of the song. He didn't even flinch, used to their pokes and pinches.

"You better miss Mich," Kelly declared.

"I could die right now," Britt added, so simply that it almost sounded true.

"Of course I miss her," Parker said. He waited for a second before he added, "But, I mean, I don't mind only having to feed three of you instead of four of you tonight . . ."

And then all their hands were on him, shoving him and punching him and calling him a dick, but with smiles on their faces anyway, because of what boys get away with.

Parker was smiling, too, ducking out of their reach as best as he could while he drove too fast on their dark, winding roads. And between the song playing too loudly, and the girls hissing about what an ass he was, no one even cared about the end of what he said. The part where he finished with "But, yeah, I miss her."

Levi's house wasn't raging that night. It was one of their weeknight parties, now that school was out, the kind of thing that only the guys on the team and the girls they preferred got invited to. The kind of thing that the kids who bused in never got a text about, would never even know had happened.

The playlist was on as they hung out in Levi's basement while some people shot pool by the sliding back door, and some people played Circle of Death around the coffee table, and some others used the long edge of the wet bar for beer pong. They poured shots that were too big into red plastic cups and choked as they held out their cups for more, celebrating nothing besides their existence and each other.

"Come grab some more cups with me," Levi said, clapping his hand on Parker's shoulder as he stood up from the oversized sectional.

"Yes, sir." Parker followed Levi to the basement steps, even though they both knew this wasn't about cups. When they'd been talking on the phone that afternoon, Levi had said they could start talking about the transition tonight.

At the top of the steps, Levi closed the basement door, leaving the voices and music behind them. On the main level of the house, you could barely hear anything that was going on downstairs, which was good. Levi's parents were home that night, but they were usually pretty chill as long as a bunch of noise didn't wake them up.

"Beer?" Levi offered, walking to his refrigerator.

"Yeah, I'll take one." Parker waited against the island as Levi pulled two cans of beer from the top shelf. He tossed one to Parker, who caught it with one hand.

"Let's talk outside for a minute."

Parker smiled as he followed Levi through the kitchen to the sliding door that would lead to the back deck. Parker was at this house almost as much as he was at his own, with all the times Levi had the guys over after practice, to chill on weekends, to watch game tapes. "You trying to get me drunk and take advantage of me right now?"

Levi laughed, sliding open the door. "I know Mich is out of town, but I suggest you get reacquainted with your hand tonight if you're having those kinds of fantasies."

Parker laughed, too, as Levi slid the screen door closed behind them.

"Yo, let me know if you want me to leave Kelly here tonight," Parker offered as they each sat in the basket-woven chairs. "No reason why you can't get it in just because I can't."

"Yeah, right," Levi said, spinning his Seton Girls baseball cap from forward to backward as he kicked his feet up on the patio table. "You know Kel's not putting out until she gets a ring on her finger." He popped the top of his beer and smirked. "Or at least the passcode to my phone."

Parker smiled, popping the tab to his beer, too. "It's not like you don't have other options, man."

But Levi shook his head. It was weird to a lot of the guys on the team, including Parker, and they'd ride Levi about it sometimes. Kelly was cute and all, but to make like some born-again virgin for his entire senior year when girls would drop to their knees for him in a heartbeat? And to be Varsity quarterback and not contribute to the vault once, the entire time he held the position?

"Bro, don't you just want to get your dick wet sometimes?" Parker asked.

Levi chuckled to himself and swigged his beer. "What about you, big man? You gonna be exercising your options tonight?"

And Parker knew exactly what Levi was referring to, even though Levi would never say it out loud. Never risk making it the kind of real that they couldn't unsay one day, if Parker needed him to. Because that's what brothers do.

"We'll see," Parker murmured.

And that night, as the brothers they'd been for the past three years—since the moment Parker Adams joined the Seton Academic football team—they settled in under the stars, peering across the darkness at their classmates' houses, at the lit bedroom lights of everyone who hadn't been invited tonight. This world that needed the both of them, more than most people even realized.

"You been talking to Coop?" Levi asked.

"Hell yeah," Parker answered. "Yo, he's hype, dude. He's been waiting for this for almost thirteen years."

Levi smiled. "You scared?"

And Parker sucked his teeth. "Scared of what?"

"It's a lot to know, man. It's a lot to manage. And that first negotiation . . ." Levi sat back in his chair like he'd just barely survived a heart attack. "That was the scariest shit of my life."

Parker leaned forward on his knees, like he was too eager to stay still. His knee bounced as he stared at Levi and asked, "How much do I have to work with, man? Like, are we talking hundreds of tapes at this point, thousands? Tens of thousands? I mean, I know that sounds crazy, but you know as well as I do that it's not *that crazy* if you think about who we're talking about. Trojan should be asking these dudes to do a fucking commercial for them at this point—"

"I'll show you," Levi said. "But it's not a tonight kind of thing. We need computers, I need the sign-in sheets . . . We'll do it soon. But not tonight."

Parker nodded, eyebrows furrowing. "Cool, cool, yeah, of course." Parker sat back in his seat and laughed a little. "Sorry, dude, I'm just fucking ready, you know what I mean?" He took a deep breath and went back to looking out onto all those big Seton houses again. They were hypnotizing, in a way.

"We lost a drive," Levi said, his voice hollow and lifeless against the perfect night air.

Parker faced him. "What?"

"Back in April. It was Zach's, and we have no idea where the hell it is. It went missing the same night we had that huge party and there were dudes from Billingsley there and from St. Mary's there and pretty much all of Seton showed up. We looked everywhere for it for three days. We never found it."

Parker stared at him, his lips parted like he'd fallen asleep with his eyes open. His voice was a whisper but a shriek at the same time. *"Dude, what the fuck am I supposed to do with a missing flash drive? This entire fucking empire collapses if we don't know where that shit is!"*

"I know. Trust me, I didn't sleep for, like, two weeks, and I know. But it's been three months now, and it hasn't turned up. A whiff of it hasn't even turned up, and I'm starting to think it won't. One of their guys probably snatched it and now he sleeps with it under his pillow every night and is just as scared to get caught with it as we'd want him to be."

Parker's breaths were shallow, and his neck got red, a nervousness that wasn't normal for him. "You really think so?"

Levi pushed his tongue through his cheek until it bulged. "I pray to God every night that's what it is."

Parker jumped when he felt the vibration against his hip. He pushed his fingers through his hair and mumbled, "Fuck, it's Mich."

"Go answer her."

He hesitated, but he pushed back from the table with his buzzing phone in his palm. He looked at it as he slid open the screen and walked back inside. He closed the screen door behind him, made a fist like he was about to punch the wall, and froze.

Because there was Britt, leaning against the kitchen island with a beer of her own, watching.

He pressed the side button on his phone and ignored Michelle's call.

"What are you doing up here by yourself?" His eyes held her like she was fragile enough to break.

"Bianca's in the bathroom."

"Where's Kelly?"

"With Bianca."

They watched each other as Parker rounded the island slowly, carefully, the way you approach a wild animal so she doesn't spook.

"How long have you been up here?" he asked.

"What, am I not allowed to go anywhere without your blessing now?"

"You look sketchy as hell, just standing here. How long have you been standing here?"

But she didn't answer. She just swigged.

He stopped right in front of her, and then he asked, "What did you hear?"

And being the sassy, gorgeous brat that she was, she watched his eyes and brought her beer can to her mouth. "What do you think I heard, Parker?"

Before he could fully back her into the kitchen island, and plant his hands on either side of her to keep her where she was, Bianca and Kelly spilled out of the powder room.

So Parker had to let her go.

That night was the first of one of their last together, at least as the way they were. The parties would keep on happening, Seton's doors would open again in the fall, but this senior class and their Varsity football all-stars wouldn't be there anymore. They'd be off to their colleges, learning who to be in a world where *Seton* didn't precede itself, and it couldn't be used anymore as an adjective, and a definition, and an identity, all in one. It'd be Parker and his team, instead. Parker and his senior class. Until another year went by, and they were gone, too.

Seton kids always drank more in the summertime, and maybe that was why. A complicated effort to make the best final memories that they could through all the nights they couldn't remember in the morning. So, Levi took out whiskey and 100-proof vodka, and they played pong with liquor instead of with beer, and they pulled out their blunts and shared them with each other while they laughed and sang and did all they could to forget that this couldn't be forever.

And sometimes, that works, when your mind is in a good place once it starts to go numb. But Parker's wasn't. Anyone could tell how distracted he was. His head clearly spinning, trying to process, trying to decide. If he could still have the year that was destined for him, that was all but promised to him, while there was a missing drive. If there was a way that he could get it back somehow, through whatever means necessary. Barter for it or bribe for it or bash somebody's head in.

He waited thirty seconds before he followed Britt up the basement stairs. They'd left a room where they wouldn't be missed, now that everyone was officially too drunk and high to care. Even Kelly and Bianca were distracted, caught up in a new round of Circle of Death with Levi's free hand nestled between Kelly's thighs.

The kitchen light was out, and Parker waited in the darkness, leaning against the wall across from the powder room. The kind of drunk that makes the room spin if you ever close your eyes.

There was a flush and the light flicked out and then the door opened. Britt stopped when she saw him standing there.

"You finished?" Parker asked.

"Were you waiting? Can't you guys just gaze at the stars and piss off the deck?"

He grabbed her wrist as she tried to walk back to the basement. And she tensed up. "I'm not trying to piss, I'm trying to talk to you." When she wouldn't turn around, he pulled her closer. And she stumbled, begrudgingly, back to where he was.

"Parker, I don't want to talk right now."

"Why not?"

"Because you're drunk."

"But you'll want to talk in an hour when it's time to get something to eat, right?" He smiled, like he just wanted her to come closer, the way he smiled whenever she was being a pain in the ass. "You know it's true. So, what is it? What *do you* want from me tonight?"

"Have you talked to Mich since we've been here?"

"Yeah." He pulled Britt closer by the belt loops of her tiny shorts, his pointers anchoring a solid hold that she'd have to rip her jeans to break. He took a slow sniff of her neck. He always went for her neck.

She slammed her foot down on his and he yanked it back. "Damn it, Parker. Can't you just go get an Evian and a sponsor already?"

"*Hey,*" he soft-reprimanded, spinning in a quick move so that she was the one against the wall now. He shuffled his feet to keep his own balance and raised his eyebrows at her as he pointed up to the sky.

Or the level where Levi's parents slept.

They both knew the rules as well as anyone else. *She was as Seton as he was.* And this was the quiet floor. It was always hell if Levi's dad came down.

"What were you doing up here earlier?" he asked, unfazed by her outburst—used to them, even.

"For the millionth fucking time, Bianca had to pee."

"You came up here this time without them to pee."

"Oh, don't ask me a bunch of bullshit you already know the answer to. Bianca never pees alone when she's drunk so she doesn't accidentally raid the cabinets for snacks while she's wandering unsupervised, and if you don't know that by now, take it up with a neurologist, not me."

His eyes stared down into hers, his six-foot, 200-pound frame boxing her in in a way that was almost experimental. A boy deciding whether or not to smush an ant.

He pressed her hard against the wall and studied her eyes like they would tell him something that mattered. But he finally decided to just ask. "What'd you hear, Britt?"

"Nothing worth repeating."

He ran his hand along the front of her neck, his fingers long enough to almost wrap all the way around it. He was always so into her neck. "For real?"

"Yeah."

He slid his grip up to the base of her chin until her head tilted upward, as much as she didn't want it to. "You promise?"

"Parker, I literally have no idea what the fuck you're talking about."

"Hmm." He nodded to himself, studied her face for a final moment, and seemed to decide it was the truth.

He smiled. One less thing.

And with that out of the way, he slid his lips across the part of her body that he'd always preferred and held her arms against her sides as he kissed her just like he wanted to, with Michelle not around for him to kiss instead.

And she didn't fight it. Not enough for him to care to stop, at least.

What it is.

"Honey buns?" I suggest, tossing one down the aisle to J. "Three for a dollar." (Which, for the record, is the *actual* right price for honey buns.)

We're at the Walgreens up the street from our houses with a twenty-dollar bill that Mom gave us when the bus dropped us off this evening so we could pick up some snacks for everybody. Dad works at our local power company, and today he got promoted to supervisor, which is the biggest news we've gotten in so long. It means a raise and everything. So now J's family is coming over, and we're grilling in the backyard to celebrate.

J catches the honey bun with both hands because my throw caught him off guard. "Two for you and one for me?"

"One for me, one for you, one for an emergency."

"Deal."

I smile, and he catches the next two that I throw his way.

We've already grabbed a bag of Ruffles and one of those onion dips that comes in a jar. We picked up two-liters of Coke and Sprite, and because we don't have enough for me to stock up on a new Glade PlugIn, I've decided I can at least have sugar.

I hug myself as I wander up to the checkout behind J, where Ms. Glenda is swiping our groceries and dropping them into plastic bags for five cents apiece. She smiles when she sees me walk up, but she's busy talking to J about the homecoming games this Saturday. She goes to our church, and I don't think she's ever actually been to a Seton game before, but she's been a fan ever since J has been playing, just like everyone else in our neighborhood. She's gonna listen to Saturday's games on the radio, she promises.

"I appreciate it, Ms. Glenda," J tells her as he takes our bags.

"You play hard for us, you hear?" she says, winking at me as we leave through the sliding doors.

The sky is orange and purple as the sun sets behind the Walmart down the road, the boundary our parents always gave us when we would play outside as kids. There's a fresh chill in the air, and it's officially fall—at least in the ways that matter to me. Trees are shedding their leaves, and the sun isn't out for our full ride home anymore. As we walk back toward our homes, the middle school boys who always play basketball on the Johnsons' hoop are wearing hoodies instead of T-shirts.

Something about right now feels really good. Maybe because Dad was outside waiting when the bus dropped us off in my driveway, and he picked me up and swung me around. Maybe because I had no idea he was even being considered for a promotion, but I can tell this one really matters. Maybe because there was music playing in our backyard—Smokey Robinson on the Bluetooth speaker we bought Mom last Christmas. Maybe because I love almost anything made on a grill, and the smell of smoky goodness that hit me when we first started our errand to Walgreens is already wafting my way again now.

"Do you think they're done cooking?" I ask.

"They'll be cooking all night."

The thought makes me smile. "Do you want to make plates and then sit out front so we can do some work?"

"You know Cory's gonna want to toss a ball around at least for a little bit."

"Cory's gonna overdose on hot dogs and be asleep by eight o'clock."

We're quiet for a second, our shoes scratching against our sidewalk that's just wide enough for J and me to walk next to each other. We'll be back at my house in another minute; it's coming up on the left-hand side, and J's is across the street, just three houses farther down than my own. In Seton-proper, three houses away can be practically two football fields, but it's nothing like that here. Our yards are small, and our homes just have an upstairs and a downstairs, and the temperature inside usually skews toward whatever the temperature is outside, regardless of whether we're using the heat or the air-conditioning. They all look pretty much the same, but we make them our own with trim work and flower beds, and we always nod at each other and say hey when we pass. We know one another, but everyone really knows J. They're rooting for him, even if it's from their couches while they tune in to the fuzzy local sports radio.

"Do you want a honey bun?" I offer.

"Depends. Would it be mine or the emergency one?"

"Depends. Is this an emergency?"

He chuckles and looks down at the sidewalk as we keep on walking. And then, like we're still just talking about honey buns, he informs me, "I told Parker I'd break his legs today."

My heart takes a funny beat. "Why'd you say that?"

J sighs, even more exhausted than he usually is by this time of night. "Because I meant it."

"But why did you mean it?"

"Because he pissed me off today, Alz. The way he's been losing it lately, and then how he went after Britt . . . He can't pull up on a girl like that, I don't care who she is. I don't care what she did." He kicks a rock across the sidewalk, and it scatters into the grass. "He can't just go after her like that. And he's out here talking about States . . . Coach would bench him in a heartbeat if he knew what went down today, so how's he supposed to get anyone to States then?" He shakes his head, squinting against the shine of the setting sun or maybe just at the insanity of everything that happened today. "It's just not worth it, no matter what people are saying, and I want to see him keep his head on straight, and be a fucking captain, and not risk everything because he's being a damn hothead. And you know what else killed me today, Alz? Not just the fact that he did it, but that he did it *in front of you*. That you were there, and he was seeing red, and you could've gotten caught up in the crossfire . . . He could've grabbed for Britt and gotten you instead . . . and that shit made me crazy *all day*. Because this is family. And he's supposed to be taking care of you, too. He's supposed to be looking out for you, too . . ."

I step in front of him so he'll stop walking, his arms at his sides as our plastic bags dangle from his fingertips. J had been a little off all day, but I figured it was stuff going on with the team, text messages and secrets between them about the Billingsley comment this morning. And I was so caught up thinking about Britt, and wanting her to be okay, and texting with her whenever we weren't together in the hallways that I didn't even think about anyone else, not even J. "Wait, hold on. I'm fine." I hold his cheeks between my hands. "Look at me. I'm completely fine." I have his face, but I don't have his eyes. They're cast to the side, focusing on something that's not there.

"I don't know, the whole day just messed with me."

I let go of his face and hug myself instead, and just like that, I'm back there—to the way Parker exploded in the hallway this morning, how scary it was for those minutes when a part of me accepted that whatever he wanted to do, he could. That we couldn't stop him. We weren't big enough, strong enough. "I felt like I didn't even know him today," I finally admit, and maybe that's why J can get himself to look at me now. "And you're right. Everything he did was terrible for every reason you just said. Did he at least get that when you talked to him?"

"I'm not really sure."

I bite my lip, my stomach twisting as everything suddenly hits me, my heartbeat tripping over this feeling I've never had before. Like all of a sudden, there are two of me. And I don't know when it happened or how, but there's This Me who Britt has—This Me who sat with her on Kyle's bathroom floor, and left Spence's house early with her, and was there when Parker flipped out this morning and knows how broken she deserves to be. And then there's this Other Me who J has—this Other Me who knows his hopes, and dreams, and plans, and how much Seton has already given him—given *us*—and what a big part of all that Parker really is.

One Me says, *Yes, it was completely terrifying and you should absolutely threaten his legs if he even thinks about acting like that again.*

And Other Me, because of how important and fragile Seton is for both of us, says, *No, you can't.*

I settle on "I don't want you and Parker to be in a bad place because of me."

He nods, but his eyes are laced with the kind of uncertainty that comes when I'm quizzing him on flash cards he hasn't studied. "One of them is lying, Alz."

I force myself to swallow. "What?"

"It's not possible for what Parker's saying and for what Britt's saying to be true at the same time. I mean, that's just how facts work. And I don't know, Alz. Sometimes I just think about how close they all were. How much time they spent together when none of the rest of us were around and how much could have been going on without any of the rest of us having any clue at all. I mean, their history runs so deep . . . Maybe she's pissed about something else. Maybe this is revenge, or . . . I don't know."

"J, Britt's not lying—"

"I didn't say she was—"

"You're really close to it, though. And I'm telling you, she's not. Parker did something to her—"

"But did he really make her have sex with him?" J asks.

"What do you mean, 'did he really make her have sex with him?'"

"Because Parker says he didn't touch her. Parker swears to God up and down on a Bible every day that he never—"

"The Parker who was at Spence's, and the Parker who freaked out in the cafeteria last week, and the Parker I saw today was capable of anything, J."

"I get that."

And so we stand here, at a stalemate.

"Look," J says, letting out a deep breath. "All I care about is you. I don't care about anything else. I'm not saying which one of them is lying, because I don't know. Maybe you feel like you do. But I don't. And I'm fine with that for tonight, because your dad got promoted, and we've got two honey buns and a spare, and we're home now and all of that shit is thirty miles away, okay? All I care about is you."

I walk into his chest and stay there as he wraps his arms around me and the two-liters bump me solidly in the back.

J is always good at this part. Separating *them* from *us*. *Where we go to school* from *where we live*. Who *they are* and who *we are*.

But I'm not. And as he holds me that night on our sidewalk in our neighborhood with our small houses and tiny front yards, I finally accept that that's because the same separation he's happy with, I've always secretly hated.

What it was.

<u>Around July 4, 2019</u>

Levi and Parker made the transition at the back of a Walgreens parking lot, six miles away from their homes as they sat in Levi's SUV, confident that no one who mattered would find them there. They played the music from their team playlist, songs by the greats like Tupac and Biggie, added by the greats like Cooper and Wallace and all those other quarterbacks who'd come so long before them. They had Five Guys burgers and sodas, Levi's MacBook, and a stack of maybe a few hundred papers. And Parker listened closely to the things he needed to know; he watched Levi's mouth as it moved like it might help him remember it all, because he couldn't write it down. He couldn't text in a couple of months when Levi was gone at school and Parker had forgotten something. He needed to know it and be able to do it on his own.

So he listened as Levi scrolled through the files, told him how they were saved so he could find what he wanted when he wanted it. Levi flipped through the stack, showing him the sign-in sheets that they'd kept all those years, and how they were perfectly sorted by date, in manila folders named after whoever hosted that night. Levi showed him the contracts, the ones they used for the boys on other teams who they were making their deals with, and the Excel tracker of all the guys and all their emails and all their phone numbers who'd ever gotten a drive in exchange for a Seton win. Levi role-played a couple of negotiation scenarios with Parker, because there was an art to it. And then he role-played the meeting Parker would end up having with his Varsity team, so they'd know what was going on and they'd get their own honorary drives to hold on to and look at. So they'd be ready to contribute to the vault, too. He took Parker through everything, every nuance of an almost-perfect strategy that, by birthright, ran through Parker's veins.

And in the end, Levi gave him the flash drive that Parker would need to give to J Turner in the next few days, because the incoming JV quarterback always held on to a spare.

"Do you think he'll be cool about all this?" Levi asked as they stuffed all their secrets into Parker's bright red duffel bag, *Seton Football* embroidered proudly along the side.

Parker knew he was talking about J. And with a furrowed brow, he asked, "What do you mean?"

"I don't know, man, it's just different. He doesn't live around here. Coolest kid in the world, but he doesn't have any kind of net to save him . . . His dad installs cable boxes and his mom works at a beauty salon or some shit. He's screwed if stuff gets out while he's running it. And maybe he'll be smart enough to know it." Levi peered out the windshield as Parker finished filling his bag. "I mean, sometimes I think about how J might not even *need* all this. The way he can play? Just get on the field and win."

Parker's skin got splotchy red. At the idea that J, or *anyone*, could do what they'd been doing without help. At the insinuation that J was good enough to choose himself over what they'd built for him. At the mere suggestion that what they were doing would get out one day, that what his brother had built would eventually fall apart like it wasn't genius enough to last forever. Yeah, maybe J was different. But the thing was, people had said the same thing about Levi when it was his turn, wondering if he could do it. Because he listened to James Taylor and Tim McGraw when no one was around to stop him, and spent more time trusting God than fixing things, and could spend a whole year making out with Kelly Donahue when she wouldn't even sleep with him. Levi had been different, too.

But at the end of the day, they were brothers. And it didn't matter who they were when they were alone, or how good one of them was, because above and beyond anything else, they were a part of this Seton football team.

Parker assured him, "J's gonna do it. J needs football more than any of us." Then he zipped the duffel closed and the stuff that'd been inside of him poured out instead, like a grocery bag that'd finally gotten too heavy and everything fell through the bottom. "Levi, it's a big problem that we don't know where one of those drives is. J isn't gonna fuck us up, or the guy who comes after him, or the guy who comes ten years after that. It's gonna be this missing drive. I'm telling you. I know it."

And they sat there for a moment, their drinks sweating in the cupholders.

"I know it's bad," Levi said. "But if it hasn't made its way out yet, maybe it won't. We just have to hope to God it won't."

"God isn't gonna fix this kind of shit, though. The reason why this works, the reason why we've had no issues for so long is the fact that we've got so much hanging over these guys' heads if they ever try to come for us. We have their names on contracts. We have a goddamn Excel that has every single one of their names and cell numbers and addresses *for twelve years.* And that's why we don't have to worry about those drives. But if there's a drive out there and we don't have collateral for it . . . If we lost it the same night Billing-sley was there and St. Mary's and AP? Why *wouldn't* they destroy us with it? They'd be idiots not to."

"Then why not just go ahead and get it over with?" Levi said.

"I bet whoever has it is waiting for the season to start and then they're gonna drop the bomb. I just . . . We have to scare them out of it, man. We can't just go home and try to hope this shit away."

"So how do you think that gets done?"

Parker thought for a moment. "I think we go through the Excel and hit up every guy who got a drive while you were negotiating this year. I think we tell them the deal, because they know they're just as fucked as we are if we can't find one of those drives. And we use the sign-in sheet from that night to do exactly what it was designed to do if this shit ever did happen, and tell them exactly which dudes from their school were there that night. And we let them handle it for us, but at least then we have guys on the ground keeping an eye out. And if whoever has that drive realizes it's not just Seton who's in on it but their team, too, that at least gives him a reason not to do something stupid." Parker watched him, waiting. It was a weird in-between, the transition of power. "What do you think?"

But Levi watched his eyes, and trusted Parker's gut. Maybe he was right. Maybe that drive wasn't so much missing as it was wait-ing. Ticking until it detonated and destroyed their perfect world.

"Let's do it," Levi agreed, because he had to be the one to choose. This was still his team until it wasn't. And Parker slapped his hand supportively, like the idea had been Levi's all along.

What it is.

J and I have been in my room, on my bed, for about an hour while our parents stay outside. The music is still going, and they're playing bid whist, and every now and then they erupt because J's mom reneged like she always does. J's ten minutes into one of his classic power naps, head on my stomach. I'm trying my best to focus on the words on my iPad for AP Lit tomorrow.

My phone vibrates on the bed next to me, and I assume it's Britt, because for weeks now, it's always been.

But it's Parker.

My nerves haven't fully calmed down from earlier, from everything that today has already been. But at least J can't see Parker's name on my phone, and it doesn't reignite this thing between us that we just sort of stamped out when we came back to eat burgers in honor of Dad's promotion.

My thumb hovers over my phone's lock screen, and Parker's name against his unread text shines back at me.

I make sure J's really sleeping and then I slide my thumb across the screen.

Think we can knock out the interview tomorrow?

I'm both relieved and disappointed that that's all he has to say. Or maybe it isn't. I don't know. But I have this anxiety about the moment that we're all in right now, and I can't get rid of it. It's like phantom fingers tickling my arms in the dark, that make me itch even though there's nothing there. Weeks of watching this family we all built together collapse, and I'm so eager to react. To scratch.

I write back:

Yeah

Because Parker and I need to talk. And if he's offering to do it over tacos at Julio's tomorrow once he finishes practice, then that's where we'll do it.

———————————

Parker and I walk across the blond hardwood floors, through the seating area where every table and booth is full. The loudness buzzes against my eardrum like a hovering bee, but it's not so loud that I can't hear the Shaggy song playing over the speakers—"Boombastic." Another one of those songs I know all the words to because it's been on the team's playlist since I've been at Seton.

Servers in red T-shirts and black jeans weave effortlessly through the congestion, carrying trays of food to the tables with the right numbers propped on their little metal stands. Parker squeezes the shoulder of an older man who's a couple of inches shorter than him as we slide past—probably in his forties or something, with jet-black hair and a red T-shirt that matches the rest of the staff. At first, Parker looks like he's gonna keep walking, but then he smiles when the man realizes who he is. They laugh together and slap hands and immediately start chatting the way Parker would with any of the guys at school, except in Spanish. One of the subjects Parker tested into Seton on is languages. He gives Michelle his pretty smirk and flirts with her in Spanish all the time.

"Aly, this is José. Big man manager around here." Parker slaps his shoulder again. "José, this is my friend Aly."

José smiles and takes my hand and gives it a quick squeeze. "You make sure this guy is buying for you. No splitting the check. He needs to be a man about it."

I smile. "I'll make sure to find you if he tries to stick me with the bill."

"You know I was raised better than that," Parker says, and he slips in something else in Spanish that makes them both laugh.

"I've got space out on the patio," José says. "Sit wherever you want. If you guys need a heat lamp or something, let me know and we can bring one out. Can I get you anything?"

Parker looks at me, eyebrows raised. "Margarita, mojito? They've got a full bar."

Since he's the one offering, we'll be fine, but I still feel weird about drinking in public when any one of our teachers could walk in or drive by.

"I'm okay," I answer.

And Parker offers one more time before he tells José he'll have a cerveza.

We walk up to the counter to order, Parker with his hands in his pockets as we stand next to each other and look up at the menu—an oversized blackboard with offerings written in different colored chalk—displayed behind the cash registers.

"Any idea what you want?" Parker asks.

"This is the longest menu that's ever existed without a paper version."

He keeps his gaze locked overhead. "I know. Complete insanity. What do you usually get when you come here?" His voice is as carefree as ever.

"I've only been here once, and I've never had the food."

"*What?*" That makes him look at me. "We were all here last year . . . after Terrance got that pick-six before we went back to party at Levi's."

I nod. "And I didn't eat that time."

"Wow." Parker exhales, looking back up at the board. "That's a fucking tragedy."

I hug myself and can't help but almost smile as I look back up at the menu, too.

"Is it okay if I order for you?" he asks.

"It might save us an hour."

He chuckles. "Is there anything you don't like? Or can't eat?"

"Only jalapenos."

Parker glances back down at me interestedly. "Can't or won't?"

"Isn't it all semantics anyways?"

He squints a little, smiling as he thinks about it, but he lets me be right. Come to think of it, I've never seen Parker pointlessly debate anything with a girl.

He walks up to the counter and orders us a jalapeno-free meal before he pulls out his wallet and hands over a credit card.

That's the thing about Parker, about all of this.

He really can be kind of perfect when he wants to be.

Parker and I are outside at a two-seater table with the patio pretty much to ourselves. We have a large chicken quesadilla and a giant platter of crab nachos sitting in the middle of the table for us to share. I keep the sleeves of my shirt tugged over the heels of my hands. It's not cold, but it is a little chilly when the sun dips behind a cloud.

And I guess I'm also fidgety. It's weird to be here, doing this.

The quarterback feature in *The Seton Story* is such a big part of what Seton does that Parker has been joking with me about it since the moment I got editor at the end of last year. When some of the girls were complimenting him on a new polo he wore to a party this summer, he turned to me and asked if I thought he should wear it on interview day. When a bunch of kids from one of the Seton-proper elementary schools ran up to him at the fair to take a picture, he nudged me and asked if I thought they'd read his article when it came out. When we were at the team's annual picnic, and Parker was taking a break at the table where I was sitting while every-one else was in the field playing flag football, he asked, "You think people will be surprised to find out Elmo creeps the shit out of me?"

I pull one of the chips from our heaping tower of nachos. It's heavy with creamy crab and cheese and tomato and something herby and green. "So, should we talk about States first?"

He's watching me—his gaze weighing me down like I just got drenched in a rainstorm—and it's enough to make me glance up from my plate. His green eyes pierce me like darts, pinning me where I am.

"What?" I manage to ask.

He smiles a little and shakes his head. "Nothing, I was just think-ing about how much has changed. How you're sitting here right now as this hotshot editor, and I still remember how freaked out you were when I met you on your first day at Seton. Like one of those little kids who gets separated from her parents at the mall. Hey, do you remember that first Seton party you and J came to? And you agreed to play Strip Cup because you had no idea what the fuck was going on?"

I laugh and crack my chip into pieces that can actually fit into my mouth. "And you grabbed me by the arm and dragged me away with some weird excuse about how my mom was calling."

"J would've beat my ass so bad if I'd let that happen." Parker laughs and rubs his hair, sitting back in his chair as he brings his beer with him. It's almost an afterthought, the way he adds, "I would've deserved it."

He's sitting there, in all of his Parker perfection. With his teeth that have been toothpaste-commercial-worthy since he got his braces off sophomore year, and his tanned skin from what I'm sure were flawless days he's spent on the lake or playing golf at Nappahawnick. There's something about Parker that always feels huge, and a part of me has always wondered if he knows it.

"Are we gonna talk about States?" I ask again.

He sighs. "I sort of think we should talk about the giant fucking elephant in the room before we get to this whole article thing, but you're the journalist."

I was always planning to do it, from the second I agreed to this dinner. I'd been anticipating it from the moment I kissed J goodbye as he got on the activity bus and I told him I'd call once Parker dropped me off back home. So, I'm not really sure why my mouth suddenly feels like I pulverized one of those pieces of chalk inside and swallowed it. "You guys used to love each other," is what I manage to get out, after an entire night and day of thinking about what to say. "What happened?"

He reaches for a triangle of our quesadilla, takes one bite, and it's already half gone. He chews and watches what's left in his hand. "What do you think happened?"

"I . . ." It isn't just scary to say out loud because of how long Parker and I have known each other. And it isn't even scary because of how he's been freaking out lately, because it's not like I think he's gonna do that to me. But while he sits there across the table, watching his food and not even worried about hiding the beer he's drinking in broad daylight, he feels so slippery to me. Like this fish that I don't want to touch but can't fully let go of because he's lunch, and he's dinner, and he's *everything*, and if I do this wrong, and I lose my grip, he could be gone forever.

J could lose him forever.

"I don't know," I confess. "But I do believe Britt. And I'm sorry."

"Why?" He finally takes his eyes off his food and looks into mine. "Why do you believe her?"

"I just don't think she's lying . . ."

"Did she tell you how I did it? Did she tell you when? Did she give you some kind of theory about why the fuck I even would?"

"She doesn't *have to*, Parker—"

"Yes she does," he insists, and maybe I've just never stared into Parker's eyes long enough to know any better, maybe I'm just flattering myself, but it almost feels like he cares what *I* think. Not generically about this entire disaster, but about me, specifically, in this moment, choosing Britt. "Or at least, she *should* have to. If she can say one sentence and turn my entire world upside down, turn me into some asshole guy, and I have to say *five thousand sentences* that you can choose not to believe anyway— She shouldn't get away with just saying one."

We take a second while these two little kids skip by on the

sidewalk with their mom following behind, carrying J. Crew shopping bags.

Parker nudges the quesadillas closer to me. "Eat something."

"I'm okay. I'm not that hungry—"

"Aly, come on. Please? I can't send you back to J and not even feed you. He's pissed enough at me already."

I start to eat some of my broken chip, hoping it'll make us both feel better.

"You know what the truth is?" Parker asks as I chew. "There's not a single thing I've done since I walked into Seton that I wouldn't do again." He finishes his quesadilla triangle and washes it down with a swig of beer. "I've looked out for every single one of my boys, I've gotten us through every game we've played this year, I made sure the beer was always cold and the parties were always lit. That's why this shit right now is killing me. That's why sitting here with you and hearing you say you believe Britt over me is like a fucking knife in my chest. Because I count you as a part of everything Seton's been for me. I would do all of this all over again and keep you right there with us. So I don't get what it is . . . what you think you saw one night or what I ever did to make you think I'm the kind of guy to do something like this, but that's the part that sucks, Aly. I never even did anything wrong."

I can tell him about the rage texts he sent Britt the day after Spence's party, or remind him how he body-slammed her into a locker yesterday, but I hold on to it for now. "It's not that you haven't been good to us, it's just that—"

"It's just that it hasn't been good enough to have you when it matters."

"Parker—"

"You can say it." He leans back in his chair, one arm draped over the back of it, gazing out over the shallow wrought-iron fence next to us at the parking lot full of cars. "It is what it is, right?"

"No, it's not—" And maybe it's the way my voice shakes when I say it that makes him look at me again the way that I need him to, so I know I haven't destroyed everything yet. "Parker, you have no idea how much I've been thinking about this. I couldn't even sleep last night because I didn't know how we were gonna talk about this today, or if we even would. Or if we even *should*, because on one hand, this is completely not my business, and I know that. But on the other hand, I've been with Britt while all you guys haven't been. And I can feel this huge . . . *thing* she's keeping inside. And I saw you, Parker—I saw you yesterday and the way you completely lost it, and I don't know if you get this, but that alone changed everything." I fidget with my gooey chip, holding his eyes as he doesn't blink. "The way you were on top of her, yelling at her, and Michelle couldn't even stop you—these were the two girls you've loved more than anything for as long as I've known you, and you completely ignored one while you were fully prepared to kill the other. And when J and I got home last night . . . J can literally un-complicate the most complicated situations on this planet. He can just look at me, or *anyone*, and make anything make sense. And make anything okay. But last night he couldn't look at me. And he couldn't make what you did okay. So it's not that I don't know that I was some idiot freshman who almost ended up naked at my first Seton party, or that I don't remember how it felt to know that I had you—*Parker Adams*—looking out for me no matter what. But it's that this year has been the complete opposite of what any of us has ever been to each other, and it feels like we're crashing.

Like Seton and everyone in it is just malfunctioning every second of every day."

By the time I finish, his arms are folded on the surface of the table, and he's watching me like he never has before. "I hear you."

And as he sits across from me, with all the jalapeno-free food that he ordered me sitting between us on the table, I try for the first time to really imagine it. To picture it. Him and Britt alone.

"It was hard growing up in my house." He picks at the label on his beer bottle, his pointer finger scratching against the green glass. "Coop is still the biggest star this school's ever seen, and I had to live up to that. I still do. I mean, do you know what it's like to be eight years old, waking up at five a.m. on Saturdays to make it to your early football practice so you can be home in time to practice with your second team? I had a trainer by the time I was twelve. My mom's chef has been shoving green juice down my throat and force-feeding me thirty-five hundred calories a day for as long as I can remember. People barely know this, but I had a water aerobics instructor who came to my house every day for an entire summer to work with me in our pool because my dad read some article about how it could help me keep my balance in the pocket.

"I worked my ass off, Aly. Seriously. Not everybody can do what I did, but I did it so I could show up this year and be as good as Coop. So I could be the reason why you guys get a State champion-ship *for the first time ever.* And I'm telling you, it's not easy. This shit has been hard."

The same server who brought us our food breezes by and asks Parker if he'd like another beer. He slugs the end of the one he has and tells her yeah as he hands her his empty bottle.

"Sorry, what was I saying?" Parker asks.

"How your life has been hard," I remind him.

"Right. I mean . . . okay, you wanna talk about States? Let's do it. I came into this year wanting to get us there more than anything. *I still do.* But do you know how much work that is? How hard it is to go undefeated in regular season and then make it through playoffs and then bring home a state championship? It's so hard that no one has even done it before, not even Coop. But it feels *next to impossible* when I have Britt running around trying to get in my fucking head." He cracks his knuckles absently, giving his hands something to do as he thinks. "So, I feel you, Aly—I really do—when you say everything's malfunctioning. I feel it, too. I feel like my brother reprogrammed this place to be fucking perfect, and now it's like we've been hacked. Like I used to be this certified superhero, and I had my girls, you know? B, and Kelly, and Michelle, and Britt. And I had my boys. And I took care of all of them. Of J. You, too, I think. I hope you feel like I have. But it's hard, it really is. And it's even harder with you girls . . . It's complicated. You expect us to just know what you want and what you mean . . . *No* means *Yes* or *Try harder* or *Suck my fucking face off,* depending on the day of the fucking week. What the hell are we supposed to do?" He shakes his head, and he's back to staring across the lot again. "I mean, what the hell do you expect from us?"

My fingertips are cold, like my blood can't reach them fast enough. I sit on my hands and can't take my eyes off him. "All girls or especially Britt?"

"Look, I know you and Britt have been hanging out a lot lately. Mich stares at you guys like you stole her fucking wife. And I'm not gonna act like it doesn't bug me sometimes, because it does. Because Britt's lying. Because I've always thought of you and J like my younger brother and sister, and I know you're far from home, and I never wanted you to feel like you were out here by yourselves, so I always made it a point to be nearby. Near enough so I could say, 'Yo, does J need a ride?' 'Yo, let me clear up my calendar so Aly can get this interview she's gonna need for the paper.' 'Yo, let me make sure she isn't about to get caught up in some naked drinking game . . .'" He sits back in his seat and runs his hands down his face. "So, it's been weird for me seeing you and Britt get so close the second she starts telling lies about me.

"And what I did yesterday was wrong, okay? Losing my head like that was wrong. But that doesn't make what she's doing right. And it's not fair, and it's fucking terrifying, really, that a girl like Britt—or *any* girl—has the power to ruin all my hard work with a single bullshit story." His hair wisps off his forehead in a breeze.

"It's words versus words." I don't mean to whisper, but it comes out that way.

"Well, it's the perfect Catch-22, right? Because if I didn't do it, I'm gonna say I didn't. And if I did do it, I'm gonna say I didn't. Because if I did it, and I say I did it, what the fuck good would that do me, anyways?" He scoffs. "Don't ever let anyone tell you that girl isn't an evil genius."

The way he says it is so tactical, like we're talking about chess pieces instead of one of the four most important girls in his life, and it gives me goose bumps.

"But can I tell you something? Before we do this whole interview thing? Because I care about you, Aly, for real. And I really do think there's something you need to know."

He waits, but I don't know for what. If he's waiting for me to say something, that's not gonna happen. I've been so busy spinning in his words the past five minutes that I couldn't form a sentence right now if the entire world depended on it.

"I'm willing to own the fact that the way I blew up yesterday wasn't great. Okay? Hear me when I say that. I will always own my own bullshit." He says it like he's standing on a mountaintop, making a speech that the entire universe wants to hear. But the rest of this speech, he comes back to the table for, and he says it just to me. "But I won't take back what I said yesterday. Because I swear to fucking God, that girl really is a bomb."

And then he tells me why.

It's not just what she said that night at Spence's in front of everyone, or the fact that it isn't true, but it's also about who she *is*. Who Britt has always been. To anyone who knows her. To anyone who loves her. This girl who can get anything she wants from anyone she wants. Who gets away with saying anything. Who gets away with *doing* anything. No one tells her, *No, Britt.* No one tells her, *Shut the fuck up, Britt.* No one tries to stop her. Everyone just loves her more.

But Britt *is* a bomb, he insists to me. And maybe you meet her and survive it and it's a miracle that you'll talk about forever with anyone who'll listen. Maybe that's what happens, and it feels like magic.

Or maybe the bomb goes off and she destroys you.

What it is.

Every bleacher in our stadium is vibrating; it's so loud I can't even tell if my own voice is making a sound. It's such a rush and such a relief to be in the middle of so much pandemonium, because for the first time since my dinner with Parker, these thoughts that have been punching holes in my brain have finally encountered a moment that's louder than they are.

Gina-Melissa is next to me, in Dan's old jersey from when he used to play for us last year, the same way I'm wearing J's. Once a Seton football girlfriend, always a Seton football girlfriend.

Dad, and J's dad, and my little brother are sitting on the bleachers right behind us, because GM happened to get to the field right at the same time we did today, so we all decided to sit together. They're in Seton-everything, too. The hats and the sweatshirts and the football that Cory carries with him everywhere.

It's a sea of red, and we're all on our feet, screaming together, a single giant force that matters a million times more than any of us ever would on our own. The band is slamming their drums and swaying with their horns. The Varsity cheerleaders are facing us on the track, none of them quite as pretty as Michelle as she leads them in their synchronized routine. J is with the rest of the JV guys on the bleacher closest to the field, chanting and dancing and Dougie-ing to the go-go beat. But the Varsity guys are everything in this moment, just like they always are, hopping from bleacher to bleacher, cupping their ears so we'll get louder, while Parker stands on the players' bench and faces us, beckoning us to come on, the conductor of all the mayhem.

We're already on round three of the Seton Girls cheer, which has to be the most empowering and defining thing the guys do for us. It's not the free booze at every party. It's not how they tell us we're the best in the world. But it's how they come out after halftime of every single home game we play, cheering for *us*, showing us how completely crazy they are about us, how hard they ride for all of us, how we matter just as much for Seton football as they do.

I love it so much, and today I really need it, so I scream with everyone else:

I said, the Seton Girls know what's up!
(From the front to the back)
Yeah, we know what's up!
(From the left to the right)
Yeah, we know what's up!
Because we're Seton, and the Seton Girls know what's up!
Aaayyyyeee

The referees blow their whistles and wave their arms to try and get us to stop, try and get the game started, while all the news photographers' cameras flash, trying to catch every perfect shot that they can. It's Seton homecoming, after all.

After two more rounds of chanting, our coach finally tugs Parker by the shoulder, and Parker laughs and points his finger toward the sky, spinning it around so we know we have his permission to wrap it up. And our crowd is nothing if not obedient to our QB, so we finally stop chanting, the band dies down, Michelle and her squad stop shimmering their pompoms.

The guys on Varsity hop down from the different posts they'd taken on the bleachers, back toward the bench so we can start the second half of this game. St. Mary's has been bored, watching us do Seton Girls for five minutes now. And they're also probably ready to get this over with—we went into halftime with a seventeen-point lead.

I'm not ready for it to be over yet as we all melt back into our seats for the rest of this game. I'm not ready for it to be quiet enough for me to think again, for me to feel guilty that Britt didn't even want to come today, for me to be anxious about tonight.

But it's time, and as Parker heads back to the bench where he belongs, Tad Nelson, one of our yearbook editors, stops him with a microphone. It's the same one Tad used at the beginning of the game to ask Parker what it felt like to be minutes away from kickoff of his last Seton homecoming.

Now Tad asks, "How you feeling going into second half, my man? We've got a big lead, but this would also be our thirteenth homecoming win in a row. And you know that everyone says thirteen's a real unlucky number."

But Parker just grins, his hair damp with sweat. He leans into the mic so his voice is loud and clear as he peers into the crowd at none of us and all of us all at the same time. "Unlucky my ass."

He gives Tad's shoulder two solid slaps and the stands erupt as he jogs back to the field. Somewhere on the other side of the bleachers, a chant begins, and it snakes through the rest of the crowd like a flame on a really long wick. Until everyone's saying it. Everyone in the entire world. *"We want two! We want two!"*

And it doesn't stop until Parker takes a bow.

What it was.

July 4, 2019

The calls went well at first.

Every boy answered, whether he went to Billingsley or Anderson Prep or St. Mary's or anywhere else. They were rivals on the field, and would smack-talk each other online sometimes, but there was still a camaraderie about it, about them. Boys who played football, and their parents who had money, and their Nappahawnick banquets that existed only for people like them. So, they listened when Levi and Parker called. They made a few jokes about the drives they had and the things they'd seen. They agreed to keep an ear out in their own circles, to talk to the boys from their schools who'd signed in that night. Because they were, in so many ways, the same.

And they didn't want the secret to get out either.

Every boy they called respected the conversation except for one. Brady O'Grady, who was quarterback at Iverson. Iverson was loud, but they weren't *good*. Still, Levi needed a sure thing, so he'd made a deal anyway.

Brady was also at the party the night Zach's drive went missing. His name scribbled on one of the sign-in sheets like so many others.

So, they called Brady O'Grady just like they called every other name they had. But when they told him what they needed from him, he laughed and answered, "Not my problem."

When they told him all the reasons why it was, he told them, "Call my lawyer."

And the line went dead.

Brady O'Grady was a piece of shit. A wannabe who wasn't really anybody, with parents who toted around their UCLA degrees like someone should be impressed and who ran those cheap *If you've been in an "accident" and need a lawyer because you're too lazy to get off your ass and earn your money, call us!* commercials on TV. Their faces were all over benches and bus stops in all the low-income-housing neighborhoods, and still the best they could do was get Brady a used BMW for his birthday. So, Brady was a joke, and his family was a joke, and his seven-and-three season at Iverson was a joke. At least, that's what Parker would say, whose stats—boys love stats—were objectively better in every humanly possible way.

And it was bad—bad for Seton quarterbacks everywhere and the secrets they created—for someone like Brady to not know his place.

Parker was mad enough to get Levi mad, too. Parker was contagious that way, just like his brother had been. And however he felt, whatever he thought—you caught it, too, like an outbreak.

Boys like Parker also have connections—ways of finding out the things they want to know and getting the things they want to have. So it wasn't clear, exactly, who it was that fed Parker information over those next few days. Who it was at Iverson that was texting Parker the things that Brady would never want him to know. All Brady had was state-school, ambulance-chaser parents and a pathetic used car. He didn't have the power—the grave diggers—to keep things buried.

He was a joke.

Piece of shit.

According to Parker.

"*Don't leave me . . .*" Michelle whined, both arms wrapped around Parker's neck, hanging on him like the pretty little damsel that she was as they Fourth-of-July-partied in Kyle Samuelson's basement. Every year he'd been at Seton, he'd hosted Fourth of July. His back-yard stretched on for acres, and his parents and their neighbors didn't care if they used fireworks.

"I'd never leave you," Parker coaxed her, sliding his hands ro-mantically into the back pockets of her tight jeans.

"*No*, you fucking weirdo. I don't mean it like that." She was drunk, and Michelle got mouthy when she was drunk.

Parker smiled. "What do you mean, then?"

"I mean don't leave just to get more booze," she clarified. "We don't even need more booze."

"Babe, fireworks haven't even happened yet. You drank a whole pint of tequila on your own."

"You're such a lying little—"

"Don't you agree it's my duty as a leader and the best boyfriend in the world to replenish the supply you depleted?"

She pulled like she wanted to get away, but she'd be mad if he let her go, so he didn't.

"I promise to bring him right back," Levi assured her, standing with his hands in his pockets and a smirk on his lips as he waited a few feet away.

Michelle looked at Levi suspiciously, drunkenly, and smiled when he sealed his promise with a wink. She looked back up at

Parker, who was still holding her body against his. "Will you bring the girls back a snack?"

"Whatever you guys want," Parker promised. "Talk to them, and then text me and we'll grab it."

"K." She watched his eyes for an extra second, mischievously, and he looked back into hers. But she didn't know he was lying. She never did. "You want my gum so you don't miss me too much?" She wiggled the piece she'd been chewing between her front teeth.

"You guys are so damn sick." Levi laughed.

But Parker smiled anyway, knowing it. And he stood there willingly as she laughed, too, and pushed up on tiptoes and slid her chewed 5 gum into his Colgate-commercial mouth.

He bit down on the rubbery wad to solidify the exchange and confirmed. "Am I allowed to go now?"

"Yep." She broke free and patted his cheek. "Get me food or I'll kill you." She left him to go back to her friends, the three of them busy bullying Zach and a few other guys while they attempted to play a round of beer pong.

"You think she'll miss you too much?" Levi smiled as he and Parker headed to the basement stairs.

"Nah," Parker assured him. "She was drunk belly dancing on the pool table with Britt to that 'Like a Bird' song, like, five minutes ago. She won't even remember I'm gone."

While the music blared in honor of the freedom they'd all inherited, Levi and Parker slipped out the front door armed with the information Parker had gathered over the past few days. Like the fact that Brady O'Grady's grandma was in a nursing home, and that nursing home was the same one where a bunch of the Seton kids volunteered to get their community service hours. And Brady was going to be there with her to watch the fireworks, for reasons that were beyond Parker's ability to comprehend.

Parker and Levi found Brady's used car easily when they pulled up to the nursing home that night, and even though there were barely any other cars there, they parked all the way in the back, under the leafy branches of a towering tree. And Levi and Parker sat there together, waiting, smoking the blunt they'd brought and talking about the year that was. It never felt right when another era ended and another class of Varsity players shipped off to their colleges to start the rest of their lives. Everything they ever could have asked for was right here, was what they'd already created for themselves, and while they waited that night, Parker and Levi talked about those things. Proud of what they'd done. Proud of who they were.

And when the fireworks started, they got out of Parker's truck together, and pulled their black beanies down over their ears, and zipped their black pullovers up as far as they'd go, burying their chins inside of them despite the ninety-degree heat. They grabbed their bats from the bed of Parker's truck and walked toward Brady's shitty 3 Series. They took their positions on opposite sides of it.

Levi peered over the hood at Parker, still the boss until he left. And Parker still treated him like one, respected him like one. Loved him, even.

"Fly baby fly," Levi said, his voice muffled behind the collar of his jacket.

"Fly baby fly," Parker proudly recited.

Their bats connected with the metal and the cheap tinted windows, muted by the exploding sky. They shattered every bit of glass they could, but they still didn't stop. Smart-ass, second-class little bitch. There was no way Brady was gonna disrespect them like that when Parker, or Levi, or any of their other teammates, called him and needed help.

So, fuck Brady O'Grady.

Their bats flew into his car for as long as the fireworks were there to protect them.

Parker reached into his pocket and dropped a folded piece of paper into the front seat. In black Sharpie, it read *We can do worse.*

They hadn't signed it—they weren't *idiots*—because Brady would already know the attack came from Seton. And he'd be scared, the way he should've been all along. The way nobodies like Brady should always be.

Levi and Parker jogged back across the lot to Parker's lurking truck and dropped the bats back into the bed before they climbed inside. They were sweating and unzipped their jackets, took off their hats, and Parker rolled down the windows and blasted the AC at the same time.

They sat there for a second, basking in what they'd done, in the legacy they'd saved. They stared out the windshield at the night sky, and that was when Parker admitted to Levi for the first time, "I wanna get us States this year."

Levi faced him, maybe high from what they'd just done or maybe high from the weed they'd just smoked. He laughed. "Why? You don't need it."

Parker shrugged. "I want it."

Levi's laugh died down, but his smile stayed. "Bro, no one's gonna start throwing playoff games for a drive. And they *especially* aren't handing over States. Just take your undefeated season like the rest of us. It's plenty. Trust me."

"They might. If I make the drive better. Give them the kind of shit they dream about. Pass it off to the whole team instead of just one guy. It'd be fucking legendary, bro. For all of us. You, too."

"Shit, I mean . . ." Levi rubbed his hair and rested his head against his seat. "Yeah, maybe. But *why?* We don't need it."

And Parker told him again, "Because I want it."

They'd talk about it more when it wasn't Fourth of July, when they weren't distracted by the fact that they were already heroes. Parker would tell Levi what kind of stuff he thought he could add to the drive, how he thought it could work, and why. And after listening to Parker for long enough, understanding his plan deeply enough, Levi was almost convinced that maybe it could work, too.

But that night, they'd done enough, and all that was left was to go back to Kyle's Fourth of July party with the Taco Bell order that Michelle had texted them.

Because there was no reason to ruin a perfectly good night with a bunch of girls bitching about being hungry.

What it is.

Parker's beach house is packed with anyone from Seton who could get a ride. This is what we do instead of homecoming dances, ever since Cooper came back to watch our homecoming game his freshman year in college. He tried to sit in the stands with everybody else, but he was such a celebrity by then that the team had him watch from their bench like an unofficial assistant coach. The news photographers who'd been there for the big game switched all their attention to him, and the commentator announced he was there with all the formality of introducing the pope. Cooper got a standing ovation.

It's not like I was there to see it. This was twelve years ago when I was, like, four. But I never had to meet Cooper, or see Cooper, to *know* Cooper. He's everywhere. He's that double salami sub sandwich from the deli by school (they named it "The Coop"). He's in the middle of that full team picture that's still hanging in the gym. And the stuff he did and the stuff he changed permeates everything and all of us like a religion, to this day.

So, I wasn't there, but I know the story. Seton beat Billingsley in a blowout that year, and Seton rushed the field, and the team was so excited to have Cooper there that they all ditched the dance that night and drove out to Cooper's parents' beach house—*this* beach house—to party instead. They brought half the school with them.

And they did it again the next year, when Cooper came back to watch the homecoming game again.

The third year, Seton administration threatened to cancel the dance if the team and all their friends went to the beach instead. But Cooper showed up at the game for the third year straight, and they followed him to the beach that night anyway.

So, Seton stopped having homecoming dances.

That's how it got to be this way—all of us piling into cars and riding an hour and a half away, out to the beach house that we'd be staying in for the night. It's not all of us following Cooper anymore—he stopped coming back for homecoming a long time ago. Instead, we rally behind whoever our latest version of Cooper is.

Last year, it was Levi Jackson who had us all over to his family's beach house. The games had been early that Saturday and Varsity killed Anderson Prep after a season when we'd both been previously undefeated. Everyone got to the beach by four, and it was the drunkest I've ever been in my life. Levi was invincible and Parker was his hype man, and the vibe was so good and so contagious that people didn't stop talking about that weekend for months.

So much of what happened that night is still fuzzy to me, even after all the stories J told me to try and jog my memory. I remember being on the front lawn while Levi, Parker, J, and this guy who's still the favorite to be the Varsity QB after J—Miles—stood in the street with their arms around each other's shoulders so I could take a picture. Even though the rule had always been no pictures, they figured outside of the house with no party in the background was okay. They figured this was a big enough deal to find a loophole. There was a whole drunken conversation about it, that Levi said I had to endorse because girls think better than dudes. Because the girls were to thank for everything. Because Seton had the best girls in the world.

I remember waking up way too early in the morning, still drunk, and stumbling from the upstairs couch to the bathroom in the hallway. But the light was on and the door was locked. I kind of panicked while I tried to remember where any of the other bathrooms were, but all my pee breaks over the course of the night were blending together. The door was open to the room that Parker had been given for the night, though, and I tiptoed inside to see if maybe there was a bathroom in there. There was.

On my way out of the room, I noticed there were three people in the bed. Parker in the middle and Michelle and Britt on either side of him, with his arms stretched around them and their heads on his chest. They belonged together, and they loved each other, and it made every bit of sense in the world. Even drunk, a part of me wished I belonged there, too—or somewhere like there, at least.

But I didn't, so I tiptoed back out to the hallway and fell on top of my couch-bed with J.

And I also vividly remember one other thing. It happened around the peak of the night—when everyone was drunk or high but no one had had enough to be tired yet. It was so loud. There were more people at Levi's than I'd seen at a Seton party, ever. There were people from our school who I'd never even seen at a party before. But at the end of the game, Levi had started yelling out to the crowd that the after-party was at his place. He said to DM him for the address. He said, "If you've got the gas to get there, come through!"

It was that time of night—when the people who decided to accept that invite had made it, when everything was so wild that it was like this party had a mind of its own. And we were downstairs in the living room when, out of nowhere, the football playlist stopped. Britt and Michelle were together on the other side of the room, exactly the way they should be. I'd seen both of them with Kelly and Bianca in the hot tub earlier, and now Michelle was in her white bikini bottoms and a red Seton T-shirt that she'd cut up at some point before tonight to make a crop top, with a floppy bun on top of her head and a pair of UGGs on her feet. And Britt was next to her, wearing a pair of cutoff jean shorts, a red bikini top, a backward Seton baseball cap that she stole from one of the guys at some point, for sure, and a pair of too-big Adidas slides.

Levi was with them and so were Parker and Zach. They had a mini-audience because they always did. And while the two of them stood together, hovering over a phone that they'd just plugged into the aux cord instead of the one that'd been plugged in all night, Zach smirked and commented, "You know, we handled the music at this party for years without help from either one of you."

"Handling isn't thriving," Britt commented, still studying the screen.

"Yeah, dream bigger," Michelle added, watching over Britt's shoulder.

Parker smiled and slapped Zach's shoulder. "Just the inspirational speech you needed tonight, huh, bro?"

"Hey!" Britt looked up, her eyes a kind of poison that's worth the risk. *"Levi."*

He smiled and appeased her with "Yeah, beautiful."

"We're doing this for you, you know."

Michelle smiled, the picture of perfection, even wasted. "Because we *love* you."

"Hey . . ." Parker warned.

"Kind of like how you love our Kel . . ." Michelle went on.

Levi's smile stayed while he opted not to hear the second part. "Doing what for me?"

"Zach, did you know Levi's been lying to you all these years?" Britt asked.

"He's been sacrificing his *soul* for the sake of *our* musical preferences—" Michelle insisted, and that was when Levi started laughing, and Parker started cracking up, too, and Levi said, "Aw, fuck . . ."

"Because he's a benevolent leader. He's like our fucking FDR or something," Michelle finished.

Britt smiled at Michelle with complete adoration.

Zach insisted, "Alright, Britt, catch me up."

"Levi's been putting up a huge front. All these years listening to a football playlist made up of all this pop, R&B, hip-hop stuff—"

"Masterpieces," Michelle gently corrected.

"Masterpieces," Britt agreed. "When the *entire ride here today* all we heard was banjo playing, pickup-truck-driving, grown-man-crying country music. And we think he deserves at least one night where he can hear it. Out in the open. Proudly, you know? Because we love you, too, Levi. The same way you love us."

"That much, huh?" Levi smirked.

And that was when they found the song they were looking for, and the twanging opening bars cut through the house more distinctively than any song before it. But Britt and Michelle started dancing to it like it was the same as any other song on the playlist we were used to. They didn't know all the words, but they sang the ones they did, and part of it was making fun of Levi, but another part of it was genuine and real acceptance. That they thought it was cool. That they'd make sure everyone else did, too.

They chose "May We All" by Florida Georgia Line, and J looked up at the sky next to me (like the music was coming from heaven, or something), coherent enough to recognize that this wasn't normal, and J enough to easily accept it anyway. And I smiled as I split my attention between the card game J was playing and the fun-cool-sexy bopping around that Britt and Michelle were doing across the room, and—I swear—everything in the entire world was exactly the way it was meant to be.

It sucks that Britt's not here this year.

I'm with J and a group of the guys while they laugh-argue about some kind of NFL thing. This is my third cup of the punch that the guys made out on one of the decks. It tastes like fizzy cherries, and so many of our mouths are stained red at this point that we look like we're auditioning for the fifth Twilight movie.

Through the football debate, and the music, and the people everywhere, Michelle slips out the front door in a moment that I'm pretty sure none of us is supposed to notice. She's alone when she goes, and it's one of the fastest decisions I've ever made, but I do it: I follow her.

"I love you, bye," I tell J, kissing him on the side of his head as I go.

I slip past everyone else and push through the front door, then the storm door. It slams shut, and the sound smacks the quiet street. Beach season is over. I'm sure every single one of these houses besides this one is empty.

Michelle is at the bottom of the steps, her long hair piled into a bun on top of her head. She's wearing black leggings and a Seton Girls sweatshirt. It's colder this year than it was last.

"Michelle," I call, jogging down the steps to catch up with her.

We haven't said more than two words to each other in almost two months, and I have no idea how this effort is gonna go. There's a part of me that honestly isn't even sure if this is any less than how much Michelle and I normally talk, but it's the circumstances that make everything feel so messed up.

I stop in front of her, and her *Vogue*-cover face watches mine. It's just me and her and the streetlights and our parked cars and all the thoughts that have been paddling around my mind for days now. Michelle has always been a little bit intimidating to me. She's quieter than Britt. She smiles at everyone but doesn't jump down your throat in an effort to find common ground the way Britt does. It'd be easy to get caught in a weird silence with Michelle that she doesn't care to break, and the sheer possibility makes me anxious.

"Michelle," I say again.

It takes her a second, like she's deciding on something. Like she's deciding on *me.* "Hi," she answers. Then she offers me the blunt she's been holding by her side. "Want a hit?"

"No, thanks." I swallow. "I kind of wanted to see if we could maybe talk?"

"I'm headed to Harris Teeter to get Heath bars and an apple. B likes fruit when she's drunk."

I slowly nod. The impending silence already makes me want to fake like J's calling me. "Then why the Heath bars?" I ask, just to make sure something keeps happening.

She smiles. "Because I like Heath bars."

I smile, too.

"You wanna walk with me?" she offers.

"Yeah."

Michelle walks through this town like she could do it with her eyes closed. She's been coming here her entire life, she says. She points out the street that her own family's beach house is on—"like a mile that way." She tells me we're just walking to the grocery store on the other side of the pier, and she makes it sound like it isn't too far. And as we wander past all of these giant second homes, I attempt to swallow the sadness I felt in the car, at just the thought of next year when J is the one we're all supposed to follow up here. To the house we don't have. But J swears it's fine, that the guys have already talked about it. They'll use Vic's house next year instead.

"And we'll be okay," J says.

Michelle smokes her weed like it's nothing, like she's walking through this glitzy beach neighborhood sucking on a Tootsie Pop. And when she finishes telling me where we're going, and how far it is, and pointing out the way to her own part of town, I ask her, "How are you doing?"

"Pretty shitty," she answers, and I'm surprised how easily it comes out. "What about you?"

I hug myself as we keep walking down the middle of the street. I can imagine her and Britt here, arms spread and singing at the top of their lungs. I can imagine them playing leapfrog right now for the hell of it. I can imagine them lying down on the pavement like they're in *The Notebook*, staring into the sky and counting the stars until their phones are so full of *Where r u??* texts that their only choice is to finally head back.

But it's my interview with Parker that's still in my head, the way he preached this truth to me about Britt that I'd never in my whole life encountered, not even once. How he said it from this vantage

point of being Seton-proper his whole life, and going to school with
her for years before I even knew they existed, and being a part of
that special little world that was theirs and not ours, no matter how
badly any of the rest of us wanted in.

"I kind of just wanted to talk to you," I explain. "After what
happened between Britt and Parker in the hallway. And everything,
really."

"I'm really sorry that happened in front of you." It's weird the
way she says it—not sorry that it happened at all, but sorry that *I*
had to see it.

I think again about how Britt and Michelle whispered to each
other for the few seconds they had to themselves. How desperate
Michelle sounded when she insisted that Parker wouldn't even listen to her anymore. *That he was losing his mind.*

"Does Parker get like that sometimes?" I ask.

She watches straight ahead. "Parker gets what he wants," she
says, like it answers my question, even though I'm not really sure
that it does. But I'm drunk, and she's high, and her words are already drifting into the night. So, we both just let them float.

"Are you scared?" My voice is barely loud enough to hear over
the cicadas.

Her perfectly groomed eyebrows come together, crinkling the
meaty skin right between her eyes. "How do you mean?"

"Just with everything going on . . . with all the rumors . . . or
accusations. I don't know. It's just . . ." I gnaw the inside of my lip.
"Isn't all of this kind of scary?"

"Oh." She seems to realize what I'm saying, and then she nods.
"Yes," she answers simply, like I'd asked her if she had to go to the
bathroom.

She's existed the past couple of weeks like a shadow of something that used to be real. She isn't big anymore, the way she was when she was scheming with Britt, or when she used to loop her arm through Parker's when they'd walk together down the hall. She doesn't smile the same way, ever since it's just been Bianca and Kelly, and for weeks I haven't heard her laugh—that laugh that used to ripple through the hallway or bounce from her lunch table to ours, with her head tilted back and her mouth open like she was the happiest person on earth.

"I am so, so sorry, Michelle."

"There's no reason for you to be sorry."

"It's just . . . I know I've been spending a lot of time with Britt lately," I admit. "And that everyone's been talking about her and Parker nonstop, and I just don't want you to feel like no one's seeing you, you know? Because I do see you. And I know you aren't technically alone but that maybe it feels that way, and maybe you kind of want it that way, and now I'm starting to feel like maybe I suck for crashing this walk to the store that you probably wanted to take by yourself . . ." I stop walking. "I'm just really sorry about everything that's happening."

She stops, too, flicking the nub of her blunt into the dark. Her deep brown eyes dazzle like marbles in the blue moonlight. "How come?"

"What do you mean?"

"How come you're so sorry? You're sorrier than the people who should be sorry."

I take a deep breath and the inside of my nose burns deep, the same fire breath that happens when you accidentally inhale underwater, or your heart wants to cry when your brain doesn't. This whole thing has hurt so much lately. I used to be able to close my eyes and drift through Seton mindlessly, and now it's this minefield of being on Britt's side without being Parker's enemy and keeping J unharmed somewhere in the middle of it.

I take a deep breath through my mouth instead. "Have you ever like . . . seen a weird pattern in the stars, or felt like tulips weren't even all that pretty, or known with your *entire soul* that a Summer Breeze air freshener belongs in a car and a Passion Fruit one belongs in the bedroom, but you turn to Parker to talk about it and he just can't do it? He loves you, and he wants to, and he'll listen—sure, whatever. But he has no clue in the world what you're actually talking about. So instead, you turn to Britt, or Kelly, or Bianca, and you don't even have to explain anything because they just get it? They just get *you*?" I sniff and wave a firefly away from my face. "Michelle . . . *you have that.* You don't have to imagine what that's like, because it's real. And it's not just this shoo-in, guaranteed thing that everyone gets to have, you know? Like . . . I don't really know what that's like. And I don't know if I ever will. But the thought of you guys losing this incredible thing you have is the most tragic part of any of this, I think. It's like, in the hierarchy of life, you're not supposed to lose the best thing you've ever had. You know what I mean?"

She gently closes her eyes and takes a calming breath, the poised, born-to-be-a-politician's-wife thing about her taking easy control. When she opens her eyes a moment later, they glisten like diamonds, even though they're really tears. "I believe Britt," her steady voice tells me. "I haven't said that to anyone before, but I do. And that's why I'm glad that you're there with her. There's been enough weird stuff between her and Parker . . . the way he'd look at her some nights when he thought I wouldn't notice or he was just too drunk to care. She's the most perfect person in the world, and I believe her.

"But the problem is . . ." She shakes her head and hugs herself, looking up this dark street while we stand in the middle of it. "She refuses to talk about what happened. And we can't just *not know*. I can't just go on with our life together while she has this huge secret about what actually happened between her and my boy-friend. And the Parker thing . . . Maybe I'm fucking myself over by saying it out loud, but that's seasonal for me. It's making sure he stays focused and keeps winning, because this Seton stuff is bigger than all of us. So, I have to be there with him, I have to *stay . . .*" She turns to me. "I mean, you know how it is. You date a Seton quarterback, too."

I nod because I hope that she'll keep going.

"And so I really am glad that you're with her, Aly, because I can't be. She's the one person who knows exactly who I am without me saying a word, and right now, I can't even talk to her. I don't think that's crazy, is it? I don't think that's wrong . . . I mean, could you? Could you be *best friends* with a girl who accused J of rape and then never even tried to explain what actually happened?"

"No," I realize.

Michelle nods, rubbing her arms. Comforted, I think. "So, it's good you guys aren't best friends."

I don't think she says it to be mean, so I do my best to ignore the way it stings. Maybe she's right, and you don't just get to be best friends with someone overnight, just because you text a lot or talk whenever you can. Best friends is what *they* have. What they are.

"Did she ever call you?" I ask.

Michelle's eyes narrow, analyzing me like I'm a language she only half knows. "Britt?"

"Yeah. After the Parker thing. In the hallway, she told you she would call you later. Did she?"

"She said that?" Michelle asks, shaking her head to herself. "I didn't hear it."

But she had to. Because even I did.

I don't push her, though. Not tonight. I can tell she's tired, and she has every right to be. Michelle's been pushed a lot lately. And by the way she's nibbling her lip, and staring off at nothing, I can tell her mind is already busy with the next thing.

She sighs. "Do you know what I think messes with me more than anything? The secret, yeah. And the way everyone is so committed to keeping it. But it's also how Parker's been about it. Not even when he goes crazy, but when he pretends like he's sane. Like he's super level-headed and deep. He's been in my ear nonstop like some fucking therapist about how Britt and I need to get back together. How we're only so angry because we love each other so much. How forgiving is hard but it's worth it. Like he isn't the problem. Like he isn't *the entire reason.*"

She laughs, so sad that it hurts to watch. "But." She spreads her arms and spins a single time on the ball of her foot, in the easy, unwobbly way that only girls who take dance classes ever can. "Ever since Comment-Gate, he's finally stopped acting like he's some fucking spirit guide. So that's decent." She drops her arms, and her palms clap against her thighs. "I kind of want to send that Billings-ley kid a thank-you card."

She wipes her eyes as we start walking again, slowly toward wherever this Harris Teeter grocery store is. And as we go, the stuff

Parker said at dinner starts swirling through my mind all over again, an echo since the day he took me home.

She's a bomb.

And maybe this is exactly what bombs do. Tear apart lives and families, until the only thing that's left is the mangled remains of a girl in the middle of the night who can't even decide whether to laugh or cry.

What it is.

<u>October 14, 2019</u>

Monday morning, I jog across the bus circle, through the lawn with its fluffy green grass, scattered with red and orange and brown leaves that crunch under my feet like thin glass.

It's just before seven and the sun is starting to wake up, a full two hours after J and I did to catch our bus on time. And even though campus is usually dead when we show up in the mornings, I texted Britt last night and asked if she'd be willing to get here early today. To talk.

She's sitting on the hood of her Audi, waiting for me. Her legs crossed like she's some genie or medium, and after this weekend and the past couple of days, every part of me believes she could know enough to be either.

"How long have you been here?" I call out across the distance between us as I skip-walk to get to her faster.

"Only a few minutes." She's clipped her hair back from her face with bobby pins. "I wouldn't be able to live with myself if I made you wait for me at ass crack in the morning after you basically crossed the Atlantic Ocean to get here."

I wrap my arms around her neck and squeeze. She slides her arms around my waist and hugs me back.

"What's wrong?" she whispers into my hair.

I don't want to let go but I do. We're past the okay-amount-of-time that you can hold on to another person, even by Britt's standards. "I'm going kind of crazy."

Her gray eyes are just as intense as they always are, but her face gets sad. "Why?"

"Just thinking about everything the past couple of days . . . thinking about Parker. And you. And how J's been feeling . . . I don't know. I want to talk to you about it. I've been wanting to talk to you about everything, but I don't want to make this *my thing*, you know? I know you're dealing with so much, and I just . . . I never want to be a bad friend to you."

Britt smirks and hugs her knees to her chest. "You're not a bad friend to me, Aly. I've actually been quite impressed with your girls-friend capabilities." She taps the hood of her car so I'll lean against it, and I really don't want to because this car is worth more than my life, but I do. "Talk to me. Did something happen at the beach?"

"Yeah," I admit, hugging myself as I peer across our quiet parking lot. "Michelle and I walked. And we talked. About you, and stuff. It wasn't this on-purpose thing. I don't want you to think that I like . . . went behind your back to try and talk to her when you weren't around. It's just that . . ."

"Aly, *what's wrong*?"

"I never told you this, but the night after Parker freaked out in the hallway, J freaked out, too. He was pissed that Parker would do that to you, and that he would do it in front of me, and that he'd do it and risk the season and getting benched before playoffs. And it just kind of hit me for the first time how sticky all of this is. It's webby, almost. Like a spider's web, you know what I mean? And this thing that happened between you and Parker . . . that was like somebody coming in and snipping the web. This web we're all tangled up in together because that's what Seton is, and you can't just snip one part without everything else going to shit. And it feels like that right now. It feels like we're holding on by a thread and if the thread breaks . . ."

"So what if the thread breaks?" she gently whispers.

I turn back to face her and admit, "I just get scared about where we all land."

She squints, and I'm not sure if it's because she doesn't understand me at all or the exact opposite.

"Because J doesn't think what's happening is okay," I try to explain. "That's why he got so mad at Parker after what he did to you in the hallway. And they were okay enough at the beach. Not completely normal, but they were okay enough. Except, the thing is . . . Parker *is* Seton football. And J needs Seton football. For all his plans and all his dreams, he needs what the team has built. And a part of me feels like J wasn't thinking about any of that when he went off on Parker. And he *shouldn't be.* But it's like . . ."

"It's also like maybe he should be."

I gnaw my bottom lip as her hair swings in a gusty breeze. My stomach feels like it's carrying a bag of sand. "It's webby," I softly answer.

"It's super webby," she agrees. "Can I ask what Mich said on your walk?"

I take a deep breath. "She said that she believes you."

Britt nods, and stops hugging her knees and crosses her legs again instead. "You know what? I've been thinking about this a lot, and do you know what I feel like we're all struggling with the most?" She waits for me to answer as if I might really know. After a second, she tells me, "What it means to be a 'type.' Because I think, in all of our minds, there's this huge difference between doing shit and *being the type of person* who does shit. So, it's like, *yeah, she shoplifted that one time, but she's not a shoplifter.* Or, *he gets in fights, but he's a really sweet guy.* And that is Parker Adams. That is exactly what everyone thinks of him and exactly what he thinks of himself. That, sure, he might do shit, but he's not a *shitster.* And Parker Adams is exactly the kind of guy who can look you in the eye and swear with his entire dark soul that he didn't do anything wrong because he didn't stalk me in an alley or slam me down on a bed while I cried and he slapped his hand over my mouth and had sex with me anyway. He's the exact kind of guy who would think that if I don't have a black eye and nightmares for the rest of my life, it doesn't count. Because those are the things *bad guys* do. Their type.

"But I just feel like it's so much bigger than black eyes and morning-after pills." She shakes her head to herself, squinting a little as she dares to believe she might be right. "That it has to be. And it doesn't matter if the door was wide open the whole time. It doesn't matter how unchained you ever are, how absent the gun is from your head or some guy's hands are from around your neck. If the door is open but you know you can't get up and walk out of it, that *is* force. That's, like, the greatest kind of power that exists. That is corporation-level power. And it's that kind of power—not the muscles or the dumb boy-tanks they wear—that guys like Parker will tell you isn't real. And swear they're *not that type.* But it's the realest thing in the world."

She's exactly right. That's entirely what it is, why so many of us can hear Britt but not cancel Parker. And in a way, I feel like I've been duped. Like I've fallen for the kind of logical fallacy that hangs juries every day.

"Britt, I'm so sorry."

"Don't be sorry. I'm sorry. It sucks that you've been losing your mind the past couple days and felt like you couldn't talk about it."

"That part doesn't matter."

"Of course it matters. The way you feel will always matter."

I slide onto the hood of the car with her, my feet dangling above the black concrete. "Michelle said something else that I think you should know."

"The way she feels will always matter, too."

"Even though she believes you, she told me she can't be with you right now. Because you won't tell her what actually happened. And that all she really wants from you is to know. She doesn't know how to be with you again if there's this terrible thing that happened between you and her boyfriend and you won't tell her what it is."

She takes another deep breath and gazes at the cars that are slowly starting to pull into their parking spaces. "I'm just not sure how to make this real yet," she softly admits. "Can I ask you the single most important question I'll ever ask you?"

I swallow. "Do we have enough time?"

"It's quick." She picks at her nails and won't let go of my eyes. "Do you trust me?"

"Is that the single most important question?"

"That's it."

So I swear, "Of course I trust you."

She gives me a second, like she's granting me time to take it back if I want to. But I don't now, and I never will.

"Because I want to show you something so badly," she finally says. "But I know your immediate response is gonna be to find any excuse you can to convince yourself I'm lying. It's gonna be instinctive, and reactive, and I get it. But once I say it, I can't unsay it. And you can't not believe me. Because I can't lose another friend right now."

It's finally here. The moment that didn't happen on Kyle's bathroom floor, and didn't happen on her bedroom floor, and didn't happen when Kelly showed up at our lockers begging for it, or the countless times I can only imagine that Michelle wished it would happen for her. That moment is now, and I don't know why it's now, but this feels like the biggest deal I've ever been asked to make. Life changing, potentially, the way most things are with Britt.

But I don't care.

So I tell her, "No matter what, you're not gonna lose me."

What it is.

October 14, 2019 (continued)

Britt and I skip class, and she takes us to A Coffee Shop first for the calories she insists we need. For herself, she gets bacon, egg, and sun-dried tomato cream cheese on a bagel the size of a volleyball and an iced chai latte. I'm not hungry, but Britt has selective hearing when it comes to words she doesn't like, so I end up with an orange juice and a chocolate muffin that weighs at least two pounds.

Her house is chilly when we get there, but I'm used to that now. Aside from the maid who comes and cleans every day, she pretty much lives alone during the week while her parents travel for work. So, she keeps the thermostat where she likes it—on a cool sixty-seven degrees—and accessorizes me appropriately so I don't go into hypothermic shock.

Today she gives me a hoodie to go over my long-sleeved shirt.

We settle in her kitchen, with its dazzling white countertops and sophisticated black cabinets. Britt climbs onto her giant island and sits on it with crossed legs as she unwraps our paper bags. I slide onto one of the island stools and suck the pulpy, eight-dollar orange juice from a straw. I'm so thirsty that it burns on its way down.

She picks up half of her breakfast sandwich and unhinges her jaw like a cobra as she takes a bite.

We watch one another as she chews and I suck my orange juice, and after a few seconds, her fingers on one hand are drifting toward my cheek. "Do you know you have a beauty mark?" She places her pointer about an inch below the corner of my left eye. "It's small but it's perfect." She brings her hand back.

I touch the spot where I can still feel her finger. "Thanks. My mom has a bunch of them."

"I love that. I love when skin has marks."

"Should we talk about stuff?" I ask.

"You don't like your muffin?"

I break off a piece because we won't get anywhere until I do. "Should we talk about stuff?" I try again.

She watches herself rip a piece of bacon from her sandwich before she makes herself look at me again. "Parker did make me have sex with him. This summer, one random night while Michelle was out of town. He's been drunk and come on to me before . . . grabbed my ass when no one was around to stop him, or smelled my neck, stupid shit like that. He's been drunk enough to grab my face and kiss me a couple times . . . not like he's in love with me." She drags her finger along the side of her bagel and gathers a glob of cream cheese. "Not like this is some unrequited soul-mate drama, but Parker just has this thing about him. This itch to control stuff. And be the boss of everything. And he comes off like he's cool playing second fiddle to Michelle and Kelly and Bianca and me, like he's just this good-dude-chauffeur-meets-takeout-delivery-guy when we want one. But he's hella manipulative. It's all just a front. That's how it was when he would kiss me. Like it was just to let me know who was really running this shit."

"Does Michelle know?"

"It didn't get really bad until this summer. Until he started stroking himself in prep to be our new quarterback." She traces the sweating rim of her iced chai. "It's funny, because the only reason Parker had sex with me the night he did is because he was so freaked out that I overheard this conversation he was having with Levi, and he just couldn't go home that night without feeling like he was taking control of the situation somehow. But the thing is, Aly, I already knew they had a secret. I could have detonated months ago. And Parker's drunk attempt to control everything—to control *me*—only ended up making it worse for him, and to this day, he still doesn't even realize it."

"Wait, what do you mean you knew they had a secret?" I ask.

"Has J ever said anything to you about a flash drive?"

I barely understand the question. "Like for your computer?"

She sighs disappointedly. I clearly have no clue what she's talking about, and it feels like I failed a test before I fully realized I was taking one.

"Tell me," I insist. "Maybe I'm just not remembering."

"You'd remember," she promises. "It's easier just to show you. Hold on."

She slides off the island and disappears upstairs, leaving her half-eaten sandwich and me behind. When she comes back, her Mac-Book is tucked under her arm, a flash drive sticking out from one of the USB ports.

She climbs back onto the island and pulls the flash drive out of her computer and squeezes it in her hand. "I stole this off of Zach Willis's key chain months ago. Mainly because I wanted it. Do you remember him? He was this Neanderthal who was basically obsessed with me last year."

"Of course I remember Zach."

"Well, last summer, he invited me over to hang out, and when I got to his house, I walked in on him and a couple of the other guys on the team crowded around his computer geeking out about whatever they were watching. And when I asked what it was, they spun around looking guilty as fuck and ejected this drive so fast you would have thought it was FBI-level classified. I asked him a bunch of times what it was, but he never told me. So a few months later, I took it.

"I looked at it back then, and it was fucking terrible, but I didn't fully get it until after that night with Parker. Because he dropped Kel and B off at Kelly's, and then said some bullshit about how I needed to ride with him to pick up the food and we'd be back, and then he parked in the lot at McDonald's and started kissing me and saying all this stuff about how I needed to join him and Michelle one of these days, how we already do everything else together. How he'd show me how good it could be . . ." She hugs herself. "He's a psychopath, basically, and I don't want to talk about all the specifics, but when he finished, the drive-thru was stupid long, so he went inside, and I was just in a daze . . . I don't know. I was really fucked up about whatever the hell had just happened, and all I wanted was to get the taste of his mouth out of mine. So, I dug in the center console for some gum, and instead I found a plastic bag with like fifty of these." She dangles the flash drive between her thumb and pointer. "So, this is what I wanted to show you."

She tells me what to do as I slide the flash drive back into the USB port, my heart thudding inconsistently in my chest like the footsteps of a stumbling drunk. Her voice is almost background noise as I try to steady my trembling fingers so I can navigate a computer. She's explaining to me how the files are sorted, because there are so, so many. There are folders for each school year for the past thirteen years, and when I hover over each folder to see who the owner is, it's the corresponding Varsity quarterback for that year, every time.

Once I double-click one of the school year folders, there are even more files, listed in alphabetical order by first initial. Girls. All the names seem like they belong to one of our girls. She suggests I open hers first, so I do.

B. MacDougal, hers is called.

Inside are three files.

"Pick any one," she says.

I just choose the first.

And that's when my stomach liquifies, and bile burns the bottom of my throat. Britt's straddling some blurry guy on a bed while they make out and he slides his hands into the waistband of her jeans. I know what comes next if this tape doesn't end soon, and it doesn't—not for another ten minutes.

I X out and double click the next file, praying to God I'm gonna see kittens or test answers or *anything*. But it's her again, on a different night, in a different outfit, in the same room, with who I have to assume is the same blurry guy.

And maybe just because I'm naïve enough to believe that there's still a chance that Seton is the place I always dreamed it was, I click into the last file, too.

But it's still Britt.

I close out of her file and blindly scroll, dragging my finger down the trackpad in the folder for last school year alone, and the list goes on forever. There are at least a hundred files.

Videos.

Of Seton girls who seem completely clueless that they're having sex on camera.

An entire lifetime has gone by over the course of a single school day.

The setting sun turns the sky purple and orange as I run up the concrete walkway to J's front door. The doorbell hasn't worked in years, so I rap my knuckles against the screen, and from the outside it sounds like nothing, but I've been inside enough times when someone knocks to know it's loud enough, so I hug myself and wait and try not to cry. Not yet.

Britt offered to stay when she was dropping me off, but I told her to go and that I'd let her know. What? I'm not sure. That's the scary part. The part I don't want her here with me to find out. So even though I let her drive me home for the first time ever today, that's as far as I can let her come for now.

J's mom opens the door and smiles when she sees me, her dreads pulled back in a ponytail with a rubber band. She's in a black T-shirt and blue jeans, so she either just got back from the salon where she works or is headed there now for an evening appointment. She barely has a chance to say hello before J appears breathlessly behind her, like he was trying to get here first.

"Ma, I got it," he says, sliding past her out the door.

"You guys eating over there tonight?" she asks, referring to my house. We haven't talked about it in the midst of the few chaotic texts we did exchange today after I left school with Britt and didn't come back, but she's just doing what she would any other night. Because, to her, that's exactly what this is.

J kisses her cheek and tells her, "Yeah." Just so we can keep moving.

We head down his walkway to our sidewalk, where grass grows through the cracks. I wish we had somewhere we could go where we could be alone, or at least not be so easily observed, and I know J feels it, too.

"Wanna go to Walgreens?" he asks.

The five-minute walk has never felt so long, even though I don't notice a single thing about it. I don't know if any cars drive past or if the boys are playing basketball on the Johnsons' roll-away hoop, like always. It's just this purple-orange sky and everything Britt told me that's been stabbing my brain all day as we walk faster down this sidewalk than we ever have before, because we're reaching our quota on how much longer we can go not saying everything that needs to be said.

We walk around to the back of the store, where the parking spaces are empty and there's just a green dumpster. J stops in front of me with eyes that are the same kind of confused as a puppy's when you close a door before he has the chance to come in, too.

"Where did you go today?" he asks.

But before I can answer, and tell him everything that Britt told me, everything that Seton really is, all the ways I tried and failed to have any of the right words for her this afternoon, and how badly I hope she still wants me, or thinks I'm worth it, or *whatever*, after I sucked so bad at knowing how to make any of this better . . .

Before I have the chance to do any of that, one of the Walgreens employees comes whistling around the corner with an overstuffed trash bag. "J! How's it going, man? Yo, great game on Saturday," the guy says the second he notices us.

I'm pretty sure J doesn't know him, but he nods like he does. "Thanks, man, I appreciate it."

"What is it—one more game, two before playoffs?" The guy tosses his trash bag into the dumpster.

"One more game."

"Shit. You guys about to go into playoffs undefeated *again*. You think you'll make it to States? Y'all got cheated last year, for real, man. How the fuck is the ref about to call offensive pass interference when your man was triple covered in the end zone?"

"Hey, man, let me talk to you when I get inside, cool?"

"Oh." The guy laughs apologetically and nods at me. "Of course, man. I'll see you inside."

And guy-we-don't-know slowly makes his way around the building, swinging his arms and clapping his hands each time they connect in front of him as he goes.

J slides his hands into his pockets, smiles a little like he's embarrassed but he's not, and taps the toe of his sneaker against the toe of mine. "Fans," he apologizes.

I roll my eyes and smile for the first time in hours. "Shut up."

J laughs and keeps tapping his toe against mine, messing with me because he can. Fidgeting around because he does. "Come on, Alz, what's going on? You never skip school like that. You always said you never wanted Britt to have to drive us home. You wouldn't tell me what was up while you were texting me . . ." He peeks at me from underneath his scrunched eyebrows. "Tell me what's up now."

I look down at our shoes, too. At his incessant tapping. I haven't figured out how to say any of this to him. I'm not sure if I would figure it out if I had all the time in the world. There isn't a right way to shatter a dream. There isn't a right way to break someone's heart. And that's the part that makes my eyes start to burn, just thinking about it.

"Do you remember," I softly start, watching his toes tap mine, "when we were little, and we were playing in the street outside of our houses, and you flipped out because I wouldn't share my twenty-five-cent bouncy ball?"

"Our bouncy ball, but okay."

"And you shoved me, and I fell, and I scraped my knee and it bled? And Felicia wasn't really watching us even though she was supposed to be, and when she saw me bleeding and saw you pouting and got down to put a Band-Aid on my leg, she told you that if you were gonna make me bleed, the least you could do was hold my hand. Do you remember that?"

"I think you've forgotten some of the instigating detail over time, but I remember it."

"I kind of feel like that right now, you know? Like everything was perfect, and then one day it wasn't, and after today, it feels like we're bleeding. Really, really bad. I feel like we're literally bleeding out, and I don't know who can hold our hand right now." One of my tears rolls down my nose and drips right onto the toe of his shoe that's kicking mine. I know he sees it, but he doesn't say it.

Instead, he sighs a little, and slides an arm around my waist. He pulls me in, and I close my eyes as I rest my head against his chest. He kisses me a few strong times through my hair, and then the fingers of his free hand lace their way through mine. His chin is resting on my head when he softly assures me, "I'm always here to hold your hand."

I open my eyes as we stay how we are. "Britt told me about Parker today."

Something in him drops, the firmness in his chest sliding slowly down to his stomach. But his voice doesn't show it. "What'd she say?"

So, I tell him the story. About the night at Levi's over the summer and how it wasn't the first time he got drunk and tried to mess with her. I tell him about what happened at the McDonald's, the same McDonald's that our dads used to take us to after we watched the Seton football games as little kids.

"Do you believe me?" I ask.

"Alz, I believe everything you've ever told me for sixteen years."

"Do you believe Britt?"

I hold my breath as I wait for him to answer, as I listen to his beating heart.

His thumb is wandering aimlessly across my knuckles. "Babe, why are you crying?"

"Because there's so much more. There's so much more that happened, or is happening, and if you don't believe her already—"

"I believe *you*. Tell me anything and that's where I stand. With you. So, tell me. Okay? I fucking hate it when you cry."

"There are these flash drives," I make myself say, and I tell him all I know. All the things that Britt showed me. The videos and what they are. How many of our friends have one—Britt and even Gina-Melissa with Dan, her so-called boyfriend who's supposed to love her. The guys' faces are all blurred, or their backs are positioned conveniently to the camera. But I still know it's Dan because who else could it be?

"And when Britt was waiting in Parker's car that night for him to come back with their stupid McFlurries, she found a full bag of these flash drives, and these little contracts, or something, that guys at our rival schools signed, making a trade . . . a drive in exchange for throwing the game for Seton. For the past *twelve years*. And I just . . ." I wipe my nose on his shirt and put my head back where it was. "We were supposed to matter to each other. We always talk about how much we matter to each other. Britt was supposed to matter to Parker. You guys have a whole freaking cheer for us at football games and tell us how we're the best in the world while the Varsity team has been tricking us into making these videos so they can keep winning their games . . . cheering for us like we're a part of it because in this super-fucked-up way, we are.

"And no one knows, J . . . No one knows besides them, and Britt, and me, and now you. And I know this messes up everything for you, and I hate that more than anything. I honestly sat with Britt for hours trying to figure out how we fix this without destroying everything for you. Because I know we have this plan, you and me. It's everything, and I know that, and that's why we loved Seton so much. And why we loved *them* so much. But how do we keep loving it now? How are we supposed to love anything now?"

And as I stand there, waiting for an answer, I realize he's no longer breathing.

I pull away from his chest and look up at him, our hands still together. This is the exact part I didn't want Britt to be here for, the exact part I didn't want her to have to deal with on top of everything she's already been through. She shouldn't have to try not to trip over our wreckage, too. "Are you okay?"

He was gone for a moment, but my question brings him back. His eyebrows come together, and he reassures me in the same dismissive way he tells his mom he'll wash the dishes. "Yeah. Yeah, I'm good. I just didn't know if you were finished."

My knee can't stop bouncing while I wait for him, wait for him to tell me what's next. Because this is how J processes catastrophe. Quietly. Studiously. Like Life has become a person and the world has become a classroom, and now it's time to listen to the lesson if there's any chance at all of passing the test. And so I wait, because

I always do when he gets like this, and it'll be worth it, because it always is.

But in the meantime, it's like there's this little human lodged in my chest, who can start kicking and screaming and shaking me from the inside out at any possible moment, even though I have no idea when that moment will be. Because the thought of *what's next*, and how we go to school with all of them tomorrow, and sit next to all of them at lunch . . . how—*if*—J will be able to keep his cool after how mad he got the last time Parker acted out. I don't understand how Britt has held on to all this, alone, for months. Because I'm not even sure how J and I will make it a single day.

She's stronger than us. That's what it is.

"What are we gonna do?" I finally ask, my voice tripping in my tightening throat.

He wets his lips and takes a deep breath. "I don't know."

"Do you think the other JV guys are gonna freak out when you tell them? Are some of these guys gonna, like, go to jail? I mean, what happens to the rest of the team? You'll still get to play next year, right?" I'm asking my millions of questions; I can't stop. But there's something about his eyes as I go on, and on, and on. What's not in them: Devastation. Shock. The desire to blow up the world.

And what is: fear.

"Why aren't you talking?" I ignore the chill on the back of my neck.

"I'm thinking."

"Thinking about what?"

"*About what?*" he echoes like I've fully lost it.

"Think out loud," I insist, my voice shaking. His hand in mine might as well be hollow, and his thumb isn't fidgeting with my knuckles like it should be. I'm crying and he doesn't notice it, not the way he's supposed to. And I know J well enough to know. To just *know.*

My stomach has never been so heavy in my life. "Do you have one of those flash drives?"

His lips open a little as he watches me, but nothing comes out.

That little person in my chest . . . she's ready to blow. "J, *do you have one of those flash drives?*"

"Alz—"

"DO YOU HAVE ONE OF THOSE DRIVES?"

"Can I ask you something first?"

"No!"

"Whose side are you on?" And he says it like my answer really reserves the right to dictate his.

I shake my hand free and he tries to grab it back, but I won't let him. "What do you mean *whose side am I on? There isn't any other side to be on!*"

"There *is*, though. Because you're here right now, talking to me, trying to get answers out of me, but I can feel you still in that room with Britt, listening to whatever she has to say—"

"J, do you have a drive?"

"You can't even tell me whose side you're on!" He takes my cheeks in his hands and stares into my eyes like I'm the one in the trance. Like I'm the one who got lost. "Alz, you're coming to me with this crazy allegation about some sex tape scandal that you think me and my boys are running and expect me to be able to just give you whatever answer you want the second you ask for it, but you can't even tell me you're on my side—"

"Because we're not seven years old!"

"*That's not just some little kid shit,*" J insists, still gripping my cheeks. His hands are cold and my face is so hot. "This is *real*, and bigger than Seton, or any cool new girlfriend you're gonna make there. Alz, it's like . . . there is never a question in my mind where my loyalty lies when I wake up in the morning. If you wanna leave a party early to get an air freshener, we leave. If you want to go to some boring-ass country club and sit around and do nothing for a whole afternoon, we do it. And if Parker loses his mind and there's a chance you could've been caught up in it? I'll check him *every single time*." His grip on my face gets stronger, whether or not he notices it. "I told you on that sidewalk a week ago that I don't give a shit about any of the rest of this because I only choose you. And because there's never a doubt in my mind, there's never a doubt in yours. So, you can come to me with something like this, and want your answer more than anything, and not even hesitate about it or even realize why you're really asking it." That's when he lets me go. "Because I'm telling you, the way you're going on right now, that's all for Britt. Not for me. So, yeah, before we go down some rabbit hole of whatever this shit's about to be, I want to know whose side you're on."

We stare at each other, the silence wrapping around us like smoke. "*What?*"

"Alz, don't make me say all that shit again—"

"You want me to choose between you and Britt? After everything I just told you, you feel like that's really the point? Me. Choosing. Between you and Britt."

He looks around like he's waiting for the hidden camera crew to come out of the bushes. "*Of course* I want you to be able to choose between me and Britt! I've got the next six years of my life figured out with *you*, and Britt didn't even send you a text message for the first time until two months ago—"

"It's different, J—"

"I mean, I hope so."

That little human in my chest is slamming my sternum like a drum, and I don't know how the hell we got here. Fighting like we're little all over again, over a twenty-five-cent bouncy ball that's mine but he wants it. Except this is so much bigger, maybe even big enough to crush us. This is our school, and our future, and our friends, and our lives, and these promises he's made to his team and the ones I've made to Britt.

"I told Britt today that she'd never lose me." But I don't recognize my voice now that I'm saying it to him.

He scoffs, nodding to himself, unimpressed. "Lucky her."

And then he turns and starts walking back toward home, and he doesn't stop when I call his name, and he doesn't stop when I run up behind him and slam my fist into his back because now I'm the seven-year-old, and he doesn't stop when I stop following him.

And when I ask him a final time if one of those flash drives is his, he still doesn't answer.

What it was.

Cooper Adams graduated from Seton Academic High School twelve years earlier with a 3.1 GPA. It wouldn't have been good enough for anybody else to get into Penn, but it was good enough for him because he was a legacy, because his family had been donors for decades, and that was why they gave him a scholarship, too, saving his family the money they could have easily spent anyway. On his third day of college, at a frat party, he met Kyla Abernathy, who'd been in the midst of winning a wet T-shirt contest. She was from Tennessee and had the accent to prove it, chewed gum even when she was drinking a beer, and her blue eyes twinkled behind her sassy gaze. She came from family money, and her parents were surgeons, and Cooper decided he wanted her from the second he saw her in a white T-shirt, soaking wet and bra-less.

They dated their whole time in college, the all-American couple, according to anyone whose America only looks one way. They graduated, and once they did, they decided to stay in Philadelphia. Cooper liked the bar scene there, and the way people had gotten to know his name after he'd thrown some wild parties and started a little underground cheating ring for all of his friends and anyone who was willing to give him a hundred bucks. He didn't play football at Penn; he wasn't on the team and never tried to be. Seton football was a pastime for him, one that he was genetically blessed enough to excel at, and as soon as he left, it was on to the next.

In Philadelphia, his dad connected him with a buddy who ran a hedge fund, and Cooper worked there for four years before he was promoted to a management position. His parents gave him the down payment for a $700,000 townhome in the city, and then gave him the $20,000 to buy Kyla's ring. They got married on an old plantation in South Carolina and posed for black-and-white pictures with a bunch of bridesmaids and groomsmen who all looked exactly the same. Blond and sandy-brown hair. Light-colored eyes. White skin.

You know. "All-American."

A lot like the way that Parker's house looked right now, except for Bianca and Michelle. Because Cooper was back, and Kyla was back, and their baby boy was, too.

McKesson. Happy birthday, McKesson.

Today, he was one year old.

It was one of the hottest days in years, the kind of day when leaving a dog in the car is a crime and the news tells the elderly to stay indoors. Ninety-eight degrees, to be exact, but the humidity made it feel like 120, or something close. Something dangerous.

But Parker's mother had the air-conditioning going on high and all the windows opened on the main floor. The glass wall that separated the indoor/outdoor dining area was slid open so that company could stroll easily between the patio with its babbling brook and the table full of appetizers. In the real world, people were sweating like they'd committed the crime of the century, but not here.

Parker was wearing khakis and loafers and a pale pink button-down, with a backward Seton baseball cap. Michelle was in a sleeveless, tailored, black-and-white cocktail dress—the kind of thing modern royals wear to tea parties. Bianca's navy-blue dress fit the theme, too.

And maybe it sort of was a tea party. This daytime, semiformal event for the fifty or so all-American people who were closest to the Adamses.

"Can I hold him?" Michelle begged, like McKesson was the keys to a new Tesla.

"Girl, yes," Kyla answered, in her unbothered, cool girl way as she flipped her blond hair in her one-shoulder maxi. She placed her baby in Michelle's waiting arms. "It'll give me a minute to have a sangria. Babe, do you want anything?"

Cooper stood next to his brother, in khakis and a white button-down, the slightly taller, thirty-year-old spitting image of Parker. Cooper held up his half-full bottle of beer by the neck as his way of saying *I'm good.*

"Guess it's easy to drink when you have both hands," Kyla snidely remarked.

Cooper smirked as she backed away. "Love you."

"I know it."

And she headed for the sangria pitchers on the table outside, getting stopped to chat by a group of aunts on her way.

Michelle bounced McKesson in her arms while he cooed at her and reached for her hair with his chubby arms. She frowned in the way that's really a smile and made eye contact with Parker as she did.

Parker laughed and swigged from his own bottle of beer, not ready for the whole baby thing. Not ready to even think about being ready, and Michelle knew it. "You gotta chill."

So Michelle turned to her friend instead and pleaded. "B, hold him . . ."

But Bianca shook her head determinedly while her big brown eyes stared longingly into McKesson's. "I can't . . ."

"You can."

"No . . ." she said, accepting him as Michelle smiled and placed him in Bianca's arms. "Ugh, I have to go to med school," she concluded.

Michelle giggled and rested her chin on Bianca's shoulder and slid her arms around Bianca's waist, scrunching her nose as McKesson babbled and grabbed for it.

Cooper gripped Parker's shoulder and squeezed. "You wanna go grab a shot of Dad's whiskey?"

Parker nodded easily, swigging from his beer. "Hell yeah."

"You girls okay watching Kess for a minute?" Cooper asked.

"I actually have to pee," Michelle said, still wiggling her fingers into McKesson's.

"I'll watch him," Bianca offered.

The powder room was next to the study, and Michelle made Parker kiss her goodbye before she disappeared inside, before Parker was free to follow his brother into the room next door.

"Are the other two coming?" Cooper asked his little brother, one hand in his pocket as his eyes skimmed the options displayed on Mr. Adams's bar cabinet. Bottles that were older than both of them.

"Kelly and Britt?" Parker assumed, resting against the wall across from all the books. Cooper had encountered the four girls together enough times, whenever he was home for the holidays. "Yeah, they're coming. They texted Mich a few minutes ago."

Cooper smiled to himself, setting his beer on an end table as he chose the most expensive Scotch they had. "Michelle's kind of crazy about Kess, huh?"

"Man, she loves anything sweet. Food. Movies. Babies. All of it."

Cooper nodded, opening the cabinet doors for glasses. "Then you better make sure to wrap it up twice with her." Parker snort-laughed into his beer and Cooper went on. "I'm serious, man. She 'forgets' to pop her pill one day and she's got you for life."

They could still hear the party from where they were—the music, the talking—but it was easier to talk in here. Not be overheard. Bumped into by an aunt or nagged by a mom or wife or girlfriend.

"So fill me in on this whole plan you have to grab States," Cooper said as he poured their liquor into two short glasses. "Because the drives you have aren't gonna get you there. They were never designed to."

"Yeah, but what if I make them better?" It was part-question, part-challenge as Parker set his empty bottle down next to a lamp.

"Better?" Cooper sounded like a smart-ass as he considered it.

Parker smiled. "Some girl-on-girl stuff?" Parker nudged him. "Group stuff?" He nudged him again. "You know, orgy shit. I could get Britt and Mich in bed tomorrow if I wanted to. I bet you a million bucks."

Cooper chuckled as he handed Parker a glass. "Big dreams, bro?"

"Coop, I fucking bet you this house," Parker eagerly insisted, this thing that always existed between the two of them. This valida-tion Parker always craved when it came to his older brother, this giddiness for Cooper to be on his side, to agree with him, to believe in him. "I bet you the Benz. I bet you my *fucking life.*"

Cooper let his thoughts marinate for a second, his head swaying a little from side to side like he was doing long division without a calculator. "You're probably right," he conceded as he smiled.

Parker smiled, too, gassed up. "I mean, we've gotta win it all this year, bro. You didn't start all this just for some kid to come up after we're gone and be the name everyone remembers because he was the first one to bring home the 'ship. And I've got J Turner on my heels . . . You know him. Dude that buses in from fucking nowhere every day and came by last Christmas?" Parker gave Cooper a second to remember, and Cooper nodded like maybe he did. "Now, do I think he really will get to States? Hell no. But could he? Maybe. And good for him. Fucking great for him, if he can get it done. He needs this sport, dude. But I wanna be first. He can take States and get some big scholarship and then go off and win a Heisman one day, if that's what it's gonna be. But not before me."

"So you're gonna make the drives better," Cooper summarized.

"I'm gonna make the drives better," Parker concluded, swigging his whiskey. "Task all my guys with it so we have loads of shit. Give a drive to every dude on the other team if they're willing to give me a playoff win. Hell, let them all join the club." He brought his glass down from his lips and swirled it a little. "And my girls will come through for me, Coop. I know it. They fucking love me. I bring home a couple of Big Macs at midnight and they drop to their fucking knees. I'm telling you, Coop. I think about all those trophies on the wall . . . Damn, I want two so bad it makes me crazy."

Cooper chuckled to himself, like he knew the feeling—what it's like to crave something so much you can't even think. "That's the best way to want anything." He tapped his delicate little glass against Parker's. "Look, man. If you want it, take it. Your plan for the drives? I love it. And remember, you don't gotta beat 'em, you just gotta win."

"Just gotta win," Parker echoed as he smiled. "Like Pops always says."

"Proud of you, man." They slapped hands, the torch they weren't holding officially moving from big brother to little. It wasn't the title of quarterback, though—it was the ability to get what they wanted out of any situation. It was what the twelve guys who'd come between Cooper and Parker were never wired to do—make the system *better*. Make it work *harder*. Not the same rinse-and-repeat strategy, but an evolution. More than just a reason to be remembered, but a reason to be king. "You better keep me posted," Cooper told him.

"I will," Parker promised. Braver now that Cooper believed in it, too.

They both swigged from their glasses. Then Cooper asked, "You heard anything else from bitch boy?"

"Not a peep. Homeboy is scared shitless. A couple of my boys over at Iverson say his little punk ass jumps every time a locker slams now."

Cooper chuckled. "You teach them not to fuck with you and they won't."

Parker smiled and licked his lips. "You think I'm good, right?"

Cooper frowned like the question wasn't worth asking in the first place. "Every guy on that team is gonna back you till the end. You deployed your resources and executed the contingency plan flawlessly. And scared the living shit out of the one guy who thought he didn't have to listen." He slapped Parker's shoulder, squeezed it in a reassuring massage. "You're good. You're out here making plans for States that no one's thought of for twelve years before you. This shit's in your blood. Have fun with it."

"Fun without me?" Michelle asked, appearing in the entryway.

Parker finished his whiskey and easily declared, "No such thing."

She folded her arms, resting her shoulder against the wall. She asked Cooper, "Should we get back before B drops your baby?"

Cooper smiled out of the side of his mouth and assured her, "He'll bounce." He finished off his whiskey, too. "He's an Adams."

What it is.

"A deductively reasoned forever."

Maybe that's the wrong way to get there. Maybe it needs to be a conscious choice. Not this result you get to because your parents will always be best friends or because your lives are already so tangled up together. Maybe forever happens when it's chosen, not assumed.

Maybe we did it wrong.

I don't know.

But it's the saddest, hardest thing in the entire world, knowing how much you know someone, even when you can't recognize him at all. Knowing that you know who he is, even when he's acting like something completely different. Something that's wrong. The only fights J and I have ever had ended in scraped knees or with both of us pouting over having to share whatever snack we wanted to have all to ourselves. We've never stopped talking, not for real. Not like now.

And lying in bed that night while I don't sleep—because how can anyone sleep on broken glass?—I just can't decide. If I really did choose Britt instead today, or if he'd chosen football, and a flash drive, and the future he never really needed me for in the first place.

Looking at my dark phone, when it should've been lighting up with all our late-night texts, I accept that maybe it's both.

Seton stands proud and unblemished the next morning while everyone lives like nothing has died. Our classmates walk up the main steps; cars full of best friends park in the closest spots they can find. And I sit at one of the picnic tables on the patio, alone. Unclaimed. Unnoticed. With this hole in my stomach that feels like it could suck me in from the inside out. And a part of me wishes it would.

But then there's an arm looping through mine, pulling me hurriedly off my ass, and as Britt wraps her arm around my shoulders, she says, "Come on. Let's go."

She walks me, determinedly, up the main steps and into our school, sliding through the bake sale and the football team's incessant playlist, and all the crowds huddled around all the food like they're looking at fossils under glass.

She leads me down the hallway, still squeezing my shoulders with her arm wrapped around them, and leads us to the newspaper office. She opens the door and flips on the light and closes the door behind us.

"Why are you by yourself?" she demands. "You're never by yourself. You're never not with J." She blinks nervously, anxiously. "Did you talk to him last night?"

She's standing in front of me, the same, perfect Britt MacDougal she's been her entire life, despite what Parker did to her this summer, despite everything she knows. She's still beautiful, she's still so fucking cool, in her hooded gray sweatshirt dress with an image of Rihanna on it and Timberlands and a black beanie. She's still good enough—*Seton* enough—to stand there like a phoenix.

And I'm so glad she's here, and I'm so scared she's here, because of what she's gonna think. Because of what she's gonna say.

"Yeah," I answer.

"And what happened?"

Beyond the closed door to this empty office, "Blurred Lines" blares and our classmates' voices merge together like a soft roar. J is out there somewhere, with his team and whatever baked goods he made after our fight last night, and I have no idea whether it's cookies or brownies or Rice Krispies treats or what. And it hits me like a fire hose how impossible that seems, and how impossible *this* seems, and I don't know why sometimes it's the littlest things like cookies and brownies that break our hearts.

"Britt, what if . . ." My knee bounces as my gaze wanders around the room, at all the fancy Mac computers and framed articles on the walls. I can't say that I start crying, because that would suggest I actually stopped at some point between now and yesterday, when really all I've done is force myself to pause in the moments that would trigger questions from my parents or judgmental stares from our bus driver. "What if we just talk to the guys and ask them to stop doing what they're doing?"

Her eyes narrow in on me like I'm speaking a language she's barely conversational in.

But I fumble on. "I mean, once they know we know, they have to stop anyways, right? They can't trick us into being recorded if we know they're doing it, and then with Parker, you should absolutely tell someone what he did to you that night. And I'll come with you. I'll be with you, I swear, and I want that for you *so bad*, so what if we just like . . . do it that way?"

Her eyebrows come together and she squints at me like I'm a million miles away. "No."

"Why?"

"Because they aren't gonna stop." She almost laughs at the sheer

stupidity of my suggestion. "Because that means we're just as bad as everybody else, giving them a pass for their shit behavior. The same way everyone does—the same way they don't have to sit on waiting lists when they should have made reservations, or they get to buy booze at gas stations when they should get carded, or they get to drive drunk and wave at the cops as they go by. They can't just do whatever they want, and act however they want, and only think about themselves, and then we just ask them to stop like they're kicking the back of our desks or something. Like they're just some nuisance. They're terrorists, Aly. They're basically a threat to society. To every girl who's on that drive. To me." She shakes her head, not getting it. "You cared about all that yesterday."

"I know, Britt, I know. And I do. It's just that . . ."

But Britt is the smartest girl in our school, and she doesn't need me to say anything. She can get it on her own. "J knew," she realizes.

My throat feels like strep, but I force myself to swallow. "I didn't say that."

"Then what are you saying?"

And the truth is that I don't know, even after I spent all night thinking about it. Even though the whole team is obsessed with each other, Varsity really is its own special world, and I can convince myself there are things that they know that the guys on JV don't. But J also wouldn't tell me whether he has a drive, and maybe it's because he was pissed, or felt like I chose Britt, or maybe it was because J always keeps his mouth shut when he doesn't want to have to lie.

So, I don't know. I haven't even decided if I *want* to know. But something about all that feels too raw, or even too *intimate*, to tell Britt.

"If we can just figure out a way to fix this without destroying everything else . . ." I argue instead.

She shakes her head, slow-paces in tiny circles, and stares at the shining red and white tiles on our floor. I can practically hear her brain clicking thousands of little pieces together. A puzzle.

Then she looks at me and declares like there's only one possible verdict, "I'm sorry, but you sound like an asshole."

My heart cracks up the middle.

"What do you want to *be*, Aly? Just some girlfriend? Who kisses her boyfriend while they sit in the front row at the movies or wear matching outfits to prom? Forever a plus-one for all his prior football commitments, no matter how shitty, or disgusting, or illegal they are? Or do you want to be a *real person*? Who owns the fact that this freaking office is yours, and you could change stuff if you really wanted to? Who knows how much she has to offer on her own, devoid of some high-school-boy bullshit?" She wets her lips as she glares at me. "You don't *need* Seton any more than you need any other school. You don't even need J. You really don't, Aly. You want him, I get that. I get how that's even harder sometimes. But I told you what I told you yesterday because I thought you'd listen, and I thought you'd care, and I thought we were girlsfriends and that that would matter to you the way that it matters to me. But you're too busy being a *girlfriend* to give a shit about me or any of the other girls on those tapes. So, good luck, Aly. Good luck asking your boyfriend if he could please stop sucking at life."

"*Stop*," I insist as she turns to go. "You can't leave me. Please, don't. Because if you go, I have no one else here." She stops before she gets too far, thank God, and looks at me again. "J isn't talking to me, Britt. We got in a huge fight, and he wouldn't even tell me if he had a drive or not, because I stood by you. And he hates me for that because it's always been me and him. And everything in me still hopes that it is, even though I know you can't understand why. But I lay in bed not texting him for the first time since we've had cell phones, and I rode in a seat by myself on the bus to school this morning because I'm alone right now, without you. And I'm just trying to figure out how it could maybe work, how maybe there could be a chance that everything he and I have doesn't have to go up in flames. Because you guys can rebuild, Britt, that's the difference. I *do* need Seton. You guys don't, but I do. So you can't just walk away right now. Please, don't just walk away right now."

I never, ever wanted to beg Britt to want me. I want her to want me on her own. I want to be her choice, the same way J always wants to be mine. And I feel it now, I think. Some of what he was feeling last night. When he was trying to remind me how I should choose. How easy he wanted it to be for me. How easy it would have been for him.

It's the same easy way I've always known that I would choose Britt, over and over again, if she'd have me. Not to replace J, not instead of J, but to fill all the voids that J can't. And brighten the moments where J doesn't belong. I never, ever wanted to beg for that, but here I am, begging.

And it feels like shit.

It's too embarrassing, too pathetic, for her to stick around. She's gorgeous and cool and the smartest girl in the whole school, and all I'm probably doing now is reminding her how many other options exist for her. It's the loneliest alone I can imagine.

But she doesn't walk away, and instead she wraps her arms around my shoulders and squeezes so tightly that it almost hurts, and she kisses the side of my forehead and doesn't let go. "Just because we fight doesn't mean I'm gone," she whispers. "That isn't how this works. We're gonna fight. We're gonna have huge, disastrous blowups—maybe even as bad one day as Kelly, Bianca, Michelle, and I are right now. But I know we're gonna get better. And I know they know it, too. Because we have to get better. Because that's the only possible way to know for sure that life isn't designed to just be complete and utter shit. So, you have to know that, too, okay? You have to know that, even if you and I fight, we're gonna make it better. You have to know that in order to make it true. You know what I believe, Aly?"

"What?" I ask, my voice muffled into her shoulder while she keeps on squeezing.

"I believe that whether you think something's over or whether you think it's not, you're right. So you always have to decide that the important stuff isn't over, okay? Or else it is. You know what I mean?"

I squeeze her, and with my eyes closed, I can almost convince myself that things are okay.

But then she brings me back, to everything that's real, to exactly where we are. "We have to do something about those guys, Aly."

And I open my eyes and promise, "We will."

What it is.

It's surprisingly easy to stay quiet when you don't know what to say.

For days, Britt and I know that we want to stop what's happening, but we just don't know how. She has a reason why not for every idea I have. We can't tell Principal Mitchell because of the parents who are donors and the ones on the school board, and they could (and would, Britt promises) sooner have him fired than let him ruin Seton football. We can't go to the police because their parents are the police, too, and big-deal lawyers who could bury this in a minute, Britt promises. We can't take it to one of the local newspapers or news crews because that isn't fair to the girls—they'll become media props, and that's not the way anyone deserves to find out that this happened to her.

So we stay quiet for days, and it's easier than I ever thought it would be.

In the days that pass, J and I still don't speak, and I never realized how much Seton noticed us until now. But ever since we haven't been together before the bell rings, or sitting together at lunch, now that Britt and I have started eating alone in the courtyard, Parker has been studying me like I'm a bug he's never seen before. I feel Michelle's and Kelly's and Bianca's eyes, too—and everyone's, honestly, as if they don't recognize me now that I'm not next to him. Britt doesn't find it as shocking as I do. She reminds me that I've been dating the next Varsity quarterback for years, and in Seton terms, I might as well have been Meghan Markle.

J looks at me, too, and his eyes are the only ones that really matter. They're sad, and they're tired, and sometimes even kind of red and puffy. Every time I see him, I want him to come over. I'll stop everything and look back at him and promise myself that if he just takes one step my way, I'll cover all the rest. But someone from the team always sweeps him away, dragging him into one of their latest debates as they walk down the halls that they own.

It's too much to have Britt pick me up for school in the mornings, but she's been driving me home at night in an effort to spare me the trauma of being in such proximity to J when we're not speaking. He still plays catch with Cory in our front yard, and our parents accept my absence for now because I insist I'm trying to work on this center spread article about Parker that needs to run in the paper next week. Which, at least for now, is true.

The timing is a complete joke, though, with everything else that's on my mind. I whine to Britt about it at least twelve times a day, asking her how the hell I'm supposed to write it. And she agrees every time in her very Britt way that our traditions are bullshit and she'd burn them all to the ground if she could.

I'm in my bedroom on my Seton-issued laptop for the third night in a row, while it's dark outside and my house has gone sleepy. My cell phone is under my pillow where I can't see it, because it hurts less when I don't see J's name pop up on the screen, and I have my notebook open to the notes I took at Julio's when Parker and I finally got around to the interview part of our dinner. All this stuff about what he's gonna miss most about Seton, where he hopes to be in ten years, his biggest regret—and no, it's not sex tapes or even sex tape–adjacent.

But my stark white Word document stares back at me on the screen, without so much as a headline after three days of trying.

I read back over the notes I took. I get to the part about how symbolic it is for him to lead the Seton Girls cheer this year because his brother was the one who started it, who really saw how much the girls meant for the first time, and I roll my eyes so hard that I'm lucky they don't get stuck.

With my pointer, I start slow-typing words I know I'm gonna delete. *Seton Girls.* I backspace and type it again in all-caps.

SETON GIRLS.

I study it, caught up in all I thought it meant to be one of us. I stare at the cursor blinking at me over and over again, patiently waiting for me to keep going. And finally, I do. My brain, after all the J stuff and shock of the past few days, suddenly starts working again for the first real time. The words spill onto the page like I'm overflowing.

It isn't easy to create change that lasts.

In fact, it's really, really hard.

But we did it, here at Seton. And we believed we did it together.

Don't you remember the stories? All the tales passed on from seniors to freshmen year after year?

Cooper Adams. Who he was. What he meant. How he came in and changed our whole entire world . . .

I stop for the few seconds it takes me to reach under my pillow and pull out my phone. I go to Britt's name and type out the text:

I know what we can do.

It's Friday night at Seton, and anyone who's anyone is crammed into the bleachers in our gym with its shiny wood floors. It has the echo that gyms always have, their own one-of-a-kind hearing situation that almost feels like I'm listening underwater. The clapping is non-stop, and my butt is vibrating against the wooden bench as the entire room fast-stomps our feet against the floor. It's our girls' volleyball team against Billingsley's, and if we win, we're going to Regionals.

On top of that, the football team officially had their last game over the weekend, and they won—a convenient opposing team fumble in the fourth quarter when we were down by one point. Britt came with me to the game last Saturday because it'd be too suspicious to my parents and J's if I just didn't show up, and she stuck her finger down her throat and gagged obnoxiously when our field goal was good to win the game. I haven't smiled much over the past week and a half, but Britt always finds a way to make me, whenever she's around.

But anyways, the point of the boys' last regular season game being last weekend is that that means they're here now, stress-free and rooting for the girls' volleyball team with the rest of us. They take up two full rows of bleachers, decked out in their Seton wardrobes with their Seton hats on backward or in one of our beanies instead. They don't have to play tomorrow because it's the bye week before playoffs, the bye week that kick-starts the Week of the Girls instead. And old me—the me who didn't know I existed like a goldfish in a fish tank while the boys tapped the glass—that me would've loved every single thing about this. How kick-ass our girls look tonight. This underwater echo chamber. The way the football team is rallying so hard right now, slapping the bleachers with their hands and yelling at the refs for any bad call. It's Seton at our absolute finest: united, group-thinking, group-acting, group-doing.

And it's terrifying.

One of our girls, Billie Washington, winds up for a big serve. The football team's voices overpower all of ours as they launch into a wave of "*Ayyyyyyyy-ohhhhhhhhh*," with their hands cupping their mouths. Billie has exactly four videos on the football team's flash drive. The two from two years ago are most likely with one of our Varsity guys she dated her whole sophomore year. The two from last year, I don't know.

But this is what I do lately. I can't stop myself. I see a girl at Seton, and if Britt's with me, I ask, "Her?" And so many times, Britt will nod and tell me, "One," or "Three," or "A lot." She's scrolled through the drive so many times at this point that she practically has it memorized.

So, yeah. It's fucking terrifying.

Britt pinches my knee as the gym peaks in loudness, and beckons me to come on. The fourth game of this match is starting, and if the Seton girls win this one, that'll be the three we need to take home the final win.

Britt and I had always planned to sneak out for the last game.

We slide through the bleachers, carefully stepping over our classmates' thudding feet, and slip out the side door of the gym. My ears are so numb that standing in the empty hallway feels like someone muted the world.

"Alright, I'll keep watch," Britt tells me. "Keep your phone where you can feel it, okay?"

I slap the back pocket of my jeans. "It's right on my butt."

"That's a lucky phone."

I smile.

She takes my shoulders in her hands. "This is the smartest idea you've ever had, and you've got this, okay?"

"Okay."

"Okay." She lets me go and promises she'll stay right where she is, keeping an eye on the hallway.

And then, like that, I'm gone.

What it is.

I sit at the giant screen in our empty newspaper office, all 2,431 words that I started typing that night in my room staring back at me in their perfectly formatted columns. They're right. There's nothing to change about anything; Britt has read them almost as many times as I have and swears they're the most poetic thing she's ever laid eyes on. It's the uprising we need. Far enough reach that the flames can rage before the cops or the boys' rich parents can contain it.

But still. The moment is now, and in this moment, I could do a whole comprehensive edit all over again. And there's no time.

I didn't turn the lights on when I came into the newspaper office, and the faint fandemonium echoes from the gym. The band is playing "Girls Just Wanna Have Fun" now.

I glance at my phone sitting next to me on this desk, but no warning texts from Britt. And I take a deep breath as I hold my mouse and scroll up and down this layout for the tenth time since I sat down. This was supposed to be Parker's story, and in a way, it still is.

That is, in a way that's gonna make him want to kill me.

But I'm finally okay with that.

Instead of running the article that Principal Mitchell thinks I'm running—the standard *Aren't Seton Quarterbacks the Best People on the Freaking Planet?!* kind of thing that he already read and signed off on when I (like I'm supposed to) gave him the printed proof earlier this week—I'm replacing it with a story about the drives. What we know about them, how it works, how long it's worked, why we're really undefeated. It's a compilation of the things Britt's told me over the past week and a half, and then the numbers: 1, 2, 3 . . . in list format with white space next to each—799 blank lines that stand for the 799 girls who have tapes. Names that I refuse to write down because I don't want to cause that pain. And the ones who are still here, once they've read the story, they'll know who they are. And it'll hurt bad enough.

So, I just made the list and left it blank, and it's so surreal to see how much space 799 blank lines takes up.

Britt says it reminds her of one of our sign-in sheets.

My phone buzzes. Once. Twice.

Game's ending

And then:

People are coming out!!

"Shit."

I save and stop thinking, stop rereading, and just do. I upload the replacement file to the cloud for the print shop that actually prints the paper and take a deep breath, like something final is happening. I don't know what's next, but once this runs on Wednesday, everything that was just broken before gets officially shattered.

So, I guess maybe that's what I breathe in. This office. The sameness. The world as I've known it, and my safe, quiet little place in it. What it was, and the things I liked.

But I don't know.

I'm not sure I'll miss it.

My phone shakes again and it shakes me, too. I shut down the computer and jog out of the office.

And just as I'm rounding the corner to get back to the hallway where I left Britt, I collide with someone else.

J.

He blinks at me, looking so Seton football, in the sweats and the hoodie and the backward hat.

My heart flips over in my chest.

"Hey," he says, out of breath for no reason. Maybe his heart stopped, too.

"Sorry," I stutter, and then I add, "For bumping into you."

And he frowns like he hates that I'd even say that—apologize to him like we're strangers or something. I hate it, too. "Alz, you bend my finger back until I scream 'mercy' just because you want the remote—don't say sorry."

"Sorry," I instinctively repeat. "I mean, not sorry. I mean." I sigh. "You know what I mean."

"I saw you leave the gym a little bit ago and not come back, so I thought maybe I'd try to find you. Can we talk?"

"Aly!" Britt calls when she notices me at the far end of the hall-way. I know she sees J, she has to, but—right now—she doesn't care. There's too much else that just happened. There's too much else she needs to know.

"Later?" I say hopefully to J, and I mean it, even though I don't regret leaving right now. As badly as I want him, I also want Britt to be right when she says that I don't need him.

I don't wait to hear what he says, and every organ I have is revolting at the possibility that maybe I just permanently ruined everything, but I have such an eagerness to get back to Britt, and tell her what I've done, what *we've* just done.

I jog to Britt, and as soon as I reach her, she takes my hand, and we run the rest of the way down the hallway, throwing our bodies against the giant red doors that lead back outside, just as the gym doors officially start to open.

It's dark outside, stars winking at us through the trees.

"*So?*" Britt insists, like I should be ashamed of myself for making her wait so long.

I smile and give her a thumbs-up.

"*Shut the fuck up.*" She grabs my cheeks in her hands and stares into my eyes. I laugh as she goes on, "Stop talking. Are you serious? You did it?"

"I did it."

"Aly Jacobs!" She leaps into my arms, and my knees buckle under her weight, and next thing I know, we're just a pile in the leaves. She barely notices, and I couldn't care less. "You are a goddamn queen. No. You are a goddamn king. Nothing overpowers your power. *You are a superpower.*"

"It took me so long because I kept feeling like I should proofread it one more time."

"Perfection is the number-one enemy of progress. We're progressing over here, and that's all that matters."

I look at her lying next to me on our bed of leaves, me curled on my side and her on her back, her arms spread as she stares happily into the sky. She almost looks as happy as she used to. Before the stuff with the files. Before the stuff with her friends.

"Did you ever talk to Michelle?" My voice isn't a whisper, but it's smaller than normal—careful. The kind of voice Mom uses to wake up Cory in the mornings. It doesn't matter if she pretended like she didn't say it, or Michelle pretended like she didn't hear it, because I know what I saw.

Britt keeps her gaze on the world over our heads, but her smile falls a little. "Why would I talk to Michelle?"

"Because you told her that you'd call," I remind Britt now as she slowly turns her head to face me. Her fluffy curls are like one of those memory foam pillows you can try out at the mall, swallowing her head in their softness. "In the hallway that day after Parker lost it. She was freaking out, and you told her you'd call. And I don't think you'd say that and not do it." Britt blinks, and so I ask, "Did you call?"

It takes her a second. If either of us shifts a millimeter, the leaves beneath us are gonna crunch. That's how dead they are. But it's quiet in a way that seems almost impossible as we stay frozen and stare into each other's eyes.

"Yeah." It's like it breaks her a little bit to admit it, but I have no idea why.

"Britt, that's really good," I promise her. "So, have you guys been talking?"

"Yeah, we've been talking."

And still, we lie there, not moving.

She's waiting on me, waiting for what's next. I think that maybe she can feel me waiting, too. That maybe, in addition to being ridiculously gorgeous, and absurdly smart, she can also sense my vibrations right now.

Everything that's happened over the past two months has been scarier than anything that I ever imagined Seton could be. The person Parker is. The things the team has been doing. This fight—or something worse—that J and I are going through. But lying here right now with Britt, I can accept it all, somehow. It aches and gives me chills like the worst flu I've ever had, but Seton is really sick right now, and I guess these are the symptoms.

Still. The hardest part to accept about any of this was the demise of Britt and Michelle. The fact that they would choose any option besides each other. That's what I'm thinking, for the millionth time; those are the vibrations I'm sending out that are loud enough for Britt to hold her breath but so soft that the leaves don't make a sound. And nothing else right now looks the way it's supposed to, nothing else makes sense, except for maybe this. That maybe Britt and Michelle are getting to be okay. Maybe they *are* okay.

"Of course you guys have been talking. You're best friends." It's one of the last things I know to be true about Seton.

"And I hate that I didn't tell you that, but the thing is . . . we're all like . . . fucking guppies around here," Britt says. "Even me—I know you think Seton-proper is different, but when it comes to who actually runs shit, it's the same for all of us. And Parker has to think Michelle and I are still broken right now. He'll go even crazier if he thinks all of us are against him. I know he already looks like a psycho, but I have no doubt he can go crazier. And yes, Michelle is my best friend, but you're my friend, too, Aly. Seriously. And I know this stupid scandal is what brought us together, but I just didn't want . . . I *don't* want that to change."

I have a million questions. Like, how long have Britt and Michelle been talking? And do Bianca and Kelly know? And how crazy *is* crazy when it comes to Parker?

But my newspaper teacher always tells us that one of the worst things a journalist can do is focus on questions when what they're really looking for is answers. So tonight, the sensation of that keyboard still lingering on my fingertips, I choose to focus on what I know about Britt, and what I know about me, and what *my* answer is. "I would've been your friend with or without this shit."

"Maybe. Or maybe not."

She's doing exactly what I expect from her now. She holds on to the things that feel fragile enough until she's ready to let them go. And I saw it with the videos, and I saw it with the Parker story, and I see it tonight with her and Michelle. But I still haven't walked away, and I'm not about to.

"You know what I think?" I offer.

"Tell me."

The school looms dark, not the majestic place we pull up to in our bus every morning or see on Saturdays at football games, but like a palace that's fallen. "I don't think secrets are always such a bad thing. I mean, yeah, there are bad ones—like the drives. But some are more like bubble wrap—just padding we wrap up in to try and protect ourselves. And I think it works, until it doesn't, and you're kind of suffocating. So, I guess what I'm trying to say is, you never have to tell me anything before you're ready. But I also never want you to feel like you can't breathe. Because the second you're ready to take a deep breath . . . I'm here."

"You may be the smartest girl I've ever known." Britt studies a blade of grass. "Thank you for trusting me."

I offer her my pinky. She looks at it interestedly, like she's used to more sophisticated forms of promise-making, like clinking shot glasses or pricking fingers to swap blood, but she tucks her bottom lip into her teeth as she links her pinky with mine. I don't have a file. Michelle doesn't either, and Britt is pretty confident that that's because Parker wasn't on Varsity yet when Britt first took one of the drives. Bianca and Kelly also don't have a file, and Britt says it's because neither one of them has had sex yet. (*Thank God*, she added at the time.)

So, it's just her, of the girls in her immediate world, who's been directly burned by this. But I swear, that part never mattered. It's all those other girls Britt's so angry for. Who Britt wants vengeance for.

She deserves, for once, to have someone fighting for her. To spare her the questions and give her their answer. And that's what I feel like I've done tonight. Been to her what she's always been to the rest of us.

"Wednesday's gonna be shit, but it's gonna be okay," I say as I let go of her pinky.

"Wednesday's gonna be shit, but it's gonna be okay," she agrees.

What it is.

Britt and I pull up to my house a little after ten, with her windows down and our milkshakes in hand, laughing so hard that my abs hurt as we scream-sing along to "Thinkin Bout You" by Ciara. The music is so loud that I can't even hear myself, that my seat actually trembles with the bass, but Britt is such a contact-high right now that I'm loopy. Or maybe I'm the contact-high. Or maybe it's the two of us together that's making this buzzy chemical reaction—like cats on nip.

Maybe we're screwed on Wednesday. But tonight, we're kings.

There's a huge Halloween party at Abby Hendrix's tonight, but we're not there because we know we're not wanted. Not in the way that matters, at least, by the people who matter to both of us most. And two months ago, I couldn't imagine missing a Seton party—not because of the booze or the games or the Monday-morning stories, but because of how much it always meant for me to belong there. To be a part of the unbreakable, unmatchable, unbeatable *Seton Academic*, with all the people I thought I knew.

Abby Hendrix. Two videos.

Britt puts the car in Park on the street outside my house, and we take a few more seconds to seat-dance until the song ends. I hug her and tell her to text me when she gets home. Or call me during her drive, if she wants. Or whatever.

"Remain obsessed with you. Got it." Britt gives me a casual salute.

"Basically, yes."

"Cool, will do." She laughs and adds, "Love you, bye."

I smile, gnawing my straw. "Love you, bye." I hop out of the car so she can leave.

Her music is still thumping as she three-point-turns her way around on our narrow street. "Motivation" by Normani comes on next, and as she drives away, and my neighborhood sleeps, I keep dancing a little while longer, sucking from my half-full milkshake. It's not until she makes the right at the end of the road that the music really fades away, and that's when I spin around to go inside.

"Shit!" I jump backward, clutching my chest.

"Oh, shit—" J jumps, too.

"What are you doing?!" I cry.

"I wasn't trying to scare you."

"I had no idea you were even here." I rub my forehead, my heart-beat slowly coming down from heart-attack levels. "Why aren't you at Abby's?"

"I had Jeff bring me back after the game."

A chorus of crickets chirp all around us, and gnats congregate around the light next to my front door. J is standing in front of me, in the middle of our walkway, in the exact same clothes I'd left him in a few hours before. He never went back to his own house after the game, I just feel it. He came here looking for me, maybe played with Cory for a little bit while he waited, and then he came outside and stayed in the dark while he waited for me some more.

"What's that?" he asks, nodding at the cup in my hand.

"A milkshake. Britt and I went to BurgerFi. It's Oreo." Before I even realize what I'm doing, I'm holding it out for him to have some.

And before he even has a chance to think about it, his mouth is on my straw and he's having a sip.

His warm brown eyes hold mine while I hold my cup and his mouth holds my straw. His eyes are beautiful. And J—he's still the cutest guy I've ever seen, in spite of anything else.

"I know you tried to talk to me in the hallway earlier, but I was finishing something up with Britt, and I just . . ."

He lets go of the straw. "It's okay."

"Did you still want to talk?"

His lips part before the words come out. "I've really missed you, Alz." He takes a deep breath. "You're my best friend."

My throat tightens, the words slamming my heart. *Best friends.* It was always such a big concept to me, every time I thought about Britt and Michelle. Like, the dreamiest thing ever except *better.* How loopy they were for each other. How destined and kindred and forever they seemed. And it hits me for the first time that that's exactly what this is. I whisper, "You're my best friend, too."

He slips his hands onto my hips and puts his mouth on mine, and every part of me somersaults into this kiss a zillion times over. Maybe it's perfect because of how much I missed it, or how much I took it for granted, or just because of how much we both mean it right now.

When it's too hard to kiss him and breathe at the same time, because my tears are starting to win out, I rest my forehead on his chest instead. He puts his forehead against the top of my hair. And we stay that way, my tears dripping onto the sidewalk every time I try to sniff them away.

His hand slides between our bodies, and it's holding a flash drive.

"J." My voice breaks, taking the drive from him and squeezing it in my hands. The whole time we weren't speaking, I almost convinced myself that he most likely had nothing to do with this. That it's so completely opposite from everything I know him to be that there was no way he was in on it. He wasn't the *type*.

But now the proof is pressing into my palm.

"How could you do this?" I ask, and his face blurs behind my tears. "*Why* would you do this?"

"After that day at Walgreens, I went home and pulled that drive out from the bottom of my sock drawer. I carried it around with me for three days before I got myself to look at it. Alz, Parker had me come by one afternoon over the summer to chill and talk about this year. Get ready for it, you know? QB to QB. And he gave me this drive. He told me they were trick plays and that he needed me to hold on to the spare the same way he did for Levi. So I took it, no questions asked. He told me to just keep it safe until next summer and then we'd sit down and go over it. But not to look at it till then so our shit stayed tight. So I didn't. Not until a couple days ago, after I talked to you."

I squint at him. "So, you had no idea what you were really protecting the past few months?"

He shakes his head. "I believed him."

"But why didn't you look as soon as I told you? Why didn't you say, 'Shit, Alz, I have a drive, too' and tell me all of that back then? We could have looked together. We could have figured this out days ago, together."

"We couldn't have, though."

"Why not?"

"Because I was still a part of that team. I still *am* a part of that team. And it took me so long because . . . I don't know. I guess I was trying to figure out how I could believe you and Parker at the same time."

I look into his eyes as they steadily hold mine. No, all the evidence doesn't point toward the validity of what he's saying, and yes, I recognize all the ways he benefits by claiming ignorance of our hell on earth. But this is the J I know, and this is the J I trust, and I believe him.

"And now that you realize you can't?" I ask.

"I realize that I never should've tried to in the first place." He kisses me again, slides his thumbs underneath my eyes, holds me against him. It's probably all in my head, but I swear the crickets sound happier now.

"I never want you to feel like I'm not choosing you, because I'm always choosing you," I say. "I love you in the stupidest, most basic way, it's ridiculous. I haven't slept on the bus to school in ten days because I don't know how to sleep next to anybody but you. I won't listen to music on Shuffle because I'm terrified one of those stupid *Rent* songs is gonna pop on, and I don't know how to listen to one without you. I love you like that, and I don't know how to prove it any more than what the past sixteen years already has, but I do. I really do. And you are always my choice."

"I've never heard you say it," he mutters against my hair.

And sadly, I realize he's right. I bite the inside of my lip. "It's not the worst time for you to say it back."

"I've said it to you a thousand times, Alz."

"You've said it to me like four or five times."

"The number of times I choose you to be on my Fortnite team even though you die *every single time* is at least forty times this year alone, Alz."

I smile up at him. He smirks and shakes his head. I offer him more of my milkshake, and he sips it from my straw.

"I still have to stop this shit the team is doing to you guys, though," J says.

And I was so busy being in love with him that, for a few minutes, I didn't even feel the flash drive in my hand.

"I did something tonight," I admit.

And that's when I tell him everything . . . the article I wrote and how I swapped it in for Wednesday's paper during the end of the girls' volleyball game tonight. How Parker isn't going to get his center spread coronation like all the Varsity QBs who came before him, but this instead. I tell J all the reasons why it had to be this way, why the cops weren't good enough and going to Principal Mitchell wasn't good enough. I let him sip my milkshake to numb the shock as I pull up my article on my phone and let him read it while we sit next to each other on my front step.

"Shit, Alz," J says, exhaustedly setting my phone down on the step between us. He scratches his head through his hat.

"Do you still choose me?" I ask nervously.

But he wraps an arm around my neck without a second thought, pulls me over and kisses me. "Still."

What it is.

I'm more scared for J than I am for myself.

But he tells me not to be. He keeps saying that the team will figure it out next year, that he can promise me that JV isn't negotiating to win their games, that he'll still be able to play football in college somewhere, just watch. But you know how sometimes you say things out loud so that it manifests that way, or just to silence the voice inside of you that's screaming the exact opposite?

Well, that's kind of how J sounds these days.

But I did believe him a little bit more on the night when we made up, while the crickets chirped and the moths searched for the light above our heads, while we sat on my front step and called Britt from my phone on speaker, because that was what J wanted to do.

This is what he said:

"I know nothing I say is gonna change the fact that you've been telling us all school year what Parker did to you and we still haven't canceled him. And it's not gonna change the fact that there are these videos of you, and that there's probably tons of guys out there who have seen them, who smile in your face and act like everything's good. You have every right to say whatever you want to whoever you want and try and take down every single one of us. You have every right to decide we're just a bunch of damn animals blindly following whatever road is gonna get us another trophy.

But from me—and I know I can't speak for all of them, not yet, at least—but from me, I fucking hate what we've done to you. And I'm sorry. And it's not gonna happen under me next year, I swear to God on everything in my life. I won't do that shit. And by the way? What you and Alz did tonight? It's more kick-ass than any undefeated season we've ever had."

And Britt, her voice crackling over the speaker as the wind from the parkway flooded her car, boldly declared, "You were always better than them, J."

But anyway. That was days ago.

The Week of the Girls is just as romantic and mushy this year as it is any other year. The boys on the team bring their girlfriends and their girl-friends flowers, and chocolates, and dress up their lockers with streamers or decorate their cars with window paint. Girls all over Seton are walking around with giant teddy bears or huge bunches of balloons, their boy-proclaimed significance overwhelming the hallways like cheap perfume.

Britt points to each one and whispers their number in my ear like a ghost. *One. Three. Seven.*

Seton really does feel haunted.

J can't afford to do Week of the Girls the way the boys who drive Beemers do, and I promise him, like I do every year, that he doesn't have to do it at all. But he wants to, maybe especially because of everything else, and so my week—comparatively—goes like this:

On Monday, he almost misses the bus because he was making me an egg and sausage sandwich on a croissant. We huddle together on the bus as I eat it, trying to prevent the waft of egg-stink, laughing at the faces people make as they sniff the air trying to figure out who dealt it. I force myself to eat three-fourths (it's only 6:00 a.m.) and fall asleep on his shoulder as he eats the rest.

On Tuesday, J has a custom Spotify playlist that he made for me. Twenty songs long and he has a reason for each one. *This is the song that was playing that time we were together and your mom's car broke down. This is the song I was listening to when you were taking a shower at my house that day and fell in the tub.* They're not the kind of romantic moments that girls get to have in movies, but as he tells me the reasons why he chose each one, I start to realize that J and I don't have a ton of romantic moments. It's just been us, living and existing devoid of all that romantic stuff, but with love instead. It's weird how it can work out that way. But I lean against his shoulder with my half of his earbuds stuck snugly in my ear, more comfortable than I've ever been with anyone or anything.

And on Wednesday—*the day*—I jog outside to catch the bus and discover J on one knee in the middle of my walkway under the dark morning sky, with his backpack on and Seton beanie on his head, cocked to the side. He's holding a three-pack box of Glade PlugIns like it's the diamond of every girl's dreams.

I laugh. "What are you doing?"

He smiles back and doesn't get up.

I reach him and rub his cheek with my hand before I sit on the knee that's propped. "Are we just gonna chill here today?" I ask.

"Nah, I've got a chem test," he answers, his snide little joke. We both know there are much bigger things waiting for us at Seton this morning than his chem test. "Stand up, I'm trying to talk to you."

I stand up and curl my lips in toward my teeth, an effort not to smile.

"Will you please be the one to clip air fresheners that are too strong onto my car vents forever?"

"They aren't too strong, they're perfect. You just have a weirdly sensitive nose," I say, taking the box from him and studying it to see what scent he got.

He gets up off his knees and slides his hands into his pockets as he studies the box with me. "I think you're just supposed to say 'Yes,' but I'll take that."

The ride to school is perfect. I fall asleep under J's arm, listening to the playlist he made for me yesterday through my half of his headphones. We hit just the right amount of traffic that prevents us from getting to Seton at 6:30 a.m. but not so much that we're late for first period. The sun is just rising as we pull in, right before 7:00 a.m.

It starts the moment J and I step off the bus. The air is thick, thick enough to slow me down. Seton is quieter than I've ever known it, as the people who are here stare at this week's copy of *The Seton Story*, holding it open to the center page or slow-scrolling what I'm so sure is the digital version on their phones. They read it in groups or by themselves, silently or whispering, and I think Hannah Wilson has tears in her eyes. She wears plaid skirts to school and is the head of three clubs. She's a really good girl, and I was shocked, too, when Britt told me her number. That she had a number at all, really.

Two.

It hits me for the first real time. What I've done. What I'm doing. I wish I wasn't second-guessing it, but I am. Not the part about standing up to what the team is doing, but maybe the how.

Maybe going rogue and abusing my position as editor and for sure getting fired in the next seven minutes sounded like a much better idea last week.

But J takes my hand and won't look at them. And, because of him, I remember to keep walking.

And then I'm bombarded by the explosion that is Britt, practically tackling me as she wraps her arms around my neck, and her kinky curls threaten to suffocate me. I squeeze her back. She promised me she'd be here early today because it's *the day*, and that she'd be with me between every class, but I'm still relieved to finally feel her.

She lets go and holds my cheeks in her hands, and her gray eyes swirl like they can hypnotize. "We've got this. We're gonna take down the fucking patriarchy and treat ourselves to cupcakes like it was nothing. You hear me?"

"K," I agree.

Britt holds on to me while she looks up at J. "How's she doing?"

J smiles a little and nudges me. "She got some sexy new Glade PlugIns this morning for Week of the Girls."

Britt's eyebrows come together. "Oh, hell yeah." She looks at me. "You got gifted your fetish, and it's not even seven a.m.? You're killing it."

"I feel like people are crying."

Britt nods and looks over her shoulder for a second but not too long, the way you dare to glance at the sun so it can't hurt you. "They probably are. I did."

Britt and J walk with me, walk through it, toward the main steps. Britt is trying to distract me, asking me what cupcakes are my

favorite so we can bake them after school, and then asking J, because he'll end up eating most of them. And while J is busy express-
ing the moral complexities of Funfetti vs. red velvet, it happens.

"Yo, Aly, what the fuck is this?"

It's Parker, with a bunch of the Varsity guys behind him, with a
rolled-up issue of our newspaper in his hand, raging in our direction
the same way he raged at Britt at Spence's, and the way he raged at
Britt in the hallway, and the way he raged at Sam Klein in the caf.
Except this time, he's raging toward me.

I've never been hit before—not by a girl, and definitely not by a
guy—but I'm willing for this to be my first time.

In the second before Parker can get to me, J shields me from
what's coming. Parker's skin is redder than I've ever seen, his eyes
glaring past J and at me like a predator.

Parker says, "Yo, I need to talk to your girl."

"You've lost your fucking mind if you think you're coming over
here this hot and I'm letting you anywhere near her."

"I've lost *my* fucking mind?" Parker shoves the newspaper into
J's chest. Hard. It's a punch, pretty much, excused by the paper he's
handing over in the process. "Your girl went full Benedict Arnold,
bro. Read this shit and weep."

J grits his teeth, and he doesn't move. "I read it. Days ago."

It's like slow motion as Parker pieces together what that means.
His eyes move from J, to me, and then to Britt, the veins in his neck
getting tighter every second. He blinks at J. "What are you, some
fucking snitch?"

And then he lunges.

It was never supposed to be J. He was never supposed to get

broken in all this. Be the casualty. I scream and try to grab him. Britt holds me back. "They'll kill you," she says, trying to push my head into her shoulder so I can't see. "They'll tear you apart."

She manages to keep me back as much as I'm screaming and crying and trying to get to J, trying to pull him free of what's become a complete brawl, so many guys on the team involved that I can't tell who's trying to help and who's trying to kill. Blood is everywhere, and somewhere at the bottom of that heap is J. They're breaking him, I can feel it. I can feel it as if they were breaking me.

It takes every security officer we have and any teacher within earshot to finally break it up. They're shoving guys with their ripped-up shirts and their bleeding faces to different parts of the courtyard just to keep them far enough apart from each other until they figure out what else to do with them. And then there's J. He's not standing up. *Why the hell isn't he standing up?* A couple of teachers are squatting over him, talking, but I can't see if he's talking back. One of the teachers says, "I think we should call a bus."

Principal Mitchell jogs over to what's left. J on the ground. Half of his football team torn apart. A school that's standing around watching and good girls with tears in their eyes. Principal Mitchell has a copy of *The Seton Story* in his hand, too. And the man who shook my hand back when I was taking my first Seton tour, the one who picked me for editor, isn't here. He doesn't even look at me when he says, "Aly, wait for me in my office."

"If J's leaving, I have to go with him—"

"Get in my office and do not move." His back is to me and Britt as he goes to the group of teachers who are with J.

Britt takes my hand to go with me. And Principal Mitchell knows it without even turning back around.

"Britt. No," he growls.

She hesitates, but she lets me go.

I walk alone, up our regal front steps, through the front doors that are always open in the morning, aching. I don't see anyone even though they're there, I don't hear anyone even though everybody's whispering. In the distance, sirens wail.

"Aly." Gina-Melissa reaches out and touches me.

I've made it into the main entryway, just a few steps before I get to Principal Mitchell's office. But her touch distracts me for a second from my misery about J, from everything that's been done.

"What is this?" She's holding one of our newspapers.

I wet my lips; my cheeks are tight from the stickiness of my tears. I have nothing left in me. All I can do is drop my shoulders and tell her, "It's the truth."

She stares at me, taking slow, shallow breaths, thinking about Dan Kiley, I'm sure. And probably about how many times he told her that he loved her, and how they danced at prom, or kissed at midnight on New Year's. How he probably said good night to her on the phone yesterday before she went to sleep.

She's shocked. She should be. I still am.

"Thank you for telling me," she whispers.

And I don't know. Maybe I'm stupid. But looking at her convinces me that this was still somehow the right thing.

Because, at Seton, we swear we're family. And maybe now, we actually have a chance to prove it.

What it was.

August 25, 2019

"God, I just hate his fucking voice," Michelle said.

Britt laughed, kicking herself forward in her swing as Michelle dangled in the swing next to her, the wood chips crunching and scattering beneath their hanging feet. Bowling had been fine. Just another one of Parker's narcissistic efforts to get everyone together again so he'd have an excuse to drink in public and hear himself talk. This time, the night before school started.

Michelle and Britt had suffered through it and played nice, and finally they were here. The place they went to skip class to never be found, where they lay in the grass and sang sacred cheers, where they smoked and laughed and hid from the world. The two of them now—alone at their park, underneath the stars.

"*I do*," Michelle went on. "It's not even just what he says but it's literally the voice that's tied to it. Like nails on a freaking chalkboard. Just listening to him makes me want to kill myself half the time."

"You can't kill yourself, Mich." Britt sighed into the night. "I need you."

Michelle sighed, too, sliding her foot to the side, tucking her ankle behind Britt's. "Same."

They'd been keeping secrets for a long time, and secrets have a way of becoming parasitic after a while. They were thinner from it, weaker from it, tired. It'd been since April—since that party at Zach's house when he ripped, like, ten peanut butter and jelly shots and all those guys from other schools showed up, too. Britt had been waiting for the moment he'd be drunk enough, or distracted enough, or stupid enough, and had tried a couple of times before, but he was never quite gone enough. Like this one time at Nappahawnick when he was buzzed on heat and wine coolers, or the night at BurgerFi, when she hoped that maybe he'd let her have his keys to drive home.

But that party at his house was the perfect night for it, because it was the kind of party that was so wild it felt like you were spinning. So, that night, while Levi walked them home, while she and her best friends danced down the middle of the street, Britt held on to a flash drive in her pocket that no one knew she stole.

Until the next morning, of course, when she and Michelle huddled under blankets in Britt's room and giggled together as they slid the flash drive into Britt's computer. To see what could've possibly been so precious that Zach would protect it the way he had.

That was back in April.

But they didn't say anything then, because they didn't know what they'd found. They knew it was bad. They knew it made them nauseous. They both cried when they saw Britt had videos. But they also knew where they lived. They also knew how things worked. So, they kept their secret, and pretended like their perfect world was perfectly fine, while they got thinner, and weaker, and more and more tired.

But then June happened—the atomic explosion that was June— and in a single night Britt discovered exactly who Parker was and exactly what the team had been doing. And she told Michelle. Everything.

Your right arm can't just not talk to the left.

They never called it rape, even when they were just lying in bed with one another. It happens that way sometimes. Labels are harder with people you know, people you love. It's the difference between calling them a person who did a bad thing or *the type of person who does bad things*.

Semantics, maybe. But not to the heart.

Michelle had hated her boyfriend for over two months now. She hated him while she rode shotgun with the windows down, she hated him on the Fourth of July, she hated him at his nephew's stupid, stuffy birthday party, at that house where the walls were always so thin. Where she could hear him from the powder room, his whole scheme to win States. His whole plan to use her. *And Britt. Again.* As soon as Britt got there, Michelle took her to Parker's bedroom, took her into his walk-in closet, closed the door behind them. They sat on the floor and she told Britt what she'd heard, pinching her fingertips anxiously as she whispered about how unbelievable he was, how pure-evil he was, how much she couldn't believe she'd ever loved him.

Britt wouldn't let her cry because her mascara would tell on her. So Michelle just pinched her fingers and stared into Britt's eyes as Britt combed Michelle's hair with her fingers and pushed it behind her ears, and Michelle whispered, "I fucking hate him."

It was the kind of hate that made her shake sometimes or go to the bathroom just to cry. That made her sick when she hadn't even eaten. And she would have slit his throat for Britt. Honestly. She really might have gone that far.

But she didn't. Because Britt had said not to.

Michelle twisted in her swing that night, so that the chains wrapped together, and then she lifted her feet and let the swing unwind. She'd rather be dizzy than stuck where they were. "Do you think that tomorrow's gonna change anything?"

"I absolutely believe that tomorrow's going to change everything."

"But what if no one cares? What if we have this epic fight, and destroy our souls pretending to hate each other, and it doesn't change a single thing? What if the guys don't try to help us, what if they find a bunch of other girls to film their fucking threesome . . . what if Parker never cops to shit? *He never cops to shit.*" Michelle shook her head, hating him and scared of him all at the same time. Like a nightmare. "He never has to."

Britt had thought about it, too. Their half-baked plan, how it could maybe even be classified as desperate. A Hail Mary pass when there was no more time left on the clock. But miracles happen when they're right. She'd read that somewhere before. "Someone's gonna see us. Someone's gonna help us."

They sat quietly for a second, with their secrets and their plans, under the twinkling sky. It took weeks of thinking, weeks of Britt promising Michelle that she was okay after what Parker did to her that night. Okay enough, at least. Weeks of Britt holding Michelle and hating that she had to call Parker her boyfriend for even another second, but she couldn't leave him. Not yet.

Because corporations are designed to thrive. And the world we live in is designed to forgive them. And all the other people—the Britts and Michelles of the world—have to play an unbeatable game to stand any chance at victory. And even then, even if they irrefutably win, money and a good enough lawyer can make anything go away.

Britt and Michelle didn't have an unbeatable plan. They had a strategy and a glimmer of hope. They had an idea (that had really been Britt's) to fake their own breakup, knowing that that kind of catastrophe was the exact kind of disaster that Seton would tune in for. They would start their own rumors about a hookup between Parker and Britt that summer, and maybe it would break him, once he saw how much it'd broken them. Maybe he'd admit to what he'd done. And once he did, maybe the guys on the team would stop thinking he was such a god all the time. Maybe they'd be weak and vulnerable without their ringleader, and listen to Britt when she brought up the drives. Maybe they'd finally feel guilty enough, shitty enough, for human nature to take over, and some of them—or even just *one* of them—would decide to make it stop.

Maybe. Maybe, maybe, maybe.

"I go through phases, you know?" Michelle asked. "About what part I'm most worried about. Sometimes it's that I won't be able to talk to you if anybody's watching. Sometimes it's what happens if we can't make them stop. Right now, it's Kel and B, though. And how fucking heartbroken they're gonna be for who knows how long."

"I know." Britt's stomach ached, feeling it, too. The residual pain that would come from theirs. "But we can't tell them."

"We can't tell them," Michelle agreed. "There're already too many people at Seton trying to keep secrets. And they'll get that, right? Once everything comes out?"

"They'll get it. We're all gonna be okay. I just know it, Mich. I know it sounds intense, but I like . . . I *feel* it."

Michelle nodded. "Who do you think it'll be?"

"What do you mean?"

"Of the guys on the team. If any of them cares enough to do something, who do you think it will be?"

Britt thought about the options, their faces flashing through her mind easily, like anything else she had memorized—the alphabet or the numbers on her mom's credit card. It was weird for something to be so familiar yet unpredictable at the same time. "I'm not sure yet."

Michelle sighed, leaning back in her swing, succumbing to the weight of their world. "Do you ever wonder what would've happened if they'd just asked us?"

"If who'd asked us what?" Britt rested her head against one of the chains and watched her best friend be perfect.

"If the guys had asked us to be recorded. Like do you ever wonder if they'd straight-up asked, if we would have done it? Because I think that, maybe, some of us would have."

And maybe she was right. Maybe if the boys had told them what they needed from them and why, there would've been girls who just stepped up, who volunteered as Seton patriots like sexually liberated Rosie the Riveters. They protected the boys every other way they could, every other way they'd ever needed them to—with sign-in sheets and no pictures at parties and forgiving their wandering mouths and hands when they were drunk and high and stupid. They could've all been in this together. They could've loved Seton and won every game forever *together*.

But no one would ever know for sure. Because the boys never cared to ask.

"Permission," Britt paraphrased, sliding her foot through the wood chips. "I think you only ask for that if you don't already have everything else."

Michelle sat up again, looking at her, believing everything she'd ever said and would ever say, always. She reached out and pushed one of Britt's curls behind her ear before she took Britt's hand and didn't let go. Their conjoined fist dangled between them as their swings rocked back and forth at different rates, as Britt's cat-eyes studied the wood chips and Michelle's explored the sky.

"If I wish on a star that tonight never ends, do you think it'll work?" Michelle asked.

"No," Britt admitted, even though their park was the most magical place they'd ever known, and that wish probably did stand a better chance here than it did anywhere else. "But it doesn't mean we shouldn't try." She waited for a second, and then she accepted, "Tonight has to end, Mich. Nothing gets better if tonight doesn't end."

And Britt knew that, deep down, Michelle understood that. Their world was an inferno, a kind of hell. And at that moment, every single one of them was on fire. Best-case scenario, this plan would work and their burns would just leave scars for eternity. But worst-case scenario—the scenario in which they did nothing—this fire would singe them alive.

"Do you know when Parker's voice was the absolute worst tonight?" Michelle asked, tugging Britt's arm a little from their gripped hands. "When he was going on and on about goddamn superpowers."

"It was basically a seizure. It was basically a complete vocal spasm that wouldn't end."

"*It wouldn't end,*" Michelle groaned back. She took a second before she softly asked, "Do you want to know what noun you are to me?"

"Hmm . . ." Britt licked her lips, considering the options. "Queen? King? Genius? Magician?"

"Girl of my fucking dreams."

"I'll take it." And then, trying not to be too sad, and trying not to be too scared, Britt looked into the sky and wondered if she could find the same star that Michelle had used for her wish a moment before. But there are millions and millions of stars.

So she settled on one that was twinkling somewhere far away, somewhere she'd rather be. And before tomorrow started, before things got too bad and they couldn't do stuff like this for a while, Britt wanted her to know: "I would swallow needles for you, Mich. For real. I would do literally anything."

"I would do anything for you, too."

And they stayed there, dangling in their swings and holding each other's hands until Britt finally said it was time for tomorrow.

What it Turned into.

Six months used to happen so fast, back when our lives were just football, and Week of the Girls, and the Season of Giving, and Seton. Back when it was easy, and it was perfect—or we thought it was, at least. But now that it's J getting used to passing a football again with a just-healed collarbone, and a general Seton-wide uprising, every day feels like a lifetime.

Britt and her friends are leaving pretty soon, off to their colleges where no one will know about Seton unless they want them to. But they won't want them to, I don't think. I used to be convinced that I'd talk about Seton for the rest of my life. That the only future I could possibly imagine would be J and me on a porch swing outside of our own mansion telling our grandkids about the best place we'd ever known and all the greatest memories we'd ever had. But things can change so fast. Life can be one thing and then suddenly it's not, or maybe it was never even that thing to begin with. So I still hope it's me and J, on that swing, telling our stories. I'm just not sure anymore exactly what those stories will be.

It's a matter of who you do or don't believe, I guess. There's this very clear line that's been drawn and three places you can be in relation to it. On Britt's side (the boys are conniving terrorists), on Varsity's side (Britt's lying), or straddling the line in its entirety (maybe the boys did a bad thing, but they're not *bad boys*). And there's this weird instability about our school, our world, these days, the same way there is when any reigning power falls. Even though, maybe they haven't really *fallen*. Their power is still there, lingering like a spaghetti sauce stain on a white rug. We just notice it now. Not as a hypothetical concept but for what it really is, and I'm still not sure whether we're luckier for it. "Do you think it's better or worse for a lobster to spend its last few seconds alive believing he's just going for a dip in a hot tub?" Britt asked, the last time I tried to talk to her about it. But she didn't know the answer and neither did I.

All the drives Britt swears she saw are gone. We don't know where they are, and a lot of people wonder if they really existed in the first place. The only ones that do exist are the one she stole from Zach Willis and the one J handed me outside of my house. And Parker's dad, who's this big-deal lawyer, dismissively insists that's because there was never a scheme to begin with, that it was just boys being boys. Girls falling for football players the way girls have since the dawn of time, and a bunch of dumb kids in love deciding to have sex and record it. He says that the girls are just spinning this whole story because what else are they supposed to say now that their teachers and parents and pastors all know that they made a bunch of sex tapes? Say that they *wanted* to do it?

The skeptics have a scary way of making me feel crazy, of making me wonder what I really do know. But that's what power is, I guess, when it comes to the big kind that Britt's always talking about. The ability to control anything they want. Even your mind.

There's an investigation now, and I tell myself that that will validate everything, that we just have to make it until then. But in the meantime, a bunch of the boys' parents have gotten together and are threatening their own lawsuit against Seton for the harassment they say their sons experienced on campus. For the pain and suffering of having to forfeit their senior season while the investigation is ongoing. Because of my article. Because of our "lies." School is supposed to be a safe space, *especially* for donors like them, and it's not anymore. *So fix it,* they demand, *or else.*

But while it's not fixed, Seton has arranged for the Varsity boys to do their coursework from home. I heard a rumor that Principal Mitchell raised hell about it, about how broken and pathetic the system must be if it was trying to pacify a bunch of students who would be eighteen in two seconds and were accused of sexual assault. And I do believe he might've been that upset, considering he never even suspended me for the article I ran. He never took away my editor position. He came into his office and gave me the longest hug ever, on the day when everything happened. But people like Britt and her friends, who will always be Seton-proper enough to know more than I do, say the school board and all the Seton parents they golf with are perfectly happy letting the boys graduate in their pajamas. So, it really doesn't matter what Principal Mitchell thinks.

To keep the boys' spirits up, their parents gift them new cars, days out on the family boat, a spring break trip to Mexico. Parker turned his comments off, but he still posts everything to Instagram for all of us to see. For all of us to know. For all of us to hate him and miss him and remember him, always.

I think about him so much more than I wish I did. Whenever I pass the trophy display by Seton's main doors. Whenever our bus drives past Julio's. Whenever J and his JV team remind us that they've chosen Britt's side of the line, or whenever I worry that Parker's gonna find a way to ruin me or J one day, even though Britt assures me he'd never do anything that makes him look so guilty, now that everyone is watching.

But right now, I can at least push Parker to the very back of my mind, almost like the wind in my face has blown him there.

Bianca took her mom's Lexus SUV so that all six of us could fit—her and Kelly in the front, GM and me in the next row, Britt and Michelle draped carelessly in the back, for sure destined to die if we crash. Which we almost have, a couple of times.

Kelly holds on to the windowsill as Bianca presses the brake extra hard to stop us from rear-ending the eighteen-wheeler we've been trailing for the past five miles. The trash from our Burger King breakfasts slides toward the front of the car.

"Easy, B, it's a GX, not an R8," Kelly insists.

"I can't see past this guy." Bianca cranes her neck in an impatient attempt to see beyond the truck in front of us. "Are we at a light?"

"Now that we've gotten into *Harvard*, who has time for silly things like speed limits and traffic laws?" Michelle asks poshly from the seat behind me.

"You know that you don't always have to reference Harvard with a British accent now, right?" Bianca smirks at her in the rearview mirror. "I mean, it's basically in Boston. Which is quite the opposite."

"Sorry, darling, what was that?" Britt croons, her leg dangling over my and GM's seat. "It's hard to hear you while I'm so busy practicing my British accent for Harvard."

Michelle giggles, and Kelly smiles and nudges Bianca. "Will you bring us back some croissants for Christmas?"

"That's France," Bianca corrects.

"Everywhere is everywhere when we're talking fake geography," Kelly dismisses.

"Will you guys really come back for Christmas?" I ask, closing my eyes as we start picking up speed again and the wind from my wide-open window slaps my face.

"Because you miss me already?" Britt asks, tickling my ear with her neon-purple-painted toes.

"Would you even *want* to come back?" GM adds, turning so her back is pressed against the door, and she can survey the front of the car and the back of the car more easily.

It's quiet for a second, the in-between feeling of where we were and where we are making every question a little harder to answer these days.

But in so many ways, I do believe that Seton is better than what it was before. The girls—we're stronger. Our nights aren't at the disposal of what the boys want us all to do. We aren't at risk of ending up on tape because we went to bed with a football player. Seton isn't our fairy tale anymore. It's real. But that also means it doesn't flow like it used to. It isn't the perfection we all loved to claim, cheer for, wrap ourselves up in and then drift off to sleep. And maybe that does make it a lot easier to say goodbye.

"Why don't you come and see us instead?" Michelle suggests.

"Yeah, like come to one of our schools each year so you get a new experience for our whole college careers." Kelly rests her head on the back of her seat and slides her oversized sunglasses from on top of her head back down over her eyes. "It's like Around the World, U.S. Colleges Edition."

"Like for Christmas, you mean?" Because I'm not sure if we're still talking about Christmas, but I know I'd never leave during it. "Or some other time? Or like . . . a few times a year but each year only one of your cities is the theme?"

"Whatever you want," Bianca replies, and she sighs as we continue our slow roll behind this truck.

But then Britt's voice tickles my ear, the whiff of her minty gum floods my nose, and she whispers so softly that it's a promise that only the two of us can hear. *"We will not lose each other."*

It's a school day, but we didn't want to be there. Britt, Michelle, Bianca, and Kelly are just a few more quizzes and a final away from graduating, and school has felt weird ever since the Varsity guys stopped showing up. Class seems kind of optional for all of us now.

Usually, we'll skip class somewhere nearby, but today Britt and her friends wanted to go to the beach. This whole idea they had to rewrite homecoming. It started as a mention and exploded into a full commitment in the span of ten seconds as they fed off one another and ultimately decided. They told GM and me to come, and it was one of those moments that they weren't going to lose. Their gray magic swirled and intoxicated our souls, and before we even knew it, they made our choice for us.

We're close now. Out my window, I can see the water, and the road has been one lane for the past ten minutes. At any point, I'm expecting us to turn off and park and then . . . I don't know. We don't even have bathing suits.

And that's when Michelle gasps so suddenly from the back seat that I spin around to make sure she isn't hanging out the window.

"HOLY. SHIT." Kelly bolts up like she's been electrocuted.

Bianca's fingers are instantly bumping up the volume of the radio from the steering wheel, and the car is flooded with synthy violins and a song I've never heard.

"B, pull this spaceship over," Britt demands. "We're getting out."

Bianca pulls onto the shoulder, lined with rocky sand, and Britt and Michelle leap over the second-row seatback so they can climb out of the doors with GM and me. Bianca turns the music up so much we can hear it over the crashing waves and we can hear it over the cars on the road rolling past at their compliant forty-five miles per hour.

I grab Britt's elbow before she can race too far away from me with the other three girls and demand, "What is happening?"

Britt faces me as she backs her way onto the sand, smiling and dragging me with her. Her long kinky curls spill wildly from beneath her orange beanie. "We heard this song for the first time like ten years ago. It's the sappiest, most romantic, boy-band shit ever. And Parker used to want to slice his ears off every time we turned it on." Her eyes sparkle at the end, like that's the best part.

She runs to join their circle, where they're already serenading each other, the Harvard baseball cap that Bianca had been wearing officially now rolled up in her hands like a microphone.

"'Baby I Would,'" GM tells me, showing me the Shazam app on her phone. "By some group named O-Town."

I listen to the words as they belt them out, clutching their chests and twirling in pretty circles and getting down on one knee for fake proposals. It's every cliché a love song has ever been, fully meant for the love of your life. But it's also absolutely perfect. This song a bunch of boys sang a million years ago, officially reclaimed now and ours.

I offer GM my hand and shrug. "Shall we?"

GM is going through so much right now. She ended things with Dan the night my article dropped. Because she's emphatically on Britt's side of the line, and because she asked us to show her her tapes, so we did. They say going to the burial can help people more immediately process a death, and I kind of think seeing those files did the same thing for her. Dan was her first everything, and I know she's broken, and I just hope this love song doesn't make all the hard parts of this breakup bubble up again right now. But she laughs and takes my hand, and like a wave that pulls you out to sea, their circle of love sucks us in.

And as we dance, all that's happened flashes through my mind like a slide show. The way my article blew up when someone posted it to IG, and for a second, the entire universe was behind us. Reposting and cyber-feuding and starting hashtags like #GirlsDeserveBetter. But after a few days, people moved on. We were forgotten, and the next Infuriating Thing grabbed the rest of the world's attention.

But in our world, Michelle still cries about Parker sometimes. And Britt has to face the doubters who like to remind anyone who will listen that she's always been dramatic and calculated and a slut. And Bianca and Kelly have to watch their best friends suffer through a different kind of hell, now that they're back together. And I ache as I look at J rotate his shoulder obsessively because ever since they broke it, it gets tight, and that's one of a million reasons why I worry about what next year will be. And GM blocks anyone who posts pictures of Dan because she can't stand to even see his face anymore.

While the rest of the world forgets.

But we smile about it most times, and dance about it now, because we're free. Because we've shattered the snow globe we all used to live in. Because life is bigger than Seton, and Britt and her friends are almost on their way to their whole new cities, and the rest of us will be, too, soon enough. Stuff keeps moving forward, and so we are, too, and that—I think—is what makes us feel strong enough to talk about everything that's happened. The stories they have that I didn't know before, to help me weave the past together even more. And then the stories that other people bring me, ever since they read my article—people at Seton now and people who left a while ago. The kind of people who've asked me to never tell anyone I've heard from *them*. Maybe because of a guilty conscience, or maybe just another attempt to save themselves.

I write it all down—what it was and what it is—so I don't lose it all in moments like this, when I'm busy skipping school and dancing and moving on. I don't know what I'm gonna do with all their stories. Sometimes, when it's quiet enough, I think about hijacking the paper again, this time when I'm the one graduating, and lowercasing all my *V*s and asking GM to proofread for me before I publish everything I know on my way out the door. I can't do it any sooner than that, because even though Principal Mitchell had my back the first time, I'm almost positive he'd fire me if I went rogue again.

"What are you doing?" GM asks, and that's when I realize my dancing isn't as crazed as it's supposed to be.

"Sorry. I was thinking."

And then Britt has my face in her hands, and stares into my eyes as the sun beats down hard enough to make everything warm. So warm that I feel like I could ignite. "Well, don't."

And she spins me around and back into this moment, and I know without any possible question that I *am* luckier now. To be on this beach. To have these girls. To know there's something else, something more and something bigger than Seton waiting for us somewhere on the other side.

Kelly attempts a deep voice meant to match the guy singing in this moment, as she strokes Bianca's cheek and means it so much when she croons, "I'll do anything for you, girl . . ."

Michelle hops on Kelly's back, despite her mini–white sundress, her long hair flopping over her shoulder. "'Cause you're the one I want in my wooorllldddd . . ."

They reach for Britt and me and GM, laughing almost too hard to sing as we form a giant human knot, and the song ends, and we stay that way.

For so long, I've known exactly what happens next. Exactly when the Seton Girls cheer will happen. What songs to expect on the playlist. The way Seton does our traditions. And with all that's going on right now, none of that predictability exists anymore. When I woke up this morning, I assumed I'd be in third period right now, but instead I'm on the side of the road by the ocean, dancing in the sand. I started my year without any of these girls, and now we're holding each other like we never want to let go.

It's the craziest feeling ever—dizzying and intoxicating and *cool*—to fully accept that, in our new reality, anything can happen. To accept that I truly have no idea what's next.

We breathe in each other's faces as we stay huddled in our lump. Commercials are playing over the car stereo now. And I wonder when we'll move. Where we'll go. How long we'll stay.

"We should have been a girl group," Michelle declares.

"We would have been *iconic*," Bianca insists.

"Huge missed opportunity," Kelly agrees. "Like, there're those twins who missed out on launching Facebook, and then there's us for never forming a girl group."

"That opportunity is still fully available," Britt assures them. "We can do whatever the hell we want. We could start that group right now and go platinum in a year, I bet."

I smile to myself because I know that, as much as Britt's joking, she also means it. And that if any one of them decided in this moment that they wanted to skip college and go to Hollywood instead, Britt would be the first one back in that car, Google Maps–ing the fastest route.

"In that case, maybe you should practice?" GM suggests.

And then the song starts over, softer than it was before because this time it's coming from GM's phone.

"*Yessss!*" Bianca cheers as we unknot ourselves, and they twirl and sing all over again.

"*Hell* yes." Kelly drops her neck and lets the sun beat down on her face.

Michelle takes GM's hands, her pretty smile beaming as she tells her, "You're a genius. Be our agent?"

Britt takes my hand next and lifts it in the air as she spins beneath it. "And *you* be our manager."

And maybe I will be. Maybe I'll be their manager, and GM will be their agent, and we'll get back in that car and head straight for California. Maybe J's team will be undefeated anyway next year, and he'll get some amazing scholarship to play for a school out west so he can meet me there. Maybe the Parkers of the world will finally get what's coming to them, and the girls will be pop stars, and I'll do way more with my stories than just publish them in our school newspaper one day. Maybe this song will end and everything else will start.

But for now, we just keep dancing.

Acknowledgments

Firstly, I have to thank God for this incredible life and for blessing me with all the people I'm about to thank next.

To my parents, thank you for raising me to be confident and stay humble. To be faithful and always grateful. To be good to others, always. Thank you for believing in my stories even though I'd never let you read them (until now!). Thank you for always believing in me and loving me more than what's probably even fair. I love you, too.

To my family, thank you for being the most incredible family I could ask for. For always cheering for me, remembering me, and caring for me. Thank you for being proud of me and please know that I am so proud of you, too. Proud of your kindness, and your wisdom, and all the things you do. Proud to call you mine.

Grandma, I know you're not here to read this, but I know you'll know it's happened, and that you're so, so happy it has. And that makes me so, so happy, too.

I want to say thank you to our doctors and care teams, those who take care of our bodies so our souls can thrive. We're a family that both practices and has greatly benefited from modern medicine; it's the reason why some of us are still here today to see this moment and read these words. So I am so deeply grateful to those teams of magical humans who have fixed us up and kept us well.

To Ann, my incredible, huge-hearted agent. Thank you for your partnership, and your support, and your emojis. Thank you for listening to my impromptu ideas about books and so much else. Thank you for loving this story before it even existed, when I was just a writer with a partially written manuscript that you took a chance on. Thank you so much for believing in this story. But, more than that, thank you for—from the very, very start—believing in me.

To Andrew, my amazing and amazingly talented editor. Thank you for the pixie dust you sprinkled upon my words. For understanding this story and opening my mind to all the ways we could make it even better. Thank you for being so damn GOOD at what you do. I can't imagine bringing this book to life with anyone else.

To the teams at Prospect Agency, Dutton, and Penguin, thank you for everything you've done for me and do for others. There's so much happening that I don't see that transforms my Word document into a book on shelves, and I am so thankful for all of your skill, support, and commitment to this story. You've helped me achieve one of my biggest dreams and you will always feel like fairy godmothers to me.

To my friends, I am forever grateful for how we've protected each other, chosen each other, loved each other. Thank you for showing me so clearly at such a young age what *soul mates* means and what friendship is. How beautiful and complicated and perfect it can be. Our stories inspired this story. And to Amy, I miss you every day.

And lastly, to anyone else who has picked up this book: I hope you find good people, I hope you find your people, and I hope you cherish them always.

Thank you all, from the absolute bottom of my heart, for reading my words.

Xo Charlene

Credits

DUTTON BOOKS AND PENGUIN YOUNG READERS GROUP

ART AND DESIGN
Anna Booth
Kristin Boyle

CONTRACTS
Anton Abrahamsen

**COPYEDITORS AND
PROOFREADERS**
Rob Farren
Anne Heausler

EDITOR
Andrew Karre

MANAGING EDITOR
Natalie Vielkind

MARKETING
James Akinaka
Christina Colangelo
Brianna Lockhart
Felicity Vallence

PRODUCTION MANAGER
Vanessa Robles

PUBLICITY
Anna Elling

PUBLISHER
Julie Strauss-Gabel

PUBLISHING MANAGER
Melissa Faulner

SUBSIDIARY RIGHTS
Micah Hecht
Kim Ryan

SALES
Susie Albert
Jill Bailey
Andrea Baird
Maggie Brennan
Trevor Bundy
Nicole Davies
Tina Deniker
John Dennany
Cletus Durkin
Eliana Ferreri
Drew Fulton
Sheila Hennessey

Todd Jones
Doni Kay
Steve Kent
Debra Polansky
Colleen Conway Ramos
Mary Raymond
Jennifer Ridgway
Judy Samuels
Nicole White
Allan Winebarger
Dawn Zahorik

**SCHOOL AND LIBRARY
MARKETING AND
PROMOTION**
Venessa Carson
Judith Huerta
Carmela Iaria
Trevor Ingerson
Summer Ogata
Megan Parker
Rachel Wease

LISTENING LIBRARY
Rebecca Waugh

PROSPECT AGENCY
Ann Rose
Mikaila Rushing